# The ... who Rained

ALI SHAW

Atlantic Books

London

First published in hardback and export and airside trade
paperback in Great Britain in 2012 by Atlantic Books, an imprint
of Atlantic Books Ltd.

1 2 3 4 5 6 7 8 9

A CIP catalogue record for this book is available from the British
Library.

Hardback ISBN: 9-780-85789-032-0

Export and Airside Trade Paperback ISBN: 9-780-85789-033-7

Printed in Italy by 🐾 Grafica Veneta S.p.A.

Atlantic Books
Ormond House
26–27 Boswell Street
London
WC1N 3JZ

www.atlantic-books.com

*For Iona*

# The Man
## who
# Rained

'These our actors,
As I foretold you, were all spirits, and
Are melted into air, into thin air,
And, like the baseless fabric of this vision,
The cloud-capped towers, the gorgeous palaces,
The solemn temples, the great globe itself,
Yea, all which it inherit, shall dissolve,
And, like this insubstantial pageant faded,
Leave not a rack behind. We are such stuff
As dreams are made on.'

William Shakespeare, *The Tempest*

# 1

## THE CLOUD-CAPPED TOWERS

The rain began with one gentle tap at her bedroom window, then another and another and then a steady patter at the glass. She opened the curtains and beheld a sky like tarnished silver, with no sign of the sun. She had hoped so hard for a morning such as this that she let out a quiet cry of relief.

When the cab came to take her to the airport, water spattered circles across its windscreen. The low-banked cloud smudged Manhattan's towers into the atmosphere and the cab driver complained about the visibility. She described how dearly she loved these gloomy mornings, when the drizzle proved the solid world insubstantial, and he bluntly informed her that she was crazy. She craned her neck to look out of the window, upwards at the befogged promises above her.

She did not think she was crazy, but these last few months she had come close. At the start of the summer she would have described herself as a sociable, successful and secure twenty-nine-year-old. Now, at the worn-out end of August, all she knew was that she was still twenty-nine.

At the airport she drifted through check-in. She paced back and forth in the departures lounge. She was the first in the boarding queue. Even when she had strapped herself into her seat; even as she watched the cabin crew's bored safety routine; even as the prim lady seated beside her twisted the crackling wrapper of a bright boiled sweet; even with every detail too lucid to be a dream, she still feared that all the promises of the moment might be wrenched from her.

Life, Elsa Beletti reckoned, took delight in wrenching things from her.

Elsa's looks came from her mother's side of the family. The Belettis had given her unruly black hair, burned-brown eyes and the sharp eyebrows that inflected her every expression with a severity she didn't often intend. She was slim enough for her own liking most months of the year, but her mother and all of her aunts were round. At family gatherings they orbited one another like globes in a cosmos. She feared that one morning she would wake up to find genetics had caught up with her, that her body had changed into something nearly spherical and her voice, which she treasured for its keen whisper like the snick of a knife, had turned into that of a true Beletti matriarch, making every sentence into a drama of decibels.

Her surname (which she gained aged sixteen, after her mother had kicked her father out) and her physique were all she had inherited from the Belettis. She had always considered herself more like her dad, whose own family history existed only in unverified legends passed down to him by his grandparents. One ancestor, they had told him, had been the navigator on a pilgrim tall ship. He had coaxed the winds into the vessel's sails to carry its settlers over unfathomable waters en route to a new nation. Another was said to have been a Navajo medicine man, who had survived the forced exodus of his people from their homeland and helped maintain under oppression their belief in the Holy Wind, which gave them breath and left its spiral imprint on their fingertips and toes.

Elsa's mum said that her dad had made both of those stories up. She said he had done it to pretend that his sorry ass was respectable.

She said his ancestors were all hicks and alcoholics. She said it all again on the rainy afternoon when she kicked him out of the house and he stood in the falling water like a homeless dog.

Then, this spring, he had left them for a second and more final time.

The plane took off with a judder. At first all Elsa could see through the window was grizzled fog. She pinched her fingertips together to keep herself calm. Then came the first tantalizing break in the grey view. A blur of blue that vanished as quickly as it had come, like a fish flickering away through water.

The plane rose clear.

If the world that she left below her had looked like this, she could have been happier in it. Not a world of packed dirt under cement streets and endless houses, but one of clouds massed into mountains. As far as she could see white pinnacles of cloud basked in the bright sun. Peak after peak rose above steamy canyons. In the distance one smouldering summit flickered momentarily like a blowing light bulb: a throwaway flash of lightning some two hundred miles to the south. She wished it were possible to make her home in this clean white landscape, to spend her days lying on her back in a sun-bright meadow of cloud. Since that was impossible, she was giving up everything for the next best thing. Somewhere remote, where she could rebuild herself.

'Ma'am?'

She turned, irritated, from the view of the world outside to that of the aeroplane aisle and the air hostess who had disturbed her. After the majesty of the cloudscape, the domesticity of the plane infuriated her. The plastic grey cabin and the air hostess's twee neckerchief. People loafing in their seats as if in their living rooms, reading the airline's free magazine or watching whatever came on TV. A little girl wailed and Elsa thought, *Yes, me too.*

The air hostess outlined the choice of set meals, but Elsa told her she wasn't hungry. The hostess smiled with good grace and pushed her trolley further down the aisle.

The plane turned away from the country of her birth, from the glass-grey city blocks and the gridlocked avenues, from the concrete landing strips, from the ferry terminals and the boats jostling in the cellophane sea. She felt no sadness in saying goodbye to all that, although she had bitten back tears before boarding. Against Elsa's wishes, her mother had appeared at the airport to wave her off, sobbing into a handkerchief. She had brought with her another unwelcome sight: a pair of presents wrapped in sparkling red paper. Elsa had tried to refuse them – she wanted to leave her old life behind her entirely – but had ended up cramming them into her luggage regardless.

It had been years since Elsa had properly connected with her mother. Their telephone conversations were dutifully recited scripts, both of them dutifully reciting their lines. Their infrequent meet-ups took place in an old diner, where her mum would order Elsa the same muddy hot chocolate and slice of pecan pie which she had consumed greedily as a child. These days, the mere sight of that glistening slab of dessert felt fattening, but Elsa always forced it down. She hoped that by playing along, she might, some day, bring this repeating scene to a close and let the next commence. But they had been stuck in the same tired roles ever since her mum had kicked her dad out; and Elsa feared that her mother had thrown the remaining acts out into the rain along with him.

This past spring, the first sunshine and the cherry blossom had brought with it news that had shattered her life as she had known it. Her cell phone had rung, hidden somewhere in Peter's Brooklyn apartment. She and Peter had searched for it, lifting up cushions and rummaging in pockets, while it teased them with its disembodied tone. At last Peter had found it beneath a pile of magazines and tossed it to her. She had been breathless when she answered.

'Is this Elsa Beletti?' A slow, Oklahoman accent.

'Yes. Yes it is.'

'My name is Officer Fischer of the Oklahoma Police Department. Are you on your own, Elsa?'

'No. My boyfriend's with me.'

'Good. That's good.' And then a deep breath. 'Elsa, I am terribly sorry to have to tell you—'

She'd hung up and dropped the phone. After a second it had started ringing again, vibrating and turning around on its back. In the end Peter had answered and talked briefly with the officer, and then hung up and wrapped his arms tightly around Elsa.

Her dad had been found in the wreckage a tornado had made from his car – his lungs collapsed, his femurs shattered – a hundred miles west of the windswept little ranch on which he had raised his only child.

A jolt of turbulence and the seatbelt signs lit up. The plane was entangled in clouds. Elsa gazed out at the grey view. After a long while, it fissured open and she could see a line of ocean like a river at the bottom of a crevasse. Then the plane shot clear, and below it the wide sea shuffled its waves.

For some hours the world stayed unchanged. Then abruptly the sea crashed against a tawny coast. The land below was a devastated wild country, with drought-dried hills and pockmarked plains. A settlement passed beneath, its scattered buildings like half-buried bones. A tiny red vehicle crawled like a blood spider between one nowhere and the next. Then, for a while, there was only brown rock and brown soil.

She still had all the letters her dad had written her after he'd been kicked out. He'd stopped writing when he ended up in jail, and people said they found it difficult to comprehend how a man behind bars couldn't find the time to pen a few words to his only child. But Elsa understood him where others could not. She understood how his mind shut down indoors.

She'd seen it as a kid, when an afternoon storm had lifted the gutter off the ranch's barn, twirled it in the air like a baton, then flicked it at him. It broke his leg. Being holed up in the house while it healed made him catatonic. 'I'm weather-powered, see,' he mumbled once, and it was the best way to describe him. One blustering day he decided his broken leg had healed. He rose from his armchair and drove into the empty distance of the prairie. She remembered pressing her hands to her bedroom window to watch the dust trails rise up behind his departing truck. Then the wind scuffed them out. She could imagine him in whichever blasted patch of wilderness he had headed to, stepping out of the vehicle to turn his palms up to the sky, wind and rain prancing about him like dogs around their master.

Her dad had raised her to love the elements with a passion second only to his, but life in New York had weatherproofed her. Only at her dad's funeral, as the spring winds wiped her tears dry and carried his ashes away into the air, did it feel as if that passion had been uncovered again. It was her inheritance, but it had knocked a hole through her as if through a glass pane. All summer long she had been dealing with the cracks it had spread through the rest of her being.

A pylon came into hazy view below. Then another. Then more, running in a little row towards the dimming horizon. Then came lights all aglitter and white, avenues of the first trees she'd seen in many hours, a wide blue river, roads chock-a-block with cars. Then everything reverted to rocks, plains and hilly land that looked like a sandpit from this high up. Dusk came. The speakers crackled with an announcement from the captain: they were coming in to land.

The airport floors were mopped so clean that Elsa's spectral reflection walked with her, sole to sole across the tiles. Heading for work in New York, she used to catch her reflection in traffic windows or corner mirrors in subway stations. She would pretend she'd glimpsed another Elsa, living in a looking-glass world where life had not become unbearable. *Now,* she thought as her suitcases slid on to the luggage roundabout, *I'm one of them.* A new Elsa. For a minute she was paralyzed by delight. She squeezed the handles of her cases so hard she heard her knuckles pop.

By the time she reached the arrivals lounge, jet lag had set in. She stared at the row of bored cab drivers and wondered how on earth she'd find Mr Olivier. To her relief she saw a man holding a handwritten sign that bore her name. He'd left himself too little space to write it, so its last three letters were crushed together like a Roman numeral. He was a tall black man with a self-conscious stoop, wearing the same ghastly multicoloured jumper he'd worn in the photo he'd emailed her so that she would recognize him. His hair curled tightly against his scalp and was flecked with grey. When he saw her reading his sign he smiled with toothy satisfaction and proclaimed in a voice that sounded quiet, even though he raised it, 'Elsa Beletti? You're Elsa Beletti?'

'Mr Olivier?'

'Kenneth to you.'

Funny to think that she'd first 'met' this man two months back, when she was in an Internet café in Brooklyn, bright sunlight filling her computer screen and making it hard to read the word she'd typed into the search engine: *T-h-u-n-d-e-r-s-t-o-w-n.*

The computer returned a single match – an advert for a bed and breakfast. *I'm looking for somewhere to stay in Thunderstown,* she'd written in her email, *and I'm thinking of staying for quite some time.*

Mr Olivier had emailed her back within minutes. In the space of the following hour they'd exchanged nine or ten messages.

He described how he'd left St Lucia for Thunderstown in his late twenties, about the same age as she was now. He didn't ask her why, precisely, she desired to exchange New York for a backwater of backwaters, a forgotten and half-deserted place many miles from any other town. She returned the favour by not asking why he'd chosen it over the Caribbean. She fancied she understood his responses instinctively, and that he understood hers, and that his offer to turn bed and breakfast into more permanent lodgings would prove amenable to them both.

In the arrivals lounge he greeted her by clasping both his hands around her outstretched one. His palms were warm and cushioning. She could have closed her eyes, leaned against him and fallen asleep there and then.

'I'm here,' she said with tired relief.

'No,' he laughed. 'Not yet. There's still a long drive ahead of us.'

She nodded. Yes. Her mind was wilting.

Gently, he muscled her hands off her suitcases. He carried them as he led the way to a dark car park, eerily quiet compared to the concourse. Here he crammed himself in behind the wheel of a tiny car. Elsa climbed into the passenger seat and breathed deeply. The car smelled pleasantly of wool, and when she reclined her head against the seat she felt soft fleece covering it. 'Goat pelt,' he said with a smile. 'From Thunderstown.' She turned her cheek into it, and it was downy and gentle against her skin. He started up the car and drove them slowly away from the airport complex into the frenetic urban traffic and parades of street lamps, lights from bars, illuminated billboards. Then, slowly, they left these things behind them.

The steady passing of anonymous roads made her head loll. She opened her eyes. The dashboard clock told her that half an hour had passed. They were on a highway, a line of red tail lights snaking into the distance, catseyes and gliding white headlights in the opposite lanes. Kenneth hummed almost inaudibly. Elsa thought she recognized the song.

What felt like only a moment later she opened her eyes to find the clock had rubbed out another hour of the night, and the windscreen wipers were fighting rain bursting out of the darkness. The traffic had thinned. Another car sped up as it overtook them and vanished into the distance. She rested her head back into the fleece.

When she opened her eyes again the rain had stopped. Through a now-open window the night air flowed in, fresh-smelling. Ahead appeared the giant apparatus of a suspension bridge, with traffic darting across it and its enormous girders yawning. Left and right Elsa could see winding miles of broad river and lit-up boats bobbing on creased waves. A wind hummed over the car and struck the pillars of the bridge like a tuning fork. All around them the metal hummed. Her head drooped forwards.

She dreamed about being with Peter, before he did the thing that sent her over the edge and made her realize she had to leave New York. In her dream she listened while he made white noise on one of his electric guitars, back in his Brooklyn bedroom. She sensed all the tenements, all the nearby shops and offices and the distant skyscrapers of Manhattan packing in close around them. Every window of New York City straining to eavesdrop.

She opened her eyes. The traffic had vanished and Kenneth's was the only car on the road. The only visible part of the world was locked inside the yellow wedge of the headlights. The road had no boundaries, no walls or hedgerows, and the car rocking and bouncing over potholes and scatterings of slate kept her awake. A forever road, as if there were nothing more in the universe than car and broken tarmac. Then it turned a sudden bend and for a half-moment she could see a steep drop of scree, and sensed that they were at a great height.

The road straightened and the surface evened. Her head lolled.

She opened her eyes. The headlights shimmered across nests of boulders and trunks of stone on either side. No grass, only slates splitting under the weight of the car, each time with a noise like a handclap. Eyes closing, opening. The clock moved on in leaps, not ticks. Either side of the road were trees bent so close to the earth they were barely the height of the car, growing almost parallel to the shingly ground. A wind whistled higher than the engine noise.

'Awake again,' said Kenneth jovially. But she was asleep once more.

Awake again. The moon lonely in a starless sky. Swollen night clouds crowded around it. And beneath those the silhouettes of other giants.

'Mountains,' she whispered.

'Yes,' said Kenneth with reverence. 'Mountains.'

Even at this distance, and although they looked as flat as black paper, she had a sense of their bulk and grandeur. They lifted the horizon into the night sky. Each had its own shape: one curved as perfectly as an upturned bowl, one had a dented summit, and another a craggy legion of peaks like the outline of a crown.

She lost sight of them as the car turned down an anonymous track. The only signpost she had seen in these last few awakenings was a rusting frame with its board punched out, an empty direction to nowhere.

They had followed that signpost.

'One more hour to go,' Kenneth said.

Saying anything in reply took more effort than waking up a hundred times. She drifted off again.

When she came to, the car had stopped and Kenneth had turned off the headlights. 'What happened?' she asked, rubbing sleep dust from her eyes.

He pointed past her, out of the window. She turned and

straightened in her seat, suddenly wide awake. She could no longer see the mountains in the distance. Stars were brightly visible, but only in the zenith of the night. She could not see the mountains in the distance because now she was amongst them.

Through gaps in the clouds moonlight glistened like snowfall, brightening mountain peaks where it landed and illuminating their bald caps of notched rock. Elsa could feel the mountains' gravity in her skeleton, each of them pinching her bones in its direction. Yet they were not what Kenneth had parked to show her. Ahead of them the road descended dramatically into a deep bowl between the peaks, so steep that she felt they were hovering high in the sky.

At the bottom of that natural pit shone the lights of Thunderstown.

The first time she had seen those lights had been from a plane a few years back, a passenger aircraft like the one she'd disembarked from tonight. She'd been sitting beside Peter on a second-leg flight, en route to what would prove to be a crappy holiday. He and the other passengers had slept while she leaned her head against the window and watched the night-time world drift by beneath her. And then she'd seen Thunderstown.

Viewed from the black sky, the glowing dots of Thunderstown's lights formed the same pattern as a hurricane seen from space: a network of interlocked spirals glimmering through the dark. And at the heart of the town an unlit blot – an ominous void like the eye of a hurricane. Peter had despaired because on the first few days of their holiday she'd wanted to do nothing but research the route of their flight, until at last she came upon the town's name and repeated it over and over to herself like the password to a magic cave.

Kenneth restarted the engine and they began their descent. As they drew closer to the little town, the view slowly levelled, turning the glimmering spiral into an indistinct line of buildings and street lamps disappearing into the distance. Then the road bent around a towering boulder that jutted up from the earth. Its grey bulk hid the approaching town for a second, and the headlights opened up the jaw of the night.

There was something out there in the darkness. She saw it and let out a startled cry.

The lights picked out two animal eyes. Fur and teeth and a tail. Then whatever creature it all belonged to ducked out of the beam and was lost.

'It's okay,' said Kenneth.

'Was that a *wolf*?'

He laughed. 'Just a dog, I think.'

They cleared the boulder and the buildings drew close enough to make out individual windows and doors.

'Here we are,' said Kenneth. 'Home.' He spoke that word with deliberate heaviness. An invitation as much as a statement. Elsa had never been to Thunderstown, but – sitting bolt upright, wide awake now and stiff with anticipation – she did feel a sense of homecoming.

In the first street they entered many of the houses were boarded up. They were terraced slate cottages, with rotted doors and windows locked by hobnails. 'Nowadays there are more houses,' explained Kenneth, 'than there are people to live in them. We cannot keep them all in good order, especially when the bad weather comes. Nobody lives on this road any more. But don't worry, we're not all dead and buried in Thunderstown.'

The car bumped along the road's broken surface. The final tenements in the street weren't so derelict, yet there were still no lights inside. It was late at night, but these houses would not be coming to life at dawn. Their doors looked like they could no longer even be opened, shut as tightly as the doors of tombs.

In the next street the houses were taller but still seemed strangely cowed, as if they had been compressed under the weight of the sky. Their walls had been plastered and painted, and outside one front door a lantern fended off the shadows with a reassuring glow.

Beside the lantern hung a basket full of wild mountain flowers, winking orange and yellow like the lamplight. The shutters on the ground floor had been flung wide, and through the window Elsa saw a sitting room lit by a chandelier. A thin mother in a nightgown rocked a baby in her arms, and stroked its forehead. It was a welcome sight after all the decay. The mother looked up as the car drove by, as if it were the first motor vehicle in an age of mule-drawn carts.

They passed a bar, the Burning Wick, with outer walls of sooty slate and an interior panelled with caramel wood. A bare light bulb shone inside, but the bar had long since shut for the night and its stools were stacked on its tables. Nevertheless, in the doorway an old man in a raincoat remained, cradling a bottle of something wrapped in brown paper. He wore a leather rain cap, the broad brim of which flopped down at the sides like the ears of a spaniel. He stared up mournfully at Elsa as the car passed, and then the road turned and he vanished from view.

More houses followed, some of their slate fronts painted in muted colours that brought tentative life to the streets. Then the road curved into an enormous square lit by antique lamp posts, save in a few instances where their glass heads had shattered.

Suddenly Elsa gasped. At first she had missed the square's principal landmark. It loomed so large that her tired eyes must have skipped over it, mistaking it for an intrusion from a dream.

'The Church of Saint Erasmus,' whispered Kenneth, and slowed the car down. 'Patron saint of sailors, among all things.' He chuckled. He had a habit of closing his sentences with a chuckle instead of a full stop. Elsa wound open the window to poke out her head and look up, then up further.

It was gargantuan, disproportionate to the needs of the tiny town; a massif of stone to rival any cathedral. And it was entirely unlit. The night air around it looked displaced, as if evicted from its rightful position by the immense bulk of the building. She thought of the cathedrals of New York, and how at night their chiselled stone faces were celebrated by brilliant lamps. The Church of Saint Erasmus was lit by nothing. And she could tell, even in the gloom, that it would be a very different kind of spectacle if it were. Its awe was in its darker-than-nightness, its graceless silhouette, its sad blunt steeple hardly taller than the highest point of its roof, its broad sloping sides built for girth rather than height. More like a titanic pagan megalith than a Christian church.

They turned out of Saint Erasmus Square and drove along more streets of hunched terraces and town houses. She caught some of the names: Auger Lane, Drillbit Alley, Foreman's Avenue. 'There were mines here once,' explained Kenneth. 'In fact, the whole town is built on them.'

Then they turned into Prospect Street, a name she recognized. Here, at number thirty-eight, Kenneth parked the car and turned off the engine.

It was a four-storey house, crumbling but charming. Kenneth confessed that he spent most of his life in it watching cricket matches on television. He joked that cricket and lashings of rum were all he had cared to hold on to of his old life in St Lucia. The keys he gave her for her room were large and warm, like the hand he clasped around hers when he placed them in her palm. He let go slowly, giving her fingers a squeeze.

'You are here now,' he said in a formal voice, clearly aware of how momentous the occasion was for her. A kick of adrenaline perked her up. Yes, here she was. At the start of starting over.

She grinned and left Kenneth smiling after her from the bottom of the stairs, while she ascended to the uppermost floor. Kenneth had explained how he had converted this space into a one-bed apartment some years ago, when his fully grown son came to live here and wanted a place of his own. Here stood the door: a panel of rich, varnished wood like the lid of a treasure chest. She weighed the key in her hand: its head was the size of a medallion and satisfactorily heavy. She pushed it into the lock, pausing to enjoy the tarnished brass of the door handle and the flecks of rust on the hinges, then she reached out, pinched her finger and thumb around the head of the key, and began to twist.

The mechanism of the lock made a noise like a quarter dropped into a wishing well. She opened the door and listened to the hinges sing.

She closed her eyes and remembered all the beds she'd called her own down the years. The bed she'd had as a kid, on which she used to sit with her duvet piled over her, reading with a torch the cloud atlas her dad gave her; the bed in her college dorm that she'd shared with various bugs and boys; the bed in her New York studio, narrow as a pew; Peter's bed and its soft white sheets; stretches on sofas and floors.

She opened her eyes.

Beyond the door a dark stretch of hallway into which she walked so excitedly that she half-expected the air to crackle. She felt along the wall for the light switch and clicked it on.

The walls were papered grey, with a pattern that might once have been artful but was now as broken as aeroplane contrails. In places the wallpaper peeled up where it reached the skirting boards, which ran around a floor of bare wood. At the end of the hallway hung a full-length mirror in a silver frame, like something from a fairy story.

She left her cases in the hall under a row of coat pegs, took another deep breath and closed the door to shut herself in. On either side of the mirror were two closed doors and she walked down the hallway and opened the one on her left.

So this would be her latest bedroom. A high ceiling, a wide bed with grey sheets and an antique wooden wardrobe. Big enough to fill a whole wall, its doors had been engraved with spiralling patterns that threaded hypnotically around each other. In each outer corner of the door was carved a round-cheeked face, and it was from the puffing lips of these that the swirling patterns originated. She grinned, remembering her dad clowning around in her bedroom when she was very young, flapping his arms and huffing through his impression of the great north wind. She opened the wardrobe to the smell of wood polish and the jingle of dancing coat hangers. A bunch of dried flowers hung upside down from the rail within. She opened her suitcase to unpack her clothes, but immediately had no energy to do so. Unpacking could wait until the morning, although she did deposit the presents her mum had given her (still unwrapped and in their carrier bag) into the wardrobe, before firmly closing the door. She did not want her old life coming with her to Thunderstown, however well intentioned her mother had been.

Back through the hallway, the other door led to a sitting room with a kitchenette crammed into one corner. On a small table, Kenneth had filled a vase with fresh mountain flowers, their florets all buttery yellow. A wicker armchair by the window overlooked a courtyard lit by a lamp post. Beyond its far wall were more houses, and in the distance, a triangle of something darker than the rest of the night. She hoped that the morning would reveal it to be the low spire of Saint Erasmus.

She heard a faint tinkle outside the window and pushed open the glass.

A charm dangled lightly from a rusty nail wedged into the outside sill. She unhooked it and held it in her palm. A medley of trinkets, all bound by a dirty thread: silver-barked twigs; a pair of copper coins with their faces disguised by green patinas; a bent feather and something … Suddenly she jerked her head away and dropped the charm to the floor. A canine tooth, flecks of blood dried to its roots. She reached down and retrieved it. The tooth clinked against the coins.

She tossed the whole thing out of the window and watched it fall to the courtyard below, where the old twigs snapped on the flagstones.

She yawned and returned to her new bedroom. She permitted herself to test the mattress.

Within moments she was sound asleep.

In the cold dead of night a strange sound at her window awoke her. A snuffling like some wild creature. She rolled over. Probably nothing more than the sounds of an unfamiliar house. Probably just the weather making its night-time noises.

She put it out of her mind, and sleep dragged her back into her dreams.

# 2

# AN EXECUTION

Elsa woke to a bird chirruping on the window sill and a bedroom filled with sunlight. She blinked sleep away and yawned.

Then she remembered she was not in New York.

She propped herself up on her elbows. The clock on the wall had just struck half-past nine. She sank back on to the pillows and smiled. Finally. Finally she was a world away.

When she got out of bed she stood for a while at the window, taking a long look at her corner of Thunderstown. A morning haze made the street look like a faded photograph. A yellow film of sunlight masked every crumbled facade and dusty flagstone. She smiled, washed, dressed and discovered the groceries Kenneth had thoughtfully left in her otherwise empty kitchen. After a breakfast of muesli and an apple that crumbled as sweetly as fudge on her tongue, she ventured out, ready to explore her new home. The haze was lifting, although it still hid the sun in a radiant quarter of the sky. In the east, small clouds marred the blue of the atmosphere, and the warm day seemed powerless to polish them away.

The slopes of the rolling mountains that encompassed Thunderstown had been chewed back by centuries of biting wind, until their naked slate showed through. Where grass or scrub did grow, the late summer had roasted it golden. Dried-out soil had given way to rockslides that had exposed sheer tracts of black and brown earth.

Of these mountains, four imposed themselves on the town beneath, one at each cardinal point of the compass. The largest was a crumple-peaked summit in the east. During her email exchanges with Kenneth, she had excitedly posed every question she could think of about Thunderstown, and he had told her that this massive mountain was named Drum Head. It was particularly dominating due to the way the sun caught its slopes: light threw its rocky sides into a relief like the man in the moon, so that on bright days it wore a gentle and stupefied expression made from untold tonnes of rock.

Opposite Drum Head, in the west, Old Colp climbed in a steep curve like the arched back of a cat. Its slopes were dense with a species of mottled heather that the locals called tatterfur. In the north, Old Colp's foothills gave way to the ragged lower ranges of the Devil's Diadem, a mountain with no single peak but a cluster, the points of which jabbed upwards like the teeth of a mantrap. Kenneth had said that two centuries back the Devil's Diadem had been called Holy Mountain, but he had long since forgotten the story of its rechristening. There were too many legends in Thunderstown, he had said, for anybody to remember them all.

The southern mountain was more discreet. A haze shrouded it like smoke around a bonfire. This was the Merrow Wold, piled up with so many boulders and so much stony rubble that it resembled not so much a mountain but the largest cairn ever erected. Goats had made it that way, gnashing at the soil and plant life until the earth shrugged up no more flowers and shoots, only pebbles and slates. The Merrow Wold was the most barren of all the mountains and the hardest to climb; its ground slipped and crunched underfoot like the shingle of a beach.

These four were each too giant to ever be ignored by the little town they cupped between them. Their scale made Elsa feel so slight as she wandered the flowing roads with no fixed destination, letting their tributary alleyways and shadowed passages carry her. She felt at once enclosed, as if in a maze, and exposed, as if on the plains of her childhood. A narrow street would course along between the tall walls of houses, around a tight bend, narrow and narrow further, then terminate in a dead end. Just when she'd begin to think she might wander this labyrinth forever, a sharp turn or a run of steep steps would eject her and she would be released into a brilliantly lit courtyard, wildflowers bursting up between its flagstones. But wherever she found herself, one of the four mountains would always preside.

There were more residents in Thunderstown than first met the eye, but they were furtive, like pill bugs found under a lifted slab. They were absorbed in themselves, always in a hurry to be elsewhere. She couldn't comprehend their dress code: even in this late-summer warmth the women wore shawls and the men raincoats and broad-brimmed leather caps, as if such garments were the vestments of a religious order.

The wind stalked Elsa through the town, brushing over her face and bare arms before dying away and leaving the air still. Otherwise it danced at crossroads and raised miniature whirlwinds out of the dust of poky courtyards, so that it did not feel like one wind but many, each wrestling to claim its own space and territory. At a stall where a butcher sold dried meats, the wind played the part of his assistant, brushing the purpling flesh of his meats free of flies. In another place the wind helped a woman hang out her laundry, unfurling the smocks and breeches she took from her basket to hang on the line.

In one of his emails, Kenneth had potted as best he could the town's history. He had told her of a devastating flood that once ransacked these buildings. In the dry Thunderstown streets it was difficult to imagine water bucking and roaring between the houses, but Kenneth said that great fathoms of old floodwater still lurked deep and dormant beneath the lanes and alleyways, filling old tunnels where once miners had toiled. Elsa pictured this undertow as she explored, pretending it determined her course, and in doing so she made a discovery: all of the town's roads led back to the Church of Saint Erasmus. She had to tread with determination to avoid circling back there. Streets that first appeared to bypass the church turned a corner at the last minute and offered her up to it.

Another fact remembered from her email education was that, not so long ago, an excavation in Saint Erasmus's vaults had unearthed evidence of older buildings on the site, thought to be long-lost temples to long-forgotten deities. When next her route returned her to the church, she had the spine-tingling sensation that the distant past remained close in this place. She stared up at the bluntly steepled belfry and its crucifix dark as two crossed sticks of charcoal. It was the centrepiece of an array of metalwork adorning Thunderstown's rooftops. Weathervanes in their hundreds glinted from the ridges, some depicting bestial figures, some depicting human faces with lips pursed to blow forth a breeze. Winds skipped nimbly from eave to eave, tinkering with the weathervanes as they went, like engineers toying with the dials of a complex machine.

She began to walk around the edge of the church. Then, up ahead against one of its walls, she saw a small crowd of people, all raincoats and shawls, making quite a hubbub. When she reached them, one or two heads turned to regard her, but the thing they were crowded around seemed more pressing. People murmured to each other in low, serious voices. 'Hold my hand,' asked someone of their partner. 'I can't bear it,' confessed someone else. 'Whenever will Daniel be here?' 'Yes, where's Daniel?' Elsa budged into the throng to see what the fuss was all about. A creature cowered against the blackened church wall. A dog, growling uncertainly, frightened by the townsfolk who had backed it up against the stone. Elsa couldn't tell the breed, but it was something akin to an Irish wolfhound: tall and of elegant limb, with a tousle-haired coat and silver whiskers. Its snout and ears were fox-like and she was surprised by the coincidence of its eyes, which were blue and brown-grey, just like today's sky and indefinite clouds.

The beast wore no collar, and judging by the dried dirt in its fur, Elsa guessed it was either a stray or wild. It did not seem to pose any threat, yet when it moved even a fraction towards the crowd, a man swished his walking cane so violently that it whimpered back against the masonry.

A sigh of relief rippled through the crowd and the people parted for a tall man in a broad-brimmed rain cap to pass. He had a black beard, dark eyes and a Roman nose. He carried his large frame with an authority affirmed by the gathered townsfolk, who all relaxed upon his arrival. His coarse beard began at his cheekbones and hung in black straggles down to his nape. In addition to his rain cap, which he removed as he approached the dog, he wore scuffed britches, high leather boots and a brown chequered shirt with the sleeves rolled up, showing off his brawny forearms.

The dog stopped very still upon seeing him, as if in recognition. The man crouched down so that his head was level with the dog's, whisker to whisker. He stared for a while into its peculiar eyes, then began to make a deep rumbling noise in his throat like the sound of a distant rockslide. The dog seemed relieved, bowed its head and then pushed it forwards, nuzzling it against the man's chest. The man's arms came up gently to hold the dog, one hand stroking along the flat space between its ears, the other itching the soft fur hanging from its throat.

Then his grip turned a right angle and the dog's neck snapped with a click.

The crowd took a step back, leaving Elsa foregrounded and shocked. The man stood up, punched his hat back into shape and squashed it on to his head. He crossed himself. The crowd followed suit, then gave him a brief ripple of applause while the dog's corpse flopped on the flagstones.

It lay there staring hollowly up at Elsa while she stared back in horror and disbelief. Then, as she tried to comprehend what she had just seen, a strange thing happened. Its blue eyes darkened. Its irises changed colour like paper blistering in a fire. In seconds they had charred from sky blue to singed black. A sudden breeze passed over and she shivered from confusion and fright all at once.

One or two of the crowd thanked the bearded man or clapped him on the shoulder. Then they disbanded with satisfied chatter, as if exiting a theatre.

The tall man crouched over the dead body, lifted it off the dusty floor by its ears, then hefted the carcass over his shoulder and stood up. The last of the crowd had dispersed. Elsa was alone with him, uneasy but indignant. It was the first time she had seen someone murder an animal for no reason. The man turned towards her quizzically, dog draped around his neck.

'Ma'am,' he said, and ducked his head in a half-bow.

'What ... why ...' she began. 'What did you just *do*?'

'It was wild, ma'am,' he said, as if it were self-explanatory. He tried to step around her, but she sidestepped to block him.

'You should have taken it out of town or to a kennel ... or ... or *something!*'

He frowned. He seemed to her more like something blasted from rock than something that could grow up from a child. She stood her ground nevertheless.

'You are distressed by this?' He sounded confused.

She nodded as if he were stupid, but his voice was gentler than she'd expected and he seemed to be giving serious if bemused thought to her position, all the while with the corpse lolling over his shoulders and the dog's changed eyes upturned in their sockets.

'It was wild,' he pronounced again.

'It's –' she flapped her hands, '– it was a living thing!'

He frowned, like he was preparing to disagree, but instead he said, 'You are not from Thunderstown? I would know you and your family if you were. But it is a pleasure to see a new face here.'

She clenched her fists. 'Where I'm from has nothing to do with it.'

The dog's drooping tongue and dangling legs were becoming too much, as was the man's thoughtful face amongst all that dead fur.

'My name is Daniel Fossiter,' he said softly, 'and I am pleased to meet you.'

'Elsa,' she snapped, then felt all the more infuriated for becoming even this familiar with this cruel man.

'I should explain, Elsa, about this particular species of—'

She raised her palm to him, defiantly. It was a gesture she hadn't made since high school, where it meant she didn't want to hear what he had to say, but in the wide church square Daniel Fossiter only looked intently at her palm as if he were reading it. Embarrassed, she cringed away as fast as she could. Only at the end of the road did she look back, to see him watching her patiently, the dog still slung over his shoulders as if it weighed no more than the air itself.

By the time she returned to Kenneth's house she still hadn't recovered her cool. The stairs to her apartment passed the door to his sitting room, which he had left open as he loafed on the sofa, watching a cricket match. He had pulled the curtains closed to keep the sun's glare from the television screen, but the light was too strong and brightened the room regardless, projecting the fabric's peach hue on to every surface.

Kenneth had kept the furnishings simple: a plain bookcase full of yellow-spined almanacs and a cushioned footstool in front of his deep two-seater sofa. The empty seat of that sofa was as smooth as new, but when he stood to greet her, a depression remained where he'd been sitting, imprinted by years of cricket-watching. Elsa might have thought him lazy, had not one final detail of the room given her a hint of an explanation. On top of the television was a framed photograph of a young black man, probably the same age as Elsa, wearing an orange t-shirt and jeans. He had been snapped in the middle of a fit of laughter. His hands were plastered all over with clay, a large quantity of which appeared to have just that moment exploded across his body.

'He was a potter,' said Kenneth, noticing Elsa's attention to the photo. 'Michael. My wonderful son.'

Before Elsa could say anything he frowned and tugged open a curtain. The sunlight, which had seemed so powerful projecting through the curtains, turned coy through the glass, making only the window sill lambent. Then, as clouds moved across the sun, the room became darker than it had been before.

'You look mighty unhappy, Elsa.'

She told him about the dog.

He listened with the comforting expression of a counsellor, which made his response all the more surprising. 'Elsa, I don't want to upset you further, but you must understand. It is good that the dog was killed. Such dogs bring foul luck to the town.'

'*Foul luck*? It was just a dog! A beautiful dog with blue eyes!'

'Ahh, yes.' Kenneth chuckled awkwardly. 'The eyes, you see, are the giveaway. Find one of those wild dogs at sunset and its eyes will be pink or red.'

Elsa remembered the way the blue had charred out of them upon death. It made her shiver and fold her arms.

'Tell me, Elsa. The man who killed it, was he tall? With a black beard?'

'Yeah, that was him. Daniel something-or-other.'

'Daniel Fossiter. That man is very well respected in Thunderstown. His family have been cullers as far back as anyone can remember. It would be wise to remain in his good books.'

'Cullers?'

'Mostly he kills mountain goats. He keeps the population in check to stop them destroying the plants or wandering down into town. Believe me, they will eat anything they can lay their teeth on. But his role is also a ceremonial one. Daniel is expected to kill other ...' he faltered, '*creatures*, too.'

She pictured Daniel Fossiter again. There had been an air of power about him that felt animalistic. Like a lion in the wilderness. Not wicked like a human being could be, but menacing by nature nevertheless. 'I didn't like him.'

'To tell you the truth, Elsa, I must admit that I too am sometimes uneasy around him.'

'Yeah. Exactly. Uneasy.'

She went upstairs to her apartment and sat in the wicker chair looking out across the rooftops. The clouds were all oblong lumps, nothing more than blockages to the daylight. She had liked Thunderstown better before she had encountered Daniel Fossiter in it and she wished she had not chanced upon him. She could use a day without uneasiness.

There had been no such day all summer. After her dad's funeral she had felt like she was a vase full of hairline fractures, straining to contain water. Then, one day, a month ago now, the pressure finally became too much to bear. One final crack had branched through her and she had shattered into a thousand pieces.

Peter had done it. Lord knows he was probably still searching his soul over it, for she had not been able to explain to him that she had been breaking for a long time and this was just the tipping point. She hoped he would get over it quickly. He deserved that much.

His idea had been a long weekend outside of the city. 'Let's take a tent and head out west. A breath of fresh air might do you good.' He'd organized everything, and when they made their camp late on a sunny afternoon in a woodland glade in Pennsylvania she thought yes, this is precisely the good I need. Resting her head on his shoulder, watching the flames play among the cindered logs of the fire they had built, she took deep breaths of the timber smoke and felt the luxurious heat of the late lazy sun, the quick heat from the flames and the inner heat she'd absorbed from the bottle of red wine they'd shared as they set the logs to burning. Peter opened another bottle, freed the cork with a whoop and filled her glass. The leaves swayed, feather-light. Two squirrels whirled from trunk to trunk. A bird whistled as it flapped through the glade. And then he did the thing that broke her.

'Elsa,' he said, as he reached into the pocket of his jeans. He pulled his fist out, clenched around something. He opened his hand and a ring lay there in his palm.

'Elsa … will you marry me?'

She stared at that small golden loop. Its diamond eye stared back. Her eyes followed the band's circumference, round and round and round. When she picked it up the world seemed suddenly very heavy. Leaves and blades of grass lay flattened, weighty as ornaments. She looked through the ring as if it were a spyglass and saw the woods leaning in, the twigs scratching, the bird leering beady-eyed from a bent branch. Her stomach lurched. The world changed, realigning like a dial.

'Elsa?'

She dropped the ring back into Peter's palm and choked back a sudden barrage of tears.

His eyebrows knotted. 'Elsa … Elsa, I love you.'

She wept. When they had first started dating they had agreed with cool cynicism that love was just chemical flushes and electrical signals flowing through the brain, something tacky that belonged in souvenir shops. 'Love,' she had declared once to Peter, 'is just the heart on an I Heart NYC baseball cap.' And he had agreed with her.

Yet here and now he was deadly serious about it, down on his knees and looking up at her.

And she did not love him, even if she cared for him deeply, and she did not know whether she even believed in love, and she had lost her father, and she wanted to go like he had, up with the tornado to see him in whichever place he had left the earth for, and she could not explain that to Peter and could not explain why she was falling apart like this, and she did not know anything about herself any more.

# 3

# CLOUD ON THE MOUNTAIN

The next morning, in the scorched front yard, Elsa found Kenneth Olivier hard at work digging out weeds with a trowel. He stood up straight when he saw her, dusting the bleached soil from his fingertips.

'Off exploring again?'

She nodded. She had her sunglasses and a thick layer of sunscreen on, as well as a water bottle in a bag hanging against her hip. 'I'm going up to the mountains.'

He looked reflective. 'Which one?'

She paused, then pointed. 'That one.' Three of the four peaks were visible from here. The fourth, the Merrow Wold, was hidden behind a low cloud in the south. The rest of the sky remained an unbroken blue, but that cloud above the Merrow Wold was bleached like ash. In the north the broken pinnacles of the Devil's Diadem glimmered in the sunlight, while to the east the face of Drum Head was slowly emerging. Elsa, however, pointed to the western mountain, the hump-backed rise with slopes as dark as soot.

'Old Colp,' said Kenneth.

'Yeah, that's the one. On your map it says there's a viewpoint. Near to a windmill, if my map-reading's any good.'

'Hmm. That windmill's not there any more. The wind it was milling saw to that.' He chuckled uneasily. 'Be careful up there. These mountains are full of old mine entrances. Some of them are only half-sealed.'

'Don't worry. I might look like a city girl, but I grew up in a spot even more remote than this.'

He nodded, although she could tell she hadn't convinced him. He looked embarrassed. 'I beg your pardon, Elsa, I'm just an old man, fretting. I've been fretting a lot ever since Michael went away.'

She put a finger to her lips. 'Don't worry about it.' She moved towards the street then paused. 'Where did he go? Your son, Michael?'

He smiled. It was an awkward, unhappy smile. 'I wish I knew the answer to that question. All I know is he went out for a walk in the mountains.' He cleared his throat. 'There is a bit of local folklore about how these mountains come to be here. It is said that, long ago, four storms became weary from whipping and raging through the air. So they came to settle on the earth, right here, to rest for a while. They soon fell asleep, and while they slept they began to crust over and calcify. By the time they awoke, the four storms of the sky were rock, welded solid to the ground. It's a superstitious way of explaining that there are places up in the mountains that aren't as stable as they look. Places, as the story would have it, that have kept something of their stormy origins. We found Michael's clothes folded on the bank of a mountain lake. That was the last we knew of him. We dived and dived to try to find his body, but he had just … vanished.' He sighed and rubbed his brow. 'I am sorry, Elsa. Now I have made it tough for you to go up there. But you must because you want to and the views are magnificent. And you will be perfectly safe, of course.'

'Sorry,' she said, 'to hear all of that.' She had hoped to offer more sympathy, but no sooner did she think about her own loss than a lump filled her throat.

Kenneth chuckled sadly and retrieved his trowel. 'Thank you. Now you enjoy your walk, and don't worry about any of these things.'

The lower reaches of Old Colp were covered in tussocks of grey grass or knotted heather in coarse carpets. Blossoms flowered in the tangle, and Elsa assumed they must be poisonous because the mountain goats had left them alone.

Halfway up the foothills she stopped to admire the view of the town below. The sun found the metal of the manifold weathervanes and lit them up like a bay of prayer candles. Still the windows of the Church of Saint Erasmus remained indomitably dark. The sky had sullied, thanks to the dusty cloud she had seen earlier above the Merrow Wold, which had now smeared itself northwards across the heavens.

Further uphill, the path led around a shoulder of the mountain that obscured the town. All signs of civilization were erased. Dark slates sat up like rabbits between the parched grasses and occasional contorted tree. Several times she glimpsed real hares, or rodents she didn't quite recognize, hopping after shady burrows. Then later she saw her first Thunderstown goat, a stony white creature with horns that doubled its height, peering down at her from a natural turret of boulders. It brayed as she passed, and the noise was like the echoes of long-gone landslides.

From this height she could see the rest of the mountain range, running in a jutting line of yellow and brown like an animal jawbone still full of sharp teeth. Caught between some of those peaks were twists of grey and white cloud, and when at one point she passed along a valley top, she saw a puff of mist climbing the far slopes, as sprightly as one of the goats.

When she came to the windmill it was indeed ruined. A piebald cylinder of bleached plaster and blackened stone, prized open in places by the weather. Between the path and the ruin stretched a meadow of springy brown grass, across which it looked as if a storm had blown apart the mill as if with dynamite. Some thirty feet from the main structure a broken-off sail arm had been fastened to the ground by the grass. A layer of something covered it, as dried out and leathery as a gourd. The stained canvas of the sail itself stuck hard and dark to the frame.

As a viewpoint it was everything she'd hoped it would be, offering an unparalleled panorama of Thunderstown and the surrounding mountains. They leaned in above the roofs below like card players around a table. She inhaled, and the air going into her was so clarified compared to that of the city that she burst out laughing. What relief, that her plan had come good like this. Not since she first moved to New York had a change of place so delighted her. Back then she had felt drunk at the sheer sight of Manhattan, its chaos and its possibility. This time she had feared that relocating was what her mum had warned it was: escapism. She had never been good at knowing the difference between running away and running forwards and she reckoned that with her they were probably one and the same thing. When faced with any challenge or fear she knew only to run, and only in retrospect could she tell whether she had charged in headlong or fled for her life. She wondered if this was what her dad had really meant when he described himself as weather-powered. To be in constant upheaval. Finally, she turned away from the view to investigate the ruin. An assortment of cogs and ratchets poked out of its snapped top, growing red dreadlocks of rust. She walked its circumference and found, covered in mosses that brushed loose with the lightest motion, a door so small it came up only to her breastbone. She tried the handle, assuming it would be locked, but it budged an inch before wedging against its own frame. Age and water had bent it out of shape, but she shoved it hard and it lurched open.

She ducked through the door and forced it closed behind her, its woodwork groaning as she did so. Inside the ruin it was cool, and beautifully lit by beams of sunlight bouncing between the rusted gears and splintered timbers above her. It felt like entering a shipwreck. Brighter light shone in thin shafts through chinks in the wall, drawing glowing threads in the air. Knobs of fungus protruded from bricks and beams, steeped in the orange pigment of the rust that fed them.

She stood there enjoying the noise of the fluting breeze in the decrepit mechanisms above her. She soaked up the atmosphere. She lost track of time.

Then she heard a voice.

When she got over her surprise, she tiptoed to the wall and peeked out through one of the chinks in the masonry.

A man was standing there on the grass, taking in the view of Thunderstown.

The first striking thing about him was that he was there at all. The second was that he was not only bald but entirely hairless. He had a bony, wary face without any eyebrows, eyelashes or any indication of stubble. Despite this lack of hair he still looked young, and she guessed he was several years her junior, probably twenty-three or twenty-four. He stood firmly over six feet tall and was broadly built, but his size came from neither muscle nor fat. She had the impression that his body was more like that of a sea lion, as if it were a design from a different habitat in which, if it were to return there, its shapelessness would be its grace.

He wore a shirt with the cuffs rolled up, jeans worn through at the knees and a pair of shoes so battered that his toes poked out through open lips. She had no idea how long he'd been standing there. He was all alone and talking to himself. 'I wonder what would happen to me,' he said, 'if I just let go?'

His voice was slow and nasal and deep. He looked at the windmill for a second and she caught a full view of his face and drew back from her spyhole. His eyes were close together, deep and dark. His nose was smooth and straight like a piece of folded paper. She hoped he couldn't see her through the tiny crack in the wall.

He began to pace around on the grass, moving with light grace despite his size. He stopped for a moment to gaze down at the town made miniature beneath the mountain and as he did so he looked forlorn, as if he were marooned on a desert island and staring out to sea. 'There's only one way,' he said, 'to find out.'

He took a deep steadying breath and ran his hands back over his bald scalp. He bent his back and stared up at the sky. His evident distress made Elsa feel guilty about spying. She wondered if she could sneak out of the mill and away down the mountain path, so as to allow him the privacy he must surely have come up here to find.

Then the man began to undress. Elsa looked away out of instinctive politeness, but after a moment looked back.

He disrobed methodically. With light fingers he unbuttoned his shirt and tossed it to the grass. He tugged undone the buckle of his belt, then the zipper of his fly, then kicked off his trousers. He pulled down and stepped out of his underwear.

His body was as smooth as a weathered pebble on the sea shore. He had very little complexion: he was not so much a white man as a grey one. He had a flat pair of buttocks and skin as hairless as that of his head.

He stood on the ridge between her viewpoint and the sun. His tall body was an eclipse and the light was a corona behind it. He spread his arms to strike a pose of dejected surrender.

Then, very gradually, he began to dissolve.

Like chalk washed into a blur by the rain, his outline began to distort, and almost imperceptibly he lost his form. One minute he was a man and the next he was a blurry grey silhouette. His skin became a coat of mist. The sun shining from behind him lit him up and edged him with its brilliance, wherein he stopped looking man-shaped and instead resembled a cloud formed by chance into the posture of a human being.

He broke up. His head caved in, becoming nothing more than a dented sphere of fog. His chest tore apart and the blue sky and bright sun shone through the place where his heart should have been. He disintegrated, every second less like a man and more like a cloud.

She yelled wordlessly. She fought the windmill door for a panicked, precious second, then rushed out across the meadow. She slowed to a halt only a few paces from the cloud. She had no idea what she was doing; she was only aware of her heart pounding in her ears.

'Please wait,' she whispered.

The cloud flickered with light. She jumped backwards in alarm. A fine filigree of electricity shivered through the vapour. For a second she thought it made up the shapes of arteries, the network of a person's veins. Then in a shimmer the lightning was gone.

She reached up to her cheek because something cool and moist had touched it.

Rain. It was scattering out of the cloud in a drizzle.

In her bewilderment she had forgotten to breathe. She gulped for air and in doing so let out a pent-up cry.

Then the cloud began to contract. It puckered backwards into shape. Its ragged outline either dispersed in the air or else smoothed down into flesh, covering once again a frame of arms and legs. It rebuilt the man she had spied on, and when he returned into definition he coughed and screwed up his eyes. He teetered off balance before doubling up to spew crystal-clear water on to the grass.

He whimpered, and she could tell that for the first time he was aware of her presence, and consequentially, that he was entirely naked in it. After a moment – she was still shocked – she remembered enough formality to look away while he retrieved his clothes. She heard his drenched jeans squelching on.

She turned back to him as he buttoned up his shirt. 'Um ...' she began, but had no idea what to say. 'Um, what ...' Her heart was thumping. 'What just happened?'

He didn't reply. He looked as if he didn't know how to.

'What, I mean ... oh my God, are you all right?'

He nodded. He licked his lips. His irises were grey, and tinged with the same moody purple as a thundercloud. 'I can't explain.'

She gaped at him. She felt like she deserved an explanation. A raindrop dangled on his chin. Two more hung from his earlobes. 'Tell me,' she said, 'that I'm not going mad.'

He looked down awkwardly at the grass, the leaves of which balanced so many caught raindrops that it looked as if a diamond necklace had broken there. 'I can't tell you anything,' he muttered.

'But ... but ... I saw you ...'

'I let go. There, now you know. I let go. Then I heard you calling to me and that made me come back.'

The drip on his chin fell free and dashed off the broken lip of one of his shoes. In the distance of the sky behind him, a flake of cloud was blowing north, towards the saw-toothed heights of the Devil's Diadem. *A moment ago,* she thought, *you were a cloud just like that.*

'I don't understand,' she said.

He bit his lip. 'I'm not sure we should be having this conversation. You shouldn't be talking to me. We should be frightened of each other.'

She pressed her hands over her worried heart. 'I *am* frightened!'

He deflated. Now he sounded crestfallen. 'Really? For a moment I thought that you weren't. I'm sorry I frightened you. Am I really frightening?'

She felt dizzy and had to sit down and stare at the grass, where a little golden ant was nibbling through a leaf. She felt as if, in that instant, the world had grown as limitless as it must appear to an insect. 'I'm going crazy, aren't I?'

'No. I explained. I let go.' He waited for a moment, and then he began to fidget. When he spoke again he sounded alarmed. 'Please don't tell anyone in Thunderstown that you've met me.'

She rubbed her eyes. 'It was as if I saw you turn into a cloud.'

'Yes. Yes, that's exactly what you did see. And you have to promise never to tell a soul.'

'I don't think anybody would believe me.'

'They might. In Thunderstown, they might. And they might try to get me.' Again he became worried. 'I should go now.' He hesitated, then began to walk away from her.

'Wait!'

He looked back.

She stood up. 'You can't just *go*. Not after that!'

He looked at her sadly, opened his mouth as if he wanted to say something else, then turned and kept on walking across the meadow.

'Hey! Wait! Hey!' She stomped after him. 'What am I supposed to do now?'

'Just … leave me alone, okay? Pretend you never met me. Go back to doing, I don't know, whatever you were doing up here in the first place.'

She stood there, stupefied in the sunlight, watching him walk downhill towards a stretch of the mountain full of furrows and knotted boulders. Three times, lately, life had so surprised her that she felt as if the planet itself had stopped spinning. First the news of her dad's death, then Peter's unexpected proposal, then – perhaps strangest of all – a startled minute during which she had watched a man become a cloud.

When, at the bottom of the meadow, the bald man reached the place where the path veered out of sight, he paused for a second and looked back at her over his shoulder. Then he vanished around a stack of boulders.

No sooner had he gone than she felt the urge to run, although she didn't know whether she should bolt for the safety of Kenneth's house or chase the man to get some answers. For a long minute she stood on the spot, held perfectly taut by two opposing forces. But she did not want to wonder about him forever. She set off in pursuit, the soft ground putting a spring into each pace. Past the boulders the path dropped into a gully, in which there were a great many squares and triangles of slate, but no sign of the man. Then she spotted a wet blot on one of the stones, then another, and since the sky was bare she reasoned that these must have come from his soaked clothes. She followed their direction until their clues dried up, then pressed on until she came out on to smoother slopes that were scattered with lonely trees and heads of rock. Here she stopped with her hands on her hips, surveying the mountain for some sign of him.

As she paused she saw a little house built from uneven stacks of slate and tiles, camouflaged by the shadow of a gnarly old bluff it backed up against. It was a bothy, a tiny bungalow, with just one door and one window, a wilderness shelter similar to the ones she had seen in the Ouchita Mountains, which provided mountaineers and rangers with emergency reprieve from the weather.

She approached it cautiously, for she felt sure the man would be inside. Its walls were plugged up with warty grey lichens, except for in one corner which was furred with a moss as orange as a mango. It had a stubby chimney bearing the most delicate weathervane she had seen since arriving in Thunderstown: a fox or wolf with paws stretched out mid-leap and snout raised to scent the wind. Above it the vane branched out into art nouveau curves that drew, in iron, the shape of a cloud.

She knocked on the door but got no reply, so tried the handle and found it to be locked. She thumped the wood with the flat of her palm. 'Hey!' she yelled. ' Can we talk some more?'

No answer, so she went to the window and peered in.

Someone had clearly been living there, although right now she could see nobody inside. Instead there was a table with a plate on it, and on the plate was the core of a pear, brown but not yet rotten. There were two chairs, and most remarkably given her initial assumption that this was a shelter and not a home, there were mobiles hanging from the ceiling. She twisted her head to try to get a clear view. The ceiling was thick with them. Dangling configurations of wire hung with white paper birds.

'Hey!' she yelled again, tapping on the glass. For a moment she considered breaking it, and turned around to locate a stone, but then a cold wind blew past her and she thought she heard a bark. She looked back up the mountain and saw a silver-furred animal slinking over a heap of rocks in the near distance. It vanished into a ditch before she could get a good view of it, and it did not re-emerge. Still, it had made her feel uncomfortable, and she chewed her thumbnail.

Then, because it was the only way to feel safer, she turned and picked her way back towards Thunderstown.

# 4

# A HISTORY OF CULLERS

It had been many days since Daniel Fossiter had last seen Finn Munro, the strange and weather-filled young man whom he protected in secret. Daniel had been to the bothy on Old Colp once or twice in that time, but had found the stone shelter to be empty. Probably Finn was out wandering the mountains, or lurking in one of his many dens in the foothills, and Daniel had been relieved not to have had to endure one more awkward encounter with him.

He trudged now down the path from the dusty Merrow Wold, with a dead goat slung over his broad shoulders. He had shot fifteen that morning, before the winds started digging at the shingly soil and clawing up swathes of dust that trapped him for hours in their powdery fog. By the time he had picked his way clear the best of the afternoon was behind him, but he was untroubled. It excused him from looking in on Finn for one more day. Because it was tough, just being around him. He and Finn were two leftover corners of a triangle that could no longer be drawn.

Eight years had passed since Finn's mother left Thunderstown, during which time Finn's voice had deepened and he had grown taller even than Daniel. Yet being a man was about more than gender and age. That was something Daniel's father and grandfather had always been at pains to remind him of.

He sighed and adjusted the weight of the goat on his shoulders.

The gravelly earth of the Merrow Wold crunched under his boots. Every step required his concentration, for centuries of ravenous goats had turned this soil into a slide of rubble. People had fallen to their deaths on the gentle inclines; all it took was one slip, and they would find themselves skidding and rolling down a mountainside that offered no friction or solid space to arrest their fall. They would be scraped and grated apart by pebbles.

'Betty,' he whispered. It did not lessen, his ache for her, even after those eight years. His grandfather would have mocked him for it. His father would have turned away in resigned disappointment.

On the morning she left Thunderstown, Betty had appeared at his door and asked him to look after Finn. 'Take care of him for me,' she'd said. 'You're the only one I trust to do it. And anyway, I'll be back soon.' As if there were any chance he might forget her, she sealed the request with a kiss to his lips. Often he lay awake at night remembering that kiss, the lightness of her skin, the smell of her lipstick, the tension in the muscles of her neck as she went up on tiptoes to reach him. Sometimes it seemed that the only thing in the world worth holding on to was the memory of that kiss.

Anything anyone could call 'soon' had long since passed. Eight years with no sight or sound was not 'soon'. All the same, he could not be angry, for to be angry with her he would have to conclude that she had deliberately not written or called, and he could not bear the thought that she might have discarded him so casually. Then again, he could not bear the alternative, which was that something had befallen her to prevent her from making contact, and so he did his best to skirt around such speculation. All he could allow himself was this simple, painful, longing for her return.

He plodded downhill, soles crunching on the loose earth. If you found a handful of grass up here you were lucky, and if you pulled that grass even lightly it would uproot, so thin was the Merrow Wold's dirt. The stink of goat droppings and fur were ever present in the dry air, but hard evidence of the culprits who had ruined the landscape was hard to come by. On the other mountains it was easy to spot signs of them: hoof prints pressed into baked mud or the naked blonde trunk of a tree they had stripped of bark. Here there was neither mud nor trunks. In making the Merrow Wold barren, the goats had made themselves nigh on impossible to track.

His grandfather had believed that on the fifth day the Lord had created every animal on land except for the goat. This he left to the devil, who made them in his greedy image. Upon seeing how they gobbled up the apple trees of Eden, the Lord gave them tails like knotted ropes, and these caught and snared the goats in the undergrowth. The devil was outraged, but the goats were relieved – the Lord had spared them from temptation, and for this they were grateful. This the devil could not bear. He bit off their long tails and licked out their eyes and he feasted upon them, and when he had eaten his fill he replaced their eyes with his own, so that they would never know the difference between restraint and indulgence.

More often than once, Daniel's father, the Reverend Fossiter, had told that story from the pulpit of the Church of Saint Erasmus. Should any of the congregation have needed further proof of the tale's wisdom, they needed to look no further than the way the goats' long teeth tortured the trees. Putting up shoots was an ordeal in the face of the weather that befell these mountains. Even the sun could be the enemy of leaves in need of water. Trees that survived up here bent their trunks close to the soil. Branches grew thrust out like arms in a plea for mercy. A hard enough life, then, without the goats who came to chew away what protective bark they could grow. Daniel had taken it upon himself to guard the saplings whenever he came upon them, erecting fences of ringed razor wire. Still the goats would come. He would find the razor wire red with blood where the animals had chewed it, ignoring the pain it caused them.

Once he found an old nanny dead with her jaws clenched around the blades of the fence, her beard a brownish red from the blood that had flowed from her mangled tongue. And under the shade of the tree slept her plump little kid, who had scrambled on to her rump and used her neck as a ladder to clear the fence and chew so deeply on the sapling that it hung like a snapped straw. A kid like that did not deserve to die quick with a bullet between its eyes. It deserved to suffer with a bleeding belly, to ruminate on its deeds. But Daniel was weak-willed. His father and grandfather had always said so, and he conceded it was true. He had shown the kid the mercy it had not offered the tree, and killed it with one quick squeeze of his trigger.

Daniel loved the trees. Their blossoms in the spring were as silky and fragrant as rose petals. When the winds blew the blossoms loose they rolled through the air and reminded him of that day when he and Betty stood side by side in a swirling cloud of them, and two symmetrical petals had landed on Betty's nose, for all the world like butterfly wings.

He snorted, and spat out a wad of phlegm.

He had done as she had asked and taken care of Finn, even though the boy was so unnatural that Daniel sometimes feared he was damning his own soul by doing so. He only prayed it would mean something to Betty if she came back and found he had kept his promise.

'Ah, *ahh*,' he said to himself. 'Now there's a telltale sign in your thinkings.'

*If*, he had thought. *If* she came back.

When she first left he had been so certain of her return. There were some things, he'd told himself, that were fated, and his and Betty's love was such a thing. Star-crossed, they had been. He had divined it from the feeling of his bones – just as his grandfather had read signs in goat entrails (and charged a shilling for the service).

He no longer felt such certainty. These days, his heart felt like a broken compass, always spinning after a direction it could no longer find. These days, it was as hard to maintain his belief in Betty as it was to hunt for a goat on the Merrow Wold. These days, there was just the mountains, the weather, and the stink of pelt and old dung.

He left the main path and took a tussocky fork that would skirt the edge of Thunderstown to reach the south road, where the Fossiter homestead had stood for over two centuries. Not for the first time was he letting guilt gnaw at him. True, he could not bear to consider the reasons for Betty's long absence, but he could always bear to torture himself with what he had and had not done during those eight years.

He had done as Betty had asked and looked after Finn, but he had not done so happily. He was a love-smitten fool who was incapable of refusing her, but that didn't mean he was ready to forgive Finn for being the thing he was. At best Finn was a freak of nature. At worst he was touched by the devil, just as the ravenous goats were.

Every Fossiter man back through the generations had been a culler such as he. Only his father had bucked the tradition. Whereas previous generations had been heavy drinkers, meat-eaters and womanizers, Daniel's father was a teetotal vegetarian, and as spiteful as a hornet.

Throughout Daniel's childhood his father and grandfather did not speak to one another, and when Daniel's father died of a sickness they had still not reconciled. Daniel was fourteen when that happened, and after that his grandfather raised him and recommenced in earnest the Fossiter tradition for raising boys. He taught Daniel how to shoot, how to work his way upwind of a goat, how to use the curved knife that peeled softened fat from the hide. How to cleave the meat, drain the blood without spoiling the pelt and how, once Daniel's fifteenth birthday came around, to drink. He had made Daniel eat for the first time in his life the flesh of an animal, and it had tasted as seductive and vitalizing as it had immoral.

He taught Daniel the characters of the mountains, the methods and charms for appeasing them and the ways in which a canny goat could exploit the landscapes to hide from a culler. He instructed him in the preparation of traps, the spring-loading of iron jaws that would snap clean through a leg. He taught him to carry goat droppings in his pockets to dupe the foolish beasts into trusting him as he stalked the mountainsides.

He taught him, too, about the roamy goat, the one that could only ever be sighted when the mists hung over the mountains. The one goat he must not shoot.

Nobody had ever seen two roamy goats together. Logic said there must be more than one – there had been roamy sightings for centuries. Or perhaps they were a genetic anomaly, like a white hart, born to a normal buck and its nanny. Or … or perhaps, as Daniel's grandfather vehemently maintained, it was one of a kind, an ancient beast still alive and unthreatened by cullers.

It was twice as large as a normal goat, almost the size of a bullock. Its features were nobler, its tread delicate as a deer's. Its horns were a marvel, patched grey, white and iridescent like flint. Its fleece was threaded with indigo and steel-coloured hairs, so that the shadows of its coat were a moody purple and the outline bright like a cloud's silver lining.

It would mean, his grandfather used to insist with rare vitriol, a curse on your family to shoot that goat.

Daniel's father had always taught him to obey his elders. So, after his father died, Daniel did all he could to adapt to the lifestyle his grandfather pressed upon him. Yet the character of his father had also been strong. Daniel feared God, even if he did not always believe in him. He was at times, he could admit, terrorized by God.

As a teenager he would sneak off to the Church of Saint Erasmus when he knew his grandfather would not notice, to sit in its vaulted silence staring ever upwards at the black shadows of the ceiling. There he would feel a terrible despair, barren and biblical like this land of the Merrow Wold. He would repent of all the things his grandfather had encouraged him to do, the drinking and the brawling and the savage talk.

Likewise, when he was nineteen, Daniel had wept heavingly at his grandfather's funeral, even though every other tear was one of relief that at last he was free to pick up the pieces of the previous two generations and try to understand how to be the descendent of both men at once. That was a puzzle that would prove difficult to solve.

On the night before the funeral he had wolfed a steak so rare and bloody it was near raw, then, after the burial, resumed the vegetarianism of his childhood. He had consumed the meat both in homage to his grandfather and in fear for the dead man's soul. Looking back, he could never comprehend how his grandfather had shrugged off talk of his impending torment. 'You only think that'll be,' he had once said with a wink, 'because you think you yourself are so special. But look at the goats. They think they're special too, and we cullers know that ain't true. Living by instinct only. No control over what they do and don't do. And if you think we ain't the damned same as them, well … then you're more of a fool than anyone for thinking there's a bed made up in hell for the likes of me.'

Daniel was approaching the homestead now. It was a long building constructed from sturdy beams, more like a feasting hall of old than a home to be at peace in. A sturdy fence marked out the territory of its yard, on the far side of which were an outhouse, a workshop and a disused barn. Although Daniel had lived here since his father's death, his childhood years spent at the vicarage meant that the homestead, in which so many of his ancestors had dwelt and died, had never felt his own. In fact, for a few blissful years he had left it to rot. That was when he lived with Betty in her house in Candle Street.

He had met her on the Devil's Diadem one day, while he crouched with his hunting rifle. Stalking like that, in no hurry to make the kill, was an experience as calming as the long hours of prayer his father had encouraged. The Devil's Diadem, that far up and that far wide of the path, was a deserted place. He had never encountered another human being among its barbed trees and narrow boulders. So, when the woman stepped into the clearing he had been aiming his rifle at, he very nearly placed a bullet between her eyes, as he would have done had she four legs and dainty hooves.

She screamed when she saw him, and the noise stayed his trigger finger and made him blanch.

'Please!' she cried out. 'Please don't! Please just don't!'

When he realized it was the gun she was frightened of, and that she had completely misread his intent, he dropped it and stood up slowly with his hands raised. He wasn't a man of words, but a man of doings. People often mistook him for a simpleton, thinking the same had been true of his grandfather and all the Fossiters before him, but he had his father the Reverend Fossiter's mind and his father's thinkings. Indeed, it was thinkings that hampered his tongue. So thick and flavoursome that when they came down to his mouth to be spoken it was hard to make the sounds of them, like talking with a mouthful of honey.

He managed, after stumbling over and over, to tell her his purpose. 'This gun is only for goats, ma'am.' He pointed to himself. 'I am a goat culler.'

She laughed. So lightly and freely that he sensed it was all right to smile back, then laugh too. On such rare occasions when Daniel started laughing, out came a great booming laugh that rocked back his shoulders and bent his spine and opened wide his big bearded jaw to let the deep bass laughter out, like the noise of an avalanche echoing in a chasm. They laughed together for several minutes, and later he would try to conjure that sound in his head again and again.

A friendship began between them. Unlikely, someone at church remarked. For Betty was at odds with Thunderstown, while Daniel had it in his bones. Betty often said that the place was so provincial, so small that she couldn't understand why she didn't return to the metropolis she'd come from. As for Daniel, he was so rural he found even Thunderstown's size intimidating. But this was the thing they had in common, this displacement. Two people who found it hard to belong wherever they found themselves.

Daniel had been her confidant. He had been there to listen in giant silence when she told him of the urges affecting her. She wanted a child, she would say, then would say it again. She wanted a child wanted a child wanted a child. Someone she could raise right, make fit in right, fit into the world and live a full life because of it. In response he would scratch his head and try to explain that he wished she wouldn't talk as if she were some botched job. He feared it when she talked like that, because she made it sound like all she longed for was to replace herself. He could never convey how queasy it made him, for the slowdown between his thinkings and his speakings always let the proper moment slip. All he could do was listen, confused by his sympathy, as she told him of her attempts at pregnancy, and of all the subsequent ways in which her body and medicine had failed her.

She looked as fragile as a thing made from bird bones when she told him what the doctors had said. Infertile. She spat out the word like blood and Daniel at least understood, as he watched the sobs make her jerk like a marionette, that it would have been far better for her to lose a limb, or an eye, or all her teeth than to lose this thing. Then she stepped into Daniel's arms as if walking over a cliff, and he'd wrapped them around her and sensed that if he squeezed her even in the slightest she'd be crushed to salt.

After she had confessed all this to him he climbed up on to the Devil's Diadem with just his rifle and his thoughts for company. It was a day of mists: he could see barely a stone's throw through the cloud.

Then he'd glimpsed for the first time the roamy goat, the one with silver eyes and horns like flint. The one that trod with a gentleness of spirit other goats did not possess. The one whose bleat was like an infant crying. It emerged from the mist with a faint breeze blowing in its blue-hued fur. Its eyes twinkled and its fur sparkled and it was as if there were a bond between them. It cried out and the noise reached inside Daniel's chest and squeezed his heart in ways he could not understand, and made the mist become a silver world that only they shared. He chewed for a while on nothing, and the goat chewed too, and the pinks and ambers in its iridescent horns gleamed. Then Daniel let out a great choking sigh, raised his rifle and shot the goat between the eyes.

Within minutes, the mists had cleared.

He'd carried the roamy goat dead down to the homestead, letting the weight of the animal describe itself on his shoulder blades and the spike of one of its horns tease his jugular. Down he plodded from the mountains, and once at the bottom he threw it on the counter in his workshop and he skinned it and treated the fur and did all he could to cut the shape of it well, so he could present it, finally, weeks later, to Betty as a birthday gift; a shawl of silver-blue wool that she took from him gingerly and smiled at, then wrapped around her neck. Quilted in blue goat fur, she pressed herself up against him and drew his hands around her waist, helped his broad fingers slide under the soft fabric of her skirt and along the even softer surface of her skin. She led him indoors into her house on Candle Street and undressed him. Then, when he could not make his fingers do the work, she undressed herself, the goat shawl and her skirt and her underwear dropping one by one on to her bed. They lay down on that deep pile of clothes and fur and he drowned in the feel of all her flesh pressed under all of his own.

At the memory of all this he shook his head like a stunned boxer. He blinked moisture out of his eyes. He let out a harrumph. He had reached the gate of the Fossiter homestead, and he entered the yard and crossed to the workshop, still carrying the goat he had killed that morning on his shoulders. Inside, he used the goat's horns as handles to lower its head on to a chopping block. He collected his old axe from its hook on the wall and whistled it through the shaggy goat neck so that it snicked apart the vertebrae within. He hefted the carcass and left the head staring up indifferently from the block. He hung the empty body from cords suspended from the workshop ceiling and let the blood dribble out of its neck and patter into a stained collecting trough beneath.

Not a day passed by without him remembering that night with Betty. Their lovemaking had been intense and finally ecstatic, but it was their subsequent state that had affected him so profoundly. He had lain on his back with her drifting to sleep against him and he had felt aligned. She had made geometry out of him.

In the morning she'd been in tears. 'I'm so so sorry, Daniel. I've made a mistake. It's not you, it's me. I can't explain. Sex just reminds me of how I can't have a baby. There, I've said it. You shouldn't stick with me, you should have someone better, someone undamaged.' Then he put his arms around her and told her it didn't matter, and smelled her hair while she cried against his throat. He meant it. He did not believe that sex was a prerequisite to the peace he had discovered as they lay together. Sex was just bodies. Peace was spirit. They did not sleep together again.

Yet since that night he had never found such peace. Shortly afterwards, Finn had arrived.

When Betty told him she was pregnant she said, 'I swear to God, Daniel, I swear on my mother's blood, I swear on my father's grave. I went up the Devil's Diadem during the storm, and that was all I did.'

At that he covered his face with his hands. To think – he had been the one who had put that idea into her head! He had told her, without ever thinking she would act on it, a superstition of his grandfather's. The old man had believed that if a childless woman climbed to the top of a mountain during a storm, and there in a whisper petitioned it for a child, and then drank rainwater until she was sick, then, one out of a hundred such times, she might conceive. His grandfather had believed many such things.

Daniel did not know what he found worse. The idea that she had given herself up to some infernal trick of the weather, or the idea that he had planted the suggestion in her mind. 'Betty,' he whispered, 'is there no likelihood that the child is ours?'

'No. Daniel, I'm sorry. I would have been pleased by that, but there's no way. What's happened to me is a miracle.'

Towards the end of her pregnancy he would sometimes catch himself staring morbidly at her belly, while in his own he felt his terrors kicking. He had always been caught between two fears: his father's fear of the judgements of the Lord, and his grandfather's fear of wicked spirits that could conjure squalls out of blue skies. Each man had debunked as superstition the beliefs of the other, leaving Daniel with no middle way save to abandon belief altogether, which would be the most fearful thing of all. In church he stopped praying and forced his mind to think about goats and mountains and camouflaged traps. He did this because he feared hearing the whisper of the Lord in his prayers. If the Lord asked him to do something about the baby in Betty's womb he knew he would be too weak-willed to obey. Better not to hear the command in the first place. He felt removed from God then, trapped from him as though under rubble, and sometimes he would wake up with his heart thumping in the dead of night, having dreamed about a little boy holding his hand.

At last the too-late day came. Her phone call.

'Please, Daniel, no midwife,' she gasped down the line. 'Just you. Listen to me, please. Just you.'

'Betty ... you need ... I don't know ...'

'*Please!*'

He set off at once, at a run, leaving the hide he had been tanning to spoil.

He found her sitting on her bed. At once she grabbed his forearm and squeezed so hard he felt like the bones inside it would break. She was shivering and sweat-drenched. Daniel piled blankets around her, among them the shawl he'd made, but it did no good. She was freezing cold in the hot room. She ground her teeth to stop them chattering. He saw that a layer of ice had crystallized across the bed sheet. It had tiled the fabric in a snowflake's hexagonal patterns. Even as he watched (she squeezed his arm harder still) the ice spread and sculpted itself further across the bed. Icicles creaked over the bed posts and stretched for the floor. Networks of frost coated the insides of her thighs. Then there was a thump at the window and a noise like the calling of an animal, or a wind shrieking, and he crossed himself and she arced her neck and shouted and then the baby began to emerge.

'Help me!'

Daniel went to the foot of the bed and set his jaw. He tried to remember the times in his childhood when he had helped his grandfather birth the livestock. The head came first, covered in a caul of mist. He readied his hands for the body. It followed quickly –

so small and so cold, cottoned in cloud and sparkling like hoarfrost. His fingers tacked to it as if to an ice block. It let out a noise like wind wailing across wastelands. The windows shuddered and the door latch shook. 'My baby,' cried Betty, and it took a moment for Daniel to realize that she meant the thing he held. He deposited it into her outstretched arms. At once the crying ceased. As she placed the child to her breast, the contact released a hiss like a branding iron cooled in a bucket of water. The smell of burned sugar (for all he knew the smell of hell itself) filled the air. As he stood there, dumbly watching Betty as she held and stroked and soothed, the thing seemed to settle. It took on a guise more like that of a real baby, with true flesh instead of hardened ice. Betty gave a shout of pure delight. Daniel crossed himself.

'Hello,' she whispered reverently. 'Aren't you wonderful?' And then she looked up at Daniel and said, 'A boy, Daniel! And I shall call him Finn.'

# 5

# WILD IS THE WIND

Elsa woke in the early morning to the noise of a wind gusting through Thunderstown. Only when she sat up in bed did she realize that she could no longer hear it, that perhaps she had dreamed it. Through a crack in the curtains she could see the sky filling up with the dull half-light that precedes a hot sunrise. The air had closed in overnight. Inhaling felt like breathing through a veil.

She got out of bed for some water. She drank it at the window, pulling back the curtain to gaze out at the sleeping world. Beyond Drum Head's horizon it would already be daytime, but the sun had still to labour up the far side of the mountain before its rays could reach Thunderstown. For now the streets enjoyed the last reposeful moments of the night. Even the white flowers growing up through the cracked paving looked like stars set in a stone heaven.

A breeze came in through the open window and licked the fine hairs on her forearm. She shuddered. She had the feeling she was being watched, but outside there was only the view of the rooftops, the motionless weathervanes, the steadily lightening slopes of the mountains. She tried going back to bed, but the discomforting feeling had stirred her wide awake and after a few failed attempts at sleep she made herself coffee and sat by the window to watch the day begin.

When the sunlight came it overflowed Drum Head and rolled downhill to Thunderstown. Walls turned amber and chimney pots gold. Windowpanes lit up with the reflected dawn.

Then, with a start, she realized there was something down there in the courtyard beneath her window. She sprung up from her chair, her coffee dancing in her mug.

As she looked down she saw a wild dog, padding across the flagstones, its brushy tail snaking behind it. It settled down on its haunches and lifted its silvery muzzle to sniff the air. Then it looked straight up at her, its stare inexpressive and animal.

With a cry she pulled shut the curtains. She paced around the bedroom. She slapped herself on both cheeks at once, told herself how stupid she was being, then reopened the curtains an inch.

The dog still sat there, its pink tongue lolling between its incisors and its eyes fixed on her room.

She didn't know what to do. She poured herself some cereal and stayed away from the window to eat it. She had to put down her spoon when a surge of dread rose up from her toes, overwhelmed her and then was gone again.

Once more she approached the curtains. Her hands trembled so much when she drew them open that the fabric flapped in her grip.

The dog had gone.

With a great sigh of relief she hurried to the bathroom and took a long shower. She dressed and brushed her teeth. Toothpaste dribbled over her lip and pattered into the sink. She buttoned up her jacket and ensured she had packed her keys. She checked the clock. She tried to forget about the dog, just as she had tried to forget about the man she had seen yesterday. After she had come back down from the mountain she had pictured him diffusing into cloud every time she closed her eyes. She had not wanted to be alone, and had bugged Kenneth to share a glass of wine with her.

Today would be her first day in her new job and she needed to hold herself together. She would be helping in a low-key, part-time role at the town's offices. It was a step down from her job in New

York, where she had organized other people's recipes and fashion tips and inspiring real-life stories for a newspaper's weekend magazine. It had been more like collage-building than journalism and she had loved that about it: she had been a compiler of all of America's variety and she had never failed to appreciate it. Only, back then she had been sure of herself. When the cracks started spreading, each hour at her desk became an ordeal. Every story, every snippet, every horoscope and even every word puzzle made her question who she was, confused under the weight of all the people it was possible to be. One mid-summer Monday afternoon she broke down in the office. She found it hard to even work out her notice period.

The job Kenneth had helped her find was exactly the sort of thing she needed. Something to forget about come five o'clock. It was only a short walk to the offices, which stood at the end of a dusty street running west from Saint Erasmus. They rose in a grand old heap of tanned stone, with whiskery grasses poking out of their walls, and culminated in a clock tower that unified the ramshackle wings and annexes beneath, but in which the hands of the clock had frozen long ago. Craning her neck and shielding the climbing sun from her eyes, she could just make out a wooden figure on either side of the face, attached to some kind of clockwork track. The first, a man with a rough beard and broad brimmed hat, a pickaxe held in one hand and in the other a hand bell, thrusting it out into the open air. The second wore black and leaned on a scythe.

Lily, Elsa's new supervisor, met her in a reception hall panelled with dark wood and hung with row after row of trophy goat heads. Lily was nineteen years old and her jaw wagged when she spoke, as if the things she said were chewing gum. She led the way up a flight of wooden steps that tapped under their heels with hollow echoes, to an office with a small desk allotted to Elsa.

Elsa spent most of the day at an ancient photocopier. There the hours passed so slowly that they seemed measured by the broken clock.

'So what in the world,' asked Lily when lunchtime at last arrived, 'possessed you to move here from New York?'

Lily made it sound so ridiculous that Elsa hesitated. Kenneth had treated her decision with something like reverence, so it surprised her to hear someone question it. But in this shabby office it did indeed seem ridiculous.

'I ...' she said, 'I ...' She was damned if she would belittle herself; Lily could think she was nuts if she wanted to. 'I did it to try to get my head straight. In New York my life just ... accumulated. I didn't feel like I'd chosen any of it, only wandered into it and just started living it. Then earlier this year some stuff happened and it made me realize that I needed to live a life I had chosen, to be a person I had considered being. So I came here, I suppose, to have the space to find that version of myself.'

Lily looked at her like she thought she was nuts.

When she stepped out of the offices at the end of the day, the shadow of the clock tower lay across the street. She wandered wearily into Saint Erasmus Square to sit on one of the wooden benches that faced the church. The evening heat was stirred with dust that blurred the details from the rooftops and made the sky look used and flat.

She was exhausted, tempted to lie down right there in the square and sleep, but she was determined to make something from the evening that was emerging, blown full of the scent of wood fires. She got up and walked until she discovered a bar called the Brook Horse, which spanned five storeys. It had a glorious, hand-painted sign hanging above the entrance, in which a horse swam underwater, its mane flowing behind it. A grid of eggshell cracks had split the paint, but the deep teal of the water remained vivid. The horse in the sign was no ordinary equine. Instead of hind legs its body streamlined into that of a fish, its tail fanning out gracefully to propel it through the currents.

Each floor of the bar was a cubbyhole joined to the others by a rickety spiral staircase. A group of girls who would never have been served in the States nursed pots of a sticky-looking beer on the ground floor, while on the next a woman in a raggedy shawl sewed behind a bottle of wine. The top storey overflowed on to a lop-sided balcony where Elsa sat to watch the heat haze sandpapering all sharp angles from the rooftops and chimneys. It filled the distance with its dust, and of all the mountains only Old Colp was dark enough to show through it.

She gazed across the street. A weathervane creaked and turned west. In a gutter a crow jabbed at something yellow-feathered. Further off, a wind tugged at washing strung between two rooftops. It pulled loose one sleeve of a shirt and flapped it about as if it were signalling to her.

She clutched her hands to her face. All of a sudden she was raging inside for the magic of yesterday. A man had turned to cloud and rained before her very eyes. She should have knocked that bothy door down to get answers, but instead she had run back to Thunderstown and photocopied reports for eight hours. She had to go back. She had to know.

She set off at an impassioned pace, out of town and up the broken slopes of Old Colp. She thought of all the questions she would ask the man. She wondered if he would transform into a cloud again. Then, abruptly, she was lost.

Her passion sputtered out. She came to a halt so suddenly that she tripped. She had thought she recognized the track, the boulders and the harrowed trees that leaned like signposts, but she had no memory of the view that opened before her now: a valley full of weathered rocks and beyond them the horny foothills of the Devil's Diadem. She looked back the way she had come at a landscape without milestones. She supposed that dusk was soon due, so she begrudgingly turned to retrace her steps to Thunderstown. Then, to her surprise and horror, the track forked at the base of a valley and she could not remember which path she had come down.

As if in mockery of the morning, when she had watched the sunrise crown Drum Head then rush through the town in a golden outpouring, the dusk was brief and the sunset as fleeting as a smoke signal. A few pink bars flared across the sky while she toiled up the path she hoped would lead her back. Then the light blotted out behind Old Colp's eclipse. She shuddered. She still had no idea where she was or how to get back. The fierce desire that had driven her up here was gone with the evening light. Nearby an animal yipped, and she couldn't tell whether it was bird or beast. She scrambled onwards, pleased that the path had started to ascend, hoping that the higher ground would offer her a view she could use, but when she reached the path's crest she saw only expansive black slopes. In the sky vast clouds had spread like ink spills. The only light was a jaundiced smudge where the sun had died out behind the mountain.

She sat down forlornly on a rock. Darkness drained the land. The visible world became small and black; but beyond sight it ehoed with the tuneless symphonies of the wind. She wondered when she had last been so immersed in a night. Not since her last in her childhood home, when she was fifteen and could not sleep because all of her belongings were taped away in boxes, ready to be relocated in the morning to the new house her mum had bought. Her mother had never really liked living on a ranch in the empty prairie, so when she kicked Elsa's dad out she headed straight back to the city of Norman. It was only when they went to visit the new place, a bright wooden house in a leafy suburb, that Elsa realized how much she loved that ranch in the middle of nowhere. On her final night there, while her mother snored in the adjacent bedroom, she had slipped out of bed and crept downstairs, remembering how she had tiptoed just so as a little girl when she and Dad escaped for morning storm hunts.

That night she had wandered a long distance from the unlit ranch. As she'd sat down on springy earth, the darkness had felt like a sister. The night was kin to the lightless workings of her heart and lungs, the pitch-black movement of her blood in her veins. All of her feelings happened in darkness, in emptiness as immeasurable as the expanse of the firmament above her, of which the stars were but the foreground.

Now, in this night on the mountain, she felt that same darkness inside her again. Without the metropolitan fluorescence of New York she could feel it going into her like a thread through the eye of a needle. It suffused her and reassured her that, lo and behold, it had been in her all along. She was, at heart, just as empty as the night, and despite being so lost she was grateful for the rediscovery.

When the animal call sounded again it startled her out of herself. It howled nearer now and there could be no doubt – it was a wild dog. All at once it appeared. It prowled into the cusp of her vision. Even a few yards away its body was hard to pick out. Its fur was as dark as the night clouds. Its teeth when it bared them were moon-pale. Its eyes were freckled with white like the zodiac.

It padded to a halt and stood in front of her, panting and staring up along the length of its snout.

'Hello,' she whispered pathetically.

Its tongue flickered across its nose. It slinked past her and trotted away a few paces. There it paused and looked back, idly swishing its tail.

She stood up, hesitated for a second, then followed. It loped along at a fast pace, and in her attempts to keep up she stubbed her toes painfully on a stone and tripped through a rut in the earth. It kept moving, weaving down through pathless valleys and up slopes she had to ascend on all fours. When she reached the top of a peak she shrieked to find the dog lurking in wait for her, its muzzle point-blank to her face, its breath rancid and meaty. Then she realized that beyond the dog, at the bottom of a long and easy descent, shone the lights of Thunderstown.

She laughed to see their glowing amber spiral, so welcoming after having been so lost. Then for a second she had to shield her eyes because out of nowhere a blast of wind hit her, kicking up dust from the soil and flapping her hair against her ears. This wind did not smell fresh like an alpine breeze, but grimy like feral fur. Then it was gone and she uncovered her eyes. She turned to the dog to pat or scratch her thanks, but it had already left her. Surprised, she studied the night in every direction. It must have run off, into the darkness.

# 6

# PART WEATHER

The next morning, when she left for work, Elsa found Kenneth Olivier standing on a garden chair in the front yard of his house on Prospect Street, holding a battery-powered radio up to the sky like an offering. To its aerial he had affixed an extension bent from a coat hanger, which he now reached up to tweak an inch to the left. The adjustment changed the tone of the static crackling from the radio's speakers, but still all it would emit was a crackle and a hiss.

'Oh, hello, Elsa,' he said upon noticing her. He kept the radio held aloft. 'It's the heat we've been having, see? It's playing the devil with the reception for the test match. The television's a lost cause and the radio looks to be another.'

She had slept badly, and once she had given in and left the pretence of her sleep, it had taken her five minutes to pluck up the courage to open the curtains, afraid to find another wild dog crouching there in the courtyard. When she had finally opened them the courtyard had been bare, but her unease had persisted.

'Elsa?' Kenneth put down the radio. 'Are you feeling okay?'

'Yeah,' she said. Then, after a pause: 'I wanted to ask you about something. This might sound crazy, but … I keep seeing these dogs …' And she told him about the animals, the one who had lurked in the courtyard yesterday morning and the one who had guided her last night. She didn't tell him about the man she'd seen, although she could tell he was concerned by her ventures in the mountains after dark.

'Listen, Elsa, I tried to tell you about these dogs before. They're not like other dogs. They're different.'

'What do you mean?'

He scratched his head and looked wistfully at his useless radio.

'Come on, Kenneth. You were going to say something more than that.'

He cleared his throat. 'I don't expect you to understand. Part of them is weather.'

'Part of them is *weather*?'

For the first time since she had met him she saw a flash of irritation in his expression, although he quickly buried it. 'Well, of course you should believe in whatever you want. Perhaps this is just another superstition from a superstitious town.'

'Sorry, it's just … you can't be serious?'

'Look, Elsa, I am just trying to make things clear to you. For my part I have found the world a far more bearable place to live in ever since I stopped trying to assemble a list of things I believe in and a list of things I don't. Instead I have resolved to believe in just a single thing: my own ignorance. The world is bigger than the confines of Kenneth Olivier's head.'

'I'm sorry. I bugged you about it and then I overstepped the mark.'

He chuckled. 'Don't worry. Because if you stay here worrying, you are going to be late for work …'

They smiled at each other, then she set off for the office and her thoughts went back to her cloud man from the mountain. At work she became quickly reacquainted with the photocopier, but on her lunch break she found a bench in the church square and pulled from her bag the map she had used to find Old Colp's ruined windmill. Tonight she would be better prepared to find the bothy.

No sooner was her afternoon shift over than she had changed into her sneakers and was hurrying up the mountain. Uphill, the world became hushed. The brown mountain grass and the mounds of heather stood as motionless as the ranks of boulders that crested each ridge. The sky was a tinny blue, and barred in the north with diagonal clouds. When a bird of prey whistled overhead it sounded loud as a siren. She looked up in time to see it become a plunging black chevron landing death on some unfortunate mammal.

When she reached the wreckage of the windmill she stopped to catch her breath. She found the spot where she had watched the man turn to cloud and rain on the meadow, and she fancied that the grass was greener there. After her hurried climb it was pleasant to imagine the cool touch of water, but she was too close now to stop and daydream. She set off along the gully she had followed the man down, the slates grinding beneath her footsteps, and before she knew it she was at the bothy.

She approached the front door and rested her fingertips for a moment on its white-painted wood. She had to calm herself before she could knock, for now that she was here she was nervous at the thought of seeing him, and perhaps seeing cloud seep out of him again. It took her a moment to take control of her feelings, for her instinct was to either race away downhill or charge on into the bothy, demanding answer after answer. A measured approach was required, and that had never been her strong point.

She tapped her knuckles lightly off the wood. Her feet were shuffling nervously on the step when the door opened.

His eyes widened when he saw her. A weird pallor of shadow and light rippled across his hairless face, like the shadow of a cloud dappling across a field. She was again struck by his size and peculiar lack of pigmentation, as if he had no blood to show through his skin.

He looked like he wanted to run and hide, but to her delight she had him cornered. 'Hey,' she said.

'It's you.'

'Yes. Me.'

He tried to shut the door, but she stepped quickly forwards to block it. 'Wait! Please. I'm sorry to ambush you like this.'

'Then why are you here?'

She liked his voice. Each word was like the dry push of breath that blows out a candle. 'I suppose … I just want to know what I saw.'

'It's better for you if you don't.'

She swallowed. 'Then you're going to be seeing a lot more of me.'

He sighed and looked past her at the slopes. He was wearing those same broken-lipped shoes he'd worn before, and a pair of jeans whose denim had faded almost to white, and a shirt that had perhaps been red or orange once, but had turned with time to a bleached yellow. 'Are you alone?' he asked.

'Yes.'

'Okay … First you have to make me a promise. If I tell you all I can, will you leave me alone?'

'Sure. I promise.'

'And will you promise not to tell a soul?'

'Okay, I promise that too. I only know one person in Thunderstown, anyway.'

He nodded. Then right away he looked puzzled. 'Wait … you're not from Thunderstown?'

'New York.'

His mouth made an O. 'I'm sorry, I should have been able to tell that from your accent. But I don't hear many voices up here, let alone New Yorker ones.'

'Actually my accent's kinda Oklahoman. That's where I grew up.'

He looked confused. 'Oak-what?' he asked.

'La-homa,' she said, unable to hide her delight that he didn't know the name. It gave her the spine-tingling assurance that she had come as far away from home as she had hoped she would all summer.

'You'd better come in.' He moved inside the bothy and motioned for her to follow him. She held back for a moment on the hearth, then took a forwards step that felt like a leap of faith.

The building's low ceiling and confining walls told of its original function as a simple shelter. The main living space was no bigger than her bedroom in Kenneth's house, but it still managed to cram in a sitting area, including a pair of wooden chairs and a small eating table. A door on the opposite wall opened on to a bathroom, and a wooden stepladder fixed to the wall climbed to a bedroom converted out of a loft.

But it was the man's paper models that caught her attention. She had noticed the quantity and variety of them when she had peered in through the window, but inside she kept spotting more. As well as the countless paper birds that hung on mobiles from the ceiling – which now rippled their wings in the breeze flowing from the door as if they were real falcons riding on the thermals – there were paper animals tucked in every cranny. On shelves where in other houses books or photo frames might have been arranged, proud paper horses and paper dogs posed among paper trees with leaves twizzled out of paper branches. Unfolded sheets were stacked up on the table, and it seemed that she had caught him at work, for alongside them was a work-in-progress model: a half-formed animal she could not recognize.

He pulled out a chair for her, then sat down opposite. He was so big he made his chair look like a child's, but he sat on it as lightly as a balloon on a lap. He examined her for a moment, his gaze more direct than any she had experienced before. If someone had looked at her so directly in New York she'd have freaked out or told them where to shove it, but there was something forgivably curious about the way he regarded her. He had an unfettered manner, as if he were an animal and this was his den.

Eventually he met her eyes and she saw again that his irises were tinged with a stormy purple. Within them his pupils looked imperfect, the black of them mingling with the inner rims of his irises, just as the eye of a hurricane mixes with its cloudwall. Looking into them made her feel like one of the paper birds hanging in the breeze.

'Who are you?' she gaped.

'My name's Finn Munro,' he said.

But she hadn't really meant to ask him his name. She had meant *what* are you? How can you have eyes such as these and how did you dissolve into cloud? 'You're ...' she struggled. 'I mean ...'

'Are you going to tell me yours?'

'Elsa. Elsa Beletti.'

He took a deep breath. 'Well, Elsa, I am not like you. I am not like anybody. I used to think I was, but that was a long time ago now. I can't promise you will understand. I don't think many people could.'

'I'll do my best.'

'Like I say, I'm not normal. Even if I'd started out that way, I suppose I'd have become very strange by living alone for so long like this.'

'How long have you been here?'

'Eight years. I was only sixteen when I came here. Before that I lived in Thunderstown, in a beautiful old house on Candle Street, with my mother and with Daniel. But I did something bad, and for everybody's benefit I moved up here. Since then I've sort of stopped thinking in years, just in seasons. I've given up on birthdays and calendars.'

'Wait. Daniel? Fossiter? I've met him.'

'He was my mother's ... friend. He helped me move up here so I could stay out of trouble. After my mother went away.'

He said those last words as lightly as he could, but she knew how to spot a child's pain at their parent's exit. She wanted to offer him sympathy. My dad left home when I was sixteen, and I can still remember him going, as if it were yesterday. Stuff like that doesn't really get old.'

He looked up at her gratefully. 'Yeah,' he said, 'it's hard to forget what happened. But I have made my peace with it. I only mention it to explain that I've been up here on my own for a long while trying to come to terms with myself.'

'I still don't understand what I saw.'

'Okay, put it this way ...' He laid his hands flat on the table, beside the unfinished paper model he had left there. Up close she realized it was the start of a horse. The long head and fluid forelegs were complete, but the back of the animal remained only half-folded.

'I have a storm inside of me.'

She blinked. 'I beg your pardon?' But she had heard him clearly. Her instinct was to disbelieve it, but she had seen grey mist fuming out of him. She had to lock her ankles together beneath her chair to stop her legs from jittering.

'It's always been that way. Part of me is cloud and rain and sometimes hail and snowflakes.'

'But ...' Her mind hurt, as if she had bitten on an ice cube. Her eyes were drawn again to the half-finished paper horse, and she suddenly realized that she had entirely misinterpreted it. It *was* finished, it was just that its hindquarters, which she had assumed were in need of more folding, were not those of a horse. They were those of a fish. She shuddered. 'That's impossible,' she said.

He laughed ruefully. 'I wish it were. Then I would not have this problem. Because, in a way, it is impossible. Impossible to live like other people do. Like you. I am too ... unpredictable. The weather can change in an instant.'

He looked at his fingers. It took him a minute to continue. 'I grew up trying to be normal. My mother did all she could to make my life like that of any other little boy. In the end it didn't work out.'

'You said you did something.'

'Something happened, yes. And I ended up living on my own in this bothy, trying to keep out of sight. There are people in Thunderstown who might … react badly if they knew what was in me. So I spend all day walking the mountaintops and all evening folding animals out of paper. It's not much of a life. It means I stay safe, but there's always the weather inside of me, reminding me that things can never change. I can feel it, see, in my belly.'

She was sitting forwards in her chair. 'What does that feel like?'

'Well, it's different from day to day. Sometimes it's ice-cold, which makes me apathetic, like nothing matters in the world, and I think I wouldn't care even if I dropped down dead. Other times it's as hot and heavy as a monsoon and I can barely believe there's so much rain inside of me. That's when I'm glad that I'm up here alone, because I get soppy and ridiculous. I bawl my eyes out over the slightest things – a smashed mug, say, or a sad memory – then afterwards I wonder what I made all the fuss about. It makes it impossible to live life like an ordinary person. So, lately, I've started to wonder whether I should keep trying to be a person at all. Would I be happier if I was weather entirely? And that's what I mean by coming to terms wiht myself. With what I really am. A few times now I've built up the courage, but every time something's pulled me back. Just like you pulled me back at the windmill.'

'Me?'

'Yes. You asked me to wait.'

That caught her off guard. She remembered her strong urge for him to stay, but she had put it down to fear. She would never have thought that he would stay because of her.

They sat in silence for a moment. The paper birds flew along their painstaking orbits. The door was still ajar, and the breeze carried in a sudden fragrance of heather blossom. Finn seemed in no hurry to say anything more. She supposed you learned to cope with silence if you lived alone, in a stone hut halfway up a mountain.

'Sometimes,' she said carefully, 'I feel things I'm not able to define. I'm not, um, part weather, but I mean … I feel things I don't recognize, feelings for which there are no words in the dictionary. Sometimes they frighten me, if I'm honest, and … well, I'm not saying it's the same as what you've just described … I guess I'm just saying that, maybe, you don't have to feel so alone about it.'

She scratched her cheek. It was an artificial gesture created to give her hands – turned suddenly fidgety – some occupation. She looked sharply around the bothy. She was not used to talking about her emotions with strangers. In fact, she was not used to talking like this with anyone.

'Did you just try to say,' he asked quietly, 'that you feel like that too?'

A brisk nod. She forced herself to laugh. 'Well, we have become awfully serious, for two total strangers!'

Again he regarded her with that level, scrutinizing stare, so unacceptable in a bar or café or subway car. Hell, even Peter had never had the nerve to look at her as if he could see into her like that, as if she were as insubstantial a thing as she had seen Finn turn into.

'You're different to the people in Thunderstown,' he said.

She shrugged, still embarrassed. 'The world's a big place.'

'Thank you,' he said, 'for telling me that.'

Suddenly she was talking again. 'I just started feeling this stuff. It was a bolt from the blue. My dad died, you see, and that put everything out of perspective. Or into it, I can't decide. He used to have a picture on his wall of a hurricane seen from space. I found it again after he died, when I went through all his things. A little eye of emptiness wrapped up in a whole lot of bluster. That's me, right there, I thought. But I was frightened that, if I let the bluster die away, all I'd be left with was the emptiness at the middle of it all.'

She stopped as abruptly as she'd started. She was surprised to have blurted out so much of herself.

She tapped the table like a judge calling for order. 'This is crazy!' she declared, high-pitched. 'What are we talking about? It's impossible! You aren't made out of weather! You can't be!'

He was taken aback. 'But you saw for yourself.'

'It must have been a trick. One that isn't funny any more. You have to tell me how you did it. Tell me what you did to me!'

He looked hurt. 'I didn't do anything to you. I didn't even know you were there until you asked me to stay.'

She stood up and straightened out her top. 'Look,' she declared, 'this has gone too far. Tell me the truth about what happened and I'll leave you in peace.'

He scowled, then he stood up too, and went to the sink. There in a rack some cutlery was drying in the sun. He grabbed a knife and spun around with the blade raised.

She panicked and backed towards the door.

Then he turned the knife point down and used its tip to prick his forefinger. He tossed it aside and raised his hand. She could clearly see the little cut at the centre of his fingerprint, but no blood welled out of it. Instead, it hissed. It whistled like a punctured tyre. She felt its tiny breeze flowing across her cheek.

'So,' he said curtly, 'all of your questions have been answered. And now you can keep your promise.'

'What promise?' She had more questions now, although she did not know how to phrase them.

'To leave me alone.'

She could see she'd upset him. She wished she hadn't acted in the way she just had, but she had been so suddenly frightened. She tried to apologize but she was no good at it and she only mumbled something ineffectual. In the end she had no choice but to give a feeble goodbye wave and leave the bothy.

A few paces across the scraggy mountainside she looked back and hoped to see Finn at the door watching her go. But he had closed it soundlessly behind her and he was not even at the window.

# 7

# OLD MAN THUNDER

It took the morning sun a long time to light and heat the Fossiter homestead. As it crept westward shafts of it shone in at angles, highlighting the cobwebs and the painted frowns on the portraits of deceased patriarchs. In a pool of such light, Daniel Fossiter was on his knees, saying, 'Are you dead? Have you died, Mole?'

Mole, his dog, lay on the wooden floor with her paws stretched forwards and her good eye firmly shut. Her bad eye – the one in which she had been blind since birth – remained open, marbled black and blue like the shell of a mussel. She had not moved all morning and he could not detect her breathing.

If he was not such a damned sentimental old fool he would long ago have given her one last favourite meal, then led her outside. As it stood, he had let her reach this infirm stage, where every day seemed like her last.

'Mole?' he whispered. 'Are you still in there, Mole?'

Every Fossiter who had ever walked the mountains had owned a dog, a member of a canine dynasty with a pedigree as meticulously charted as that of the Fossiters themselves. They were copper-haired, hardy pointer-retrievers, who rarely barked or played, preferring to slink after scent trails with their bellies close to the ground. Daniel had inherited several from his grandfather, but he also had his father's pair of clumsy house dogs, who had spent their lives bickering in yaps so shrill that the hunting dogs had never dared to hassle them. For some years he'd lived with this motley pack, until the time when, as if in competition, the hunters and the house dogs had each birthed a litter of puppies and he'd feared being overrun. How strange it had felt to be the sole remaining Fossiter of Thunderstown, while all around him the fur-ball progenies of his forefathers' mutts scrapped and bit and barked.

He had sold the dogs then, all bar one puppy from each litter. In truth he no longer required them in order to hunt. Tracking, trapping and sniping had all become so instinctive that he fancied he could do all three sleepwalking. When those two puppies had matured and born mongrel puppies of their own, he kept only the runt: a serious, black-furred little pup with a blind eye and a wrinkled nose. This he christened Mole.

Mole was different from the other dogs he had owned. She was like his shadow. Those other animals he had looked after well, for sure, but only in the way he might look after the upholstery of his house, or polish some inherited antique whose history he had not learned. Mole was quiet, like her hunting ancestors, but thoughtful and sombre like her master. There were times when Daniel and Mole would sit side by side on some rocky parapet in the mountains and look at each other with such reflected heaviness that he would touch his face, expecting it to be canine, and Mole's to be his reflection in a mirror.

He'd been surprised, then, when Betty met Mole and the two had been madcap together. Betty would chase the dog around the yard, and Mole would bounce after Betty, the pair creating such a tumult of yapping and laughing and rolling about on the floor that Daniel could only gape and marvel.

Now here he was, on his hands and knees, pushing a bowl of gruel closer to Mole's elderly snout, wondering if, finally, the day had come when he would need to take up his shovel and pierce the earth of the Fossiter pet cemetery.

'Mole,' he whispered, nudging the bowl even closer, 'Mole, can you hear me in there?'

Her blind eye stared blankly back at him. That eye had never shut. A strange prophecy, he supposed, of the moment when the other would become its empty equal.

She opened her good eye and he breathed out with gladness. 'Mole!' He wiped his forearm across his face.

Mole climbed groggily to her feet, whiffed the gruel for a moment, then clumsily plugged her nose into the bowl and snaffled at the food.

'Mole,' exclaimed Daniel, 'good old Mole!'

Somebody cleared their throat.

He spun around, still on his knees. A man in a raincoat and cap stood in the doorway looking down his nose at Daniel. He had a flabby pink neck which he had tried to bind back with a tight collar. Likewise his belly had been squeezed by his belt into two bulges, one above and one below his waistline. He took off his hat and smeared into place the combed hair that covered his baldness.

'I see you are hard at work, Mr Fossiter, keeping the weather at bay.'

'Mr Moses,' said Daniel, gruff and embarrassed, climbing to his feet while Mole slurped behind him. Sidney Moses had, of late, taken to keeping tabs on him.

'The door was open, so I let myself in.'

'I see that you did. And to what do I owe the visit?'

Sidney cocked his head, and his jowls wobbled down to the collar. 'To the town, Mr Fossiter. You owe it to the town. In whose employment, I might add, I see that you are currently serving.'

He smiled sarcastically and looked down at Mole, who belched upon completion of her meal and sat down in a lump.

'I also see,' continued Sidney, 'that you are still utilizing the fittest, most valiant hunting hounds available to a man of your profession. I'm certain that the goats of the mountains would throw themselves from a precipice rather than face a beast such as this.'

Daniel's nostrils flared. 'What do you want, Mr Moses? I'm sure we would both prefer it if we made this brief.'

Sidney raised his hands. 'Now, now, Mr Fossiter, you know I only jest. But if you want brevity I will cut to the chase. I was expecting your report at the beginning of this week.'

Daniel glared away down the length of the hall, along which his family in portraiture expressed their disdain. He wondered whether they were frowning at his guest or at himself, for none of those men would have suffered a bureaucrat like Sidney Moses.

Thunderstown was full of busybodies, but Sidney surpassed all the rest. He had recently obtained a high-ranking position at the town offices which, much to Daniel's chagrin, had given his interferences an air of legitimacy. Daniel had as little time for him as he would have for a mosquito, but lately Sidney had proven that he had the power to withhold the culler's bursary and had implied he might revoke it entirely.

Daniel stared down at his boots and mumbled, 'I forgot to write the report.'

Sidney sighed. 'You and I,' he said, 'are either going to work through this or come to a head. It is perfectly justifiable that a man financed exclusively by the town be asked to file a weekly report on the results of his working activities.'

'I have shot thirty-eight goats, trapped sixteen and brought down four for meat and hides.'

Sidney rolled his eyes. '*Why* is it so difficult to commit that to paper?'

'Because it is unnecessary. The townsfolk know I do my duty.'

'Nobody is calling that into question.'

Mole harrumphed, and Daniel agreed with her.

'I simply wish,' said Sidney carefully, 'to make things better. How can I explain? Perhaps by asking you: when was the last time you went out into the world beyond Thunderstown?'

He shrugged. 'Once. Thirty, maybe thirty-five years ago. That was enough of seeing the world.'

'Well … it's changed a good deal in that time. Shrunk. And it will come to Thunderstown before long.'

Daniel thought of the American girl who had confronted him in the square.

'Thunderstown,' said Sidney, 'will change. Old ways of doing things will slip away. You, for example, have not taken on an apprentice.'

'I have no son.'

'Quite. But you must have given thought to the question of who takes over when you are gone.'

The truth was that he'd thought about it less than he should have. He could not imagine Thunderstown without a Fossiter. His family had been culling here since the first foundations of the streets were laid, and it seemed impossible that it would fall to him to terminate such an ancient tradition.

'Whether we like it or not,' said Sidney, 'we are approaching a moment when our old ways of doing things will be challenged. That is why I've been pressing you, Mr Fossiter, for reports and schedules. Not to question your sense of duty, but to make the most of it. What if we harnessed this moment of transition, and used it to our advantage? What if the great work of your family could be concluded?' He gestured to the grim-faced oil paintings. 'Think how proud you would make them.'

Daniel shook his head. He knew where this was going. Sidney always came to it eventually.

He looked down at Mole, who was staring into space, and wished she were still young enough to bite and growl. For when Sidney started talking about the future, he became like a fanatic in a trance. Where before he had only irritated Daniel, now he unnerved him.

'Old Man Thunder,' said Sidney in a half-whisper. 'The catch to end all catches. The one that eluded all of your forefathers.'

'Old Man Thunder is a bedtime story.'

'Is he, though? Only last week, somebody told me they'd seen a bald man walking on Drum Head.'

Inwardly Daniel cursed Finn for being so careless. Outwardly he did his best to be indifferent. 'None of us are getting any younger, Mr Moses, and half the men of Thunderstown have watched their hair desert them. It was probably just Abe Cosser, searching for a lost sheep.'

'Abe Cosser was the man who saw him.'

Daniel shrugged. 'If he were real, one of my fathers would have caught him. But not one of them ever even saw him.'

'But what if your fathers never caught him because they never had the tools? If we organize, Mr Fossiter, and if we bring in the newest technologies, I believe we can flush him out. Then, at last, the town will be safe from the weather.'

Daniel stared across the room at the picture of his grandfather. Painted before his hair had turned white and his skin had wrinkled from the bone, he looked in the portrait the spitting image of his grandson. As did every other man glowering from the hallway walls. He remembered his grandfather concluding wistfully that Old Man Thunder did not exist, just as each and every Fossiter before him had concluded it, after hoping it was true and searching for him in vain. Old Man Thunder, the legend went, was a storm cloud that had become a man. He was the master of the wild dogs, the rider of the brook horse, the herdsman of the mountain goats, and more. It was said he once lived, bald and wizened, on the spot where Saint Erasmus now stood, but he had been driven up into the mountains by the first of Thunderstown's settlers. There he still roamed, inciting the weather, scheming to reclaim the land from the townsfolk.

It was said that if the culler were to put a bullet in Old Man Thunder, then the weather would stop forming into devilish beasts and the town would be reprieved. As such, each young Fossiter had dreamed about being that gunman, then in old age called time on the fantasy and declared Old Man Thunder to be nothing but a bogeyman.

Unlike his family, Daniel had been content to dismiss the story of Old Man Thunder from an early age. He had believed in his grandfather's rebuttal, and seen nothing in the mountains to question it. Only when Finn was born did the details of the legend creep back into his thinkings. In the first months of his life, Daniel had watched nervously as Betty nursed this bawling, wizened creature, and he had thought that it matched very well the angry, bald-headed devil of folklore.

Clearly he had done a bad job of hiding such fears, for one night Betty had sat him down and held his hand and said, 'Nothing in the world is ever like you think it's going to be,' and that maxim had dropped into his thoughts like an anchor and he had again put Old Man Thunder out of his mind. Yet here was Sidney Moses, dragging him back out again.

'No,' said Daniel. 'It is a waste of all our times to look for him.'

Sidney had been watching him studiously. For a moment his mouth looked full of venom, but then he managed to smile and gently laid a wad of papers on the homestead table. 'I disagree,' he said, 'and I hope to bring you round. For now, please consider these documents a favour. To help you file your reports.' He put his hat back on his head and tipped it. 'Good morning, Mr Fossiter.'

Daniel nodded, and Sidney left him. He closed the door and bolted it, then took a cursory look at the papers Sidney had left. He had prepared row after row of boxes he expected Daniel to tick. Records of goats shot and trapped. Wild dogs sighted. Expenses incurred. Daniel spat on the sheets and prayed for a rockslide to tip down on Sidney, his report books, and eliminate every final trace of him.

After making sure that Mole was comfortable, Daniel filled a sack of groceries and with this and the fifty sheets of rolled white paper headed out for Old Colp. He did not take the direct path from Thunderstown, but instead embarked south into the Merrow Wold. Only once he was some distance from the town did he turn northwest and climb Old Colp's slopes from that oblique direction. This was his habit whenever he visited Finn, for he did not want a man like Sidney Moses to know where he was going. Should Sidney discover Finn, well ... he feared how things would turn out.

When at last he reached the bothy, the sun and the banded clouds dropped stripes of shadow across the dirt and the bluff the cottage backed up against. Crickets rattled in the grass, and when he knocked on the door a yellow bird shot up from the eaves and flew away with a corkscrewing bent.

He crossed his fingers and hoped that Finn would not be home. Then this awkward duty would have been avoided once again. He would leave his delivery of groceries and paper by way of a calling card.

Today he was unlucky. He heard the handle turn, and then the door to the bothy opened.

A lifetime spent tracking beasts had made Daniel keenly observant, so he did not miss the enthusiasm on Finn's face when he answered. It promptly dropped away, as if he had been expecting someone else. They greeted each other civilly, but when Daniel entered the shelter he sniffed the air as if he might smell an intruder. Nothing, and he wished Mole were young and well and with him. He took the groceries straight to the kitchenette corner, wondering why on earth the two of them still did this. Neither could conceal their disdain for these occasions. He dumped most of the supplies directly into Finn's cupboard and vegetable basket, then selected two plates (remembering how he and Betty had once eaten off these plates amid laughter) and carried them to the table along with a bunch of carrots still speckled with soil, a loaf of bread that yesterday had been fresh and springy but today had staled, and a tub of a vegetable pâté he had bought from Sally Nairn in Auger Lane.

They sat down to lunch at the table, but both positioned their chairs askance to it, so that they didn't quite face each other.

'Well,' said Daniel, 'are you going to tell me how you've been faring?'

'Good, for the most part.'

Daniel nodded and broke the bread. 'Dear Lord,' he prayed, 'bless this our sustenance, for which we give thanks.' *And,* he added in his head, *make this wretched hour speed by.*

'Amen,' they both said aloud.

Daniel dipped the end of a carrot into the pâté, sighed, and took a bite. Sally Nairn, he thought, was a fine woman – but whether she laboured over a spread, a pickle or a jam, the result always tasted of chalk and cauliflower.

'And you,' asked Finn, avoiding the spread, 'how have you been keeping?'

Daniel spared his palate with a mouthful of dry bread. 'Little has changed. There is still this business of Sidney Moses.'

'I'm sure you can deal with Sidney Moses.'

'Of course I can.'

The crunching of their molars on carrot was the only sound. Daniel liked to bring carrots to these meetings. Time spent chewing was time rescued from trying to talk. In the early days they had filled such gaps by reminiscing about Betty. She had been their intermediary before she had left, and without her they were like two foreigners abandoned by their interpreter. They had stopped talking about her for two reasons. Firstly, because the time when they expected her to return had passed. Secondly, because they discovered that their memories of her were so very different.

'Someone visited me,' said Finn, out of the blue.

Daniel swallowed his half-chewed mouthful of carrot. It wedged in his throat and he spluttered. 'Who?' he demanded when the coughing had settled.

'An American girl. She was nice.'

He pushed his plate away from him. He was no longer hungry. He had pictured in an instant the light in Sidney Moses's eyes were he to discover Finn. 'I don't much care whether she was *nice*. Surely we don't have to go back over the reasons for being up here. For keeping your own company.'

'I knew you'd take it badly. It doesn't matter, though. She won't be coming back.'

'Good. But really, Finn, you should not have opened the door to her.' He tapped his fingers nervously on the table until his memory finally offered up her face and name. Elsa Beletti, who had objected when he killed the wild dog. He became anxious. 'What did you tell her? What did you say about why you are living up here?'

Finn picked at a piece of bread. 'Nothing at all.'

'Good. That was wise. Nevertheless, I should speak to her.' He combed his fingers through his moustache and beard. 'Yes. I shall warn her not to blab to all and sundry about you.'

Finn frowned. 'She won't blab.'

Daniel bit his lip. And now he remembered the look of excitement on Finn's face when he had answered the door. 'You know who she is and who she is not, do you? You were hoping it was her when I arrived here today!'

'So what if I was?'

In an instant Daniel's head was full of blood. He gripped the table for support. 'So what? Damned well remember what you did to your mother!'

Finn shrank in his chair.

Daniel stood up and took a deep, controlling breath. He brushed with chopping motions the crumbs from his hands. 'I should see about her right away.' He took his broad-brimmed cap from the hook on which he had hung it. 'Good day, Finn.'

Yet even as he charged back down the slopes towards Thunderstown, he discovered that he was oddly grateful to Elsa Beletti. He told himself it was because she'd given him an excuse to cut short his visit, since his other reason unsettled him. Sometimes his thinkings presented him with sudden emotions or opinions that he did not recognize as his, as if they were intrusions from some other mind, carried like a tune into his own. This had been just such an unasked-for feeling, which he now snuffed out: he had been pleased to know that Finn had found somebody to smile about, for when he smiled some angle of his lips reminded him of Betty's.

# 8

# THE LIVES OF THE CLOUDS

Five o'clock in Elsa's office arrived as slowly as Christmas morning to a child. When it came she hurried at once along the winding roads that led to Candle Street and the path out of town. From there she was soon climbing Old Colp, en route to Finn's bothy. As she walked, tiny yellow birds flittered in pairs or trios around her, enjoying the softening heat of the evening. The sky remained a lazy blue, save for a scattering of cumuli in the east and a white band of aeroplane contrails disintegrating high overhead.

'Hi,' she said when Finn opened the bothy door. 'Me again.'

He was wearing a ropey old tank vest and a pair of shorts that had seen better days, as well as his bashed-up shoes with the holes in their lips. 'It's hard to get rid of you, isn't it, Elsa?'

She laughed nervously. 'I didn't really like the way we finished things last time. I thought I should come to apologize. For, you know, freaking out a little.'

He smiled ruefully. 'I suppose it's to be expected. In retrospect I'm amazed that you stayed as long as you did.'

'Well, I wish I'd at least stayed a bit longer.'

'It's probably best that you didn't. Don't take this the wrong way, but you shouldn't come up here any more. It's not that I don't like you – I wish I could get to know you better – it's just that … it's dangerous.'

She didn't want to be asked to leave again. 'Surely there's no harm in a little more conversation?'

He sighed and placed a hand on his chest. 'The harm is in here.'

She laughed. 'What kind of threat is that?'

He put his hands sheepishly into his pockets. One of them was a torn pocket out of the bottom of which his forefinger showed. 'I made something after we talked. I think I'd like to give it to you. Will you come in?'

'I'd love that.'

He turned and she followed him into the bothy.

He had been crafting more paper since last she saw him. Birds formed a mound of wings and white tails on the table. Each, she felt, was a work of art, as delicate and innovative as any origami she had seen, but Finn dug through them as if they were waste paper, sending them gliding left and right down to the floor.

'Here!' he exclaimed, and held up a different kind of model. It was a paper skyscraper, built with a pointed paper spire and a roof of stepped tiers. 'My mother showed me a photograph once, of New York. Is this right? Don't you have towers there?'

'It's …' she said, but she had to stop because her lip was trembling. She was surprised at how upset she was to see the shape of it. In New York she had barely registered Manhattan's height – she was so used to it after her first few weeks there – but this paper version felt as heavy as its inspiration. It trapped her hands at her sides and she could not move them. She was at once homesick and sick of the reminder of home. 'You don't like it?'

'It's not that.' She spoke through a tight throat. 'It's so very sweet of you, but …'

'Here.' He held it lightly on his palm for a second, then screwed it into litter. 'Gone.'

After a while she said, 'I'm really sorry. I don't know what came over me. I don't want to seem ungrateful.'

'I understand. Sometimes there are things in life that you would rather forget. I apologize. I should have made you something different.'

'No, it was lovely of you. I'm just ... a bit screwed up, that's all.'

He threw the scrunched paper model across the room and into the bin. 'Then you're in good company.'

'Do you know ... it's weird, but I felt like I was. When we were talking yesterday.'

He didn't say anything. She still hadn't got used to the silences that he was so comfortable with opening up between them. She supposed they were to be expected: he was, after all, part weather, and weather was not renowned for its verbosity. She waited a minute before he spoke again.

'Would you like to choose a paper bird instead? You can take as many as you like.'

She began to search through the ones on the table, inspecting each with the diligence of an auctioneer. 'How do you get them so lifelike?' she asked when she had chosen her favourite: a broad-winged goose with a neck straight as a ruler.

'I don't really know.'

She laughed. 'That's not a very good answer.'

He looked out of the window for inspiration. He had filled a clay jar on the sill with a spray of wildflowers, including one magnificent specimen whose dappled petals formed a yellow orb, like a world globe made out of gold. He touched its petals lightly as he thought, and she realized that *that* was how he made them, with a rare and gentle precision. 'Okay, put it this way,' he said with a shrug, 'I just fold on a hunch, and I know there's really no such thing as flight. That might sound crazy, but it's true. There's only really a kind of swimming in the air.'

She smiled. 'My dad always used to say the air was an ocean.'

'Yeah, exactly! Just like an ocean, with currents and tides. And people are like ... like the crabs and the worms on the ocean floor.'

'That's very flattering.'

'I just mean that people are stuck on the bottom level. But to other creatures those currents and tides can be climbed just like a person climbs a tree or a hill. When you understand how that works, you can fold a paper bird. I've watched a lot of birds surfing the air up here on the mountain. I actually look after a few of them.'

'You keep them? Here?'

'No, farther up the mountain.'

She placed the paper goose gently on to the table. 'Would you show me?'

'Um, I'm not sure I should.'

'Why not? You don't want to?'

'I'd love to, it's just …'

'Then what are we waiting for?'

After a moment he shrugged and got up.

They stepped outside and she followed him uphill. He walked with a centre of suspension that made him look as if he were gliding. She plodded along beside him and paused now and again to catch her breath. The recent heat had papered the boulders with dust, and so dried out the grass that their shoes left crushed footprints in the turf. In the east, congesting cumuli teased the prospect of much-needed rain.

They walked in the kind of comfortable silence she thought it took people years, not days, to learn. Then, unprompted, he began to describe how last summer a field mouse had made her nest outside the bothy and he had learned to entice her inside with a trail of white chocolate. Once he had lured her in he had crouched beside her to make model after paper model. He said he got good at her tail – a long twist of paper instead of a fold. And then when he had finished the story he fell to silence again, and it delighted her that she could resist her natural compulsion to fill it.

Then they came upon the fringe of a wiry copse. Around the trees a ditch had been dug and around that a perimeter of razor wire coiled. Clumps of fur hung from its blades.

'I'm guessing we'll be trespassing if we go in there,' said Elsa.

'No,' said Finn. 'These defences are Daniel's work. To keep goats out, not us. Goats would devour these trees in a day.'

He picked up a plank of wood and leaned it against the fence to create a rudimentary stile. He hopped over and turned to help Elsa. She enjoyed the smooth touch of his fingers as he took her hand and guided her over the step.

Under the copse's foliage the world immediately cooled and quietened. The leaves had been parched by summer into early autumn's hues, but enough still lined the branches to cast a pied pattern across the floor. Here they stopped, themselves dappled in light and shade.

'Now, just listen,' instructed Finn, holding a finger to his lips.

She heard the chirrup of birdsong, and scanning the intertwining branches saw in several places little yellow birds perched in threes and fours. One swept past her, warbling as it went.

'You see them?' he whispered.

'Yes. Of course.'

He grinned. 'They're canaries. I've put up nest boxes for them. There are thousands of them on the mountains in the summer. My mother told me a story about them once. She said that on the day the floods finished off the mines, a tradesman was selling canaries in Candle Street. The water knocked his stall down and smashed his cages open. Out flew a hundred canaries, and they hatched a hundred more and so on. Ever since then there have been wild canaries in Thunderstown.'

'That's a nice story.'

'But it's not true, because they don't hatch.'

'What do you mean? Of course they hatch.'

'No, they don't. Look over there.'

She looked along the line of his pointing finger, and saw nothing.

'You're too slow, Elsa. Wait … wait … Now! Over there!'

At first she thought it was an optical illusion. A trick of the sunlight playing on the fallen leaves. Then up out of a bright patch of loam shot a canary, to join its fellows in the boughs of the copse. She rubbed her eyes. 'What did I just see?'

'It's happening again! Over there!'

He was pointing to a spot in the leaf litter that seemed more radiant than all the rest. It was as if an ember had touched down there and set the leaves to kindling. As she watched, the glow became intense. It formed a tiny orb of light that made the roots and twigs around it gleam, and left a sunspot in her vision. It began to shimmer and skew, and then the leaves looked like fiery feathers and she heard a bird cry out.

The light rose from the leafy floor with a hiss like a sparkler. Then it shot past her ear and she felt a hot breeze bristling her hair to its roots. Its shine dimmed as it flew, until she could clearly see its wings, a beak and tail feathers steering its ascent. It fluttered on to a branch, where it preened its plumage and tested its song.

'Whuh … what just happened?'

'A sunbeam,' Finn said, 'came to life.'

She had too many questions to ask him any.

He grinned from ear to ear. 'Would you like to catch one?'

'What?'

'They're quite friendly. Come on.' And with that he grasped the lowest boughs of the nearest tree and heaved himself up its trunk.

She was surprised that such a big man could ghost so easily upwards. He grinned down at her from the higher branches and asked, 'What are you waiting for?'

She shook her head, still stunned by what she'd seen.

'We won't catch one on the ground, Elsa. They only like to perch among the branches.'

'I ... I ...'

He glided back down as swiftly as he had gone up. 'I'll help you climb. Here, grab this branch.'

She took hold of its warm bark and stared up through the foliage at a trio of canaries who had squeezed on to a twig, watching her with cocked heads and cooing as if she were the most ridiculous thing in the world.

She hauled herself upwards with no real method, lifting her feet from the ground and pushing them against the trunk to try to find a foothold. She was surprised by how light she felt, then realized that Finn had cupped one hand beneath her foot to give her purchase. For a moment she wanted to leave her foot there. Then she pushed on upwards and got up on to one of the branches, after which it became easier to climb.

Finn floated up the trunk to overtake her and lead her gradually higher, until they sat facing one another on two high wooden arms.

'Now we have to be quiet, and wait for the birds to resettle.'

She nodded, and they sat with the tide of leaves swaying back and forth around them. She knew he was looking at her and smiling, but she did not look back. She supposed that sights such as these were ordinary for him, but the strangeness had made her feel as if they had been through a momentous event together. It had always been her assumption that to connect with a person you needed to have shared so much. Yet here they were, still strangers, and she felt a connection to him as tangible as that between the branch she was sitting on and its trunk. 'Now,' he whispered, 'hold out your hands.'

She did so, wondering if he was going to take hold of them. Instead he produced from his good pocket a sachet of seeds, and placed one fat grain in her palms. Then they waited. A canary bustled through the treetops, springing and zipping from branch to branch, getting closer in stops and starts. It paused for a while on the twigs above Finn's head, leaning its head left and right, its eyes swivelling hard at Elsa. She smiled at it, in case that would help.

Then it flicked wide its yellow wings and whirred down to perch on her hands. She felt the pin-tip of its beak tapping against her skin as it gobbled up the seed.

'Catch it,' whispered Finn.

Nervously – it felt wrong to touch a wild creature – she slid her free hand over the canary and cupped it to trap the bird in her hold. It burbled at her furiously, and she yelped when its wings whirred and tickled her skin. Still she kept it trapped, and then she felt a change come over it.

'Finn … something's happening!'

'Don't worry. It can't hurt you.'

The canary had stopped struggling. It crouched still, virtually weightless in her hands. It was getting hot – not just with the compact warmth from its small heart and muscles, but with the penetrative warmth of a summer afternoon. And now around her hands a dim light glowed, getting brighter as she watched it, until golden shafts shone through the cracks between her fingers.

Some fearful switch tripped inside of her and she let go of the canary with a start. But her hands were empty and the bird had vanished, as had the light she had been holding, gone in a yellow shimmer of air. The only evidence that remained was the warmth in her palms, as if she had been holding them to a campfire.

Finn laughed and clapped his hands, but she needed a moment to compose herself. 'I … I …' she stuttered. 'I didn't kill it, did I?'

'No, of course not. You can't kill sunlight, can you? It'll come back in a minute or two. Unless the sun stops shining.'

He started to climb down from the tree. She stayed put for a moment, then scrabbled after him.

'Finn, I … I saw a dog the other night. It led me to a path and then it vanished. There was only thin air and a wind that barged back past me.'

Finn nodded. 'If you know where to look you will see other such things. They exist in these mountains. You might see a horse cantering out of a flood. You might see swifts and swallows vanishing on the breeze. Some will be manifestations of the weather. If we stayed here until sunset we'd see many of these canaries turn red, and if we stayed longer, until nightfall, most of them would disappear.'

She dwelt on this for a moment. 'So ... what about you?'

'I ...' he started. He looked so crestfallen that she had made the connection that she wanted to retract it.

After a moment she tried to prompt him. 'You said yourself that you are part weather. And I saw what happened to you at the windmill.'

'Yes,' he said.

The canaries trilled and warbled overhead. She wanted, she realized with a thrill like an electric shock, him to be the same as them. She wanted him to be weather entirely.

'You want to know,' he said slowly, 'whether I am any different from the dogs and the canaries. I ... I feel like I am, although I'm not sure if that counts. There is one big difference: these creatures have materialized out of thin air, whereas I was born and grew up. There are photos of my pregnant mother, and pictures of me as a baby and a boy. So I must be a man.'

'Of course,' she said, trying not to sound disappointed. 'Yeah, I guess that is different.'

'But ... sometimes I don't feel substantial enough to be a person. I feel too light, like I might be blown away at any moment. And I, um ... I ...'

'You can trust me, Finn.'

'I don't have a heartbeat.'

'But … that's impossible!'

'Is it?'

She held a hand to her head. She had a feeling like vertigo. 'No heartbeat,' she repeated, and she found herself staring at his chest. 'Then what keeps you going?'

He laid a palm on his breast. 'Maybe the thunder.'

She licked her lips. She felt like she was standing on the edge of a precipice, and she had to either back off or let herself fall in. 'Can you hear it?'

'Yes. Sometimes.'

And because she knew no other way, she let herself tip forwards. 'I want to listen.'

She held her breath. He looked at her as if she were mad. ' I don't want to scare you again.'

'I won't be scared this time. I know it.'

'Then … all right.'

She nodded, but did not move towards him. She was all of a sudden aware of his height and breadth, and of her own body and her hot pulse intruding through it, of a film of sweat on the small of her back, and of the air between them that had turned into a giant obstacle.

'Now?' she asked, to buy time.

'Y-yes,' he said. 'Whenever you are ready.'

She took a deep breath then plunged forwards, bending in towards his chest so fast she almost headbutted him.

His chest was firm against her ear. She felt him tensing. She closed her eyes and listened.

It was like putting an ear to a conch shell and hearing the sea: through his breastbone she could hear a noise like a distant storm. The steady strokes of falling rain, the whistling of winds, the unmistakable base notes of thunder, then a whiplash fizzle of lightning. She didn't flinch. She was as absorbed as she had been when she was a little girl, her hands and face pressed to her window to watch black clouds scud across the horizon.

'Elsa …'

His voice brought her back to her senses. Senses that were clearer now, clearer than they had been in a very long time. She felt as if she had just stepped in from a long and bracing walk.

'Elsa …' he repeated.

She stood up straight. 'Thank you,' she said.

Then she kissed him.

At first he made a feeble resistance, but she could tell he didn't want her to stop. Then he was kissing her back, wrapping his arms tightly around her even as she slid her hands over his shoulders and thought, *Maybe I'm kissing a storm. Maybe I'm kissing the thunder.*

Finn kissed with his eyes closed, she with hers open. Then after a minute he opened his too and she looked straight into those storm-tinged irises. She lost herself in the rough circles of his pupils, like the centres of a labyrinth, towards which she had been stumbling and lost for a very long time.

# 9

# THE SOLEMN TEMPLES

Sunday morning had come around, and Elsa lay in bed thinking about Finn. She'd hoped to see him again today, but he'd said they should wait until Monday. In Thunderstown, he explained, the Sabbath was still a day of rest and observance, when families would come together. Daniel Fossiter would often materialize at the bothy, driven there by guilt to share an awkward meal. Finn thought it best that, for the time being at least, the culler did not see them together.

Elsa had no intention of letting Daniel dictate who she could and could not see, but his interference was a problem for the future, one she hoped Finn would confront sooner rather than later. For the time being, she let herself be satisfied with a kiss.

A knock at the door. She yawned as she climbed out of bed. She answered, rubbing sleep dust from her eyes. Kenneth Olivier was wearing a crumpled suit with a fresh yellow flower through its lapel. His tie was as gruesomely patterned as one of his multi-coloured jumpers. Elsa was still dressed in her bed boxers and a t-shirt, and he looked embarrassed to see her in such clothes. 'I'm sorry,' he mumbled, backing away from the door. 'I thought you would be getting ready for church.'

'Er ... no. I'm not religious.'

'Oh,' he said. 'Oh, I see. Oh.' His expression fell, not because he judged her on it, but because just yesterday he'd told her with a level of enthusiasm she'd only seen him display before when talking about doosras and googlies in cricket matches that he'd become the church choirmaster, and this Sunday would be the first time his charges would sing in the service. She wished she hadn't said anything.

He blushed, apologized for disturbing her, and turned to shuffle back down the stairs.

'Wait!'

He looked back hopefully.

'The Church of Saint Erasmus?'

He nodded.

She grinned. 'Five minutes.'

She closed the door and hurried to her wardrobe. She immediately caught sight of the presents from her mother, still wrapped and in their bag, forgotten in the wooden shadows. She bit back a wash of guilt that their taped-up paper brought her, but still she would not open them.

Church, then. It had been a while. She couldn't stomach her mother's church, a place she was obliged to attend if a visit home took place over a Sunday. The way that the congregation raised their hands in the air and pulled pained spiritual expressions as they sang made her feel self-conscious, even though she liked the idea that God could be like lightning, that raising a hand might increase your chances of being struck. She hoped the Church of Saint Erasmus, that cavernous minster so closed to the elements, would prove to be different.

She'd have to dress smart, like Kenneth. Her only appropriate clothes were her office skirt and blouse, which she pulled on with regret, since they made her feel like a workday had come around early. She tied her hair up to disguise the fact she hadn't washed it, then hurried down the stairs, still stamping into her unpolished black shoes. Kenneth was waiting in the yard outside the house, whistling a hymn she half-recognized. The noise of a dull bell tolling rang out from the direction of the church. She put her arm through Kenneth's and they set off.

'Daniel Fossiter stopped by earlier, while you were sleeping,' he remarked as they walked.

'Why? I mean, are you guys friends?'

'Not really, no, although we get along all right. But this morning he had actually come looking for you. He said he'd heard I had a guest. And that she was an American girl. He's going to come back later, but perhaps you'll see him at church.'

'That's all? He was just paying a friendly visit?'

'Yes. I suppose so.'

They turned off Prospect Street and into Bradawl Alley, where the walls wore a green stain like a tidemark and every so often the pavement hopped down a few chipped steps.

'Weird,' she said. 'He didn't seem like the type.'

Kenneth frowned. 'You're still thinking about the dog you saw him kill. I don't think you should judge him too harshly for that. Daniel is dependable and decent. You'll find far worse than him in Thunderstown.'

'That doesn't paint a pretty picture.'

He chuckled. 'You wait until you see some of the folk in my choir. I'm afraid that the people of Thunderstown have good reasons for many of their beliefs. Some of the things they think are, frankly, nonsense, but others are born out of very real and painful memories. Lots of people here are old enough to remember the terrible flood that destroyed the mines, and many of them lost loved ones that day. It is important for them to know that a culler is here with them, to protect them from the weather.'

Bradawl Alley ended under a blackened stone arch, beyond which lay Corris Street, whose windows were all shuttered up. Saint Erasmus's belfry poked above the chimney stacks, its tolling bell sounding closer with every step. Behind it, Drum Head watched the town with one sleepy eye.

'What on earth,' she asked, 'could Daniel Fossiter do to protect Thunderstown from another flood?'

Kenneth chuckled. 'Nothing, of course, although the more superstitious residents would disagree. They still hope he'll catch Old Man Thunder.'

'What? Who's Old Man Thunder?'

He cleared his throat. 'Some people blame a sort of devil for the bad weather that has, in the past, devastated parts of the town. Legend has it that he lives somewhere up in the mountains. He's old and bald and wicked, although they say he didn't start out that way. They say he was a thunderstorm once, who got so lonely up in the sky that he turned himself into a man of skin and bones. Only, when he tried to speak, his words were lightning, and they set the meadows on fire. When he tried to touch another person he blew them away with a gale. He became so sad that he could not be a proper human being that he wept, and his tears became a flood that rushed down to the town, drowned the livestock and filled the mines with poisonous water.'

They walked in silence. There was no noise of bird or wind, only the clang of the church bell.

'Kenneth,' she asked warily, 'do *you* believe in that story?'

'Oh no, no. But I can understand it. Sometimes people need someone to blame.'

Corris Street arced into Saint Erasmus Square, and the colossal church appeared before them. The knowledge that she was about to enter it, not just to explore it but to be there with the worshippers, gave the building an even darker aspect. It didn't feel like a church from the modern world but some solemn temple from ancient times.

She shook her head as if to clear out her overactive imagination. It was just a huge stack of bricks and mortar. Inside there would be nothing but empty space and elderly churchgoers.

She was right, and triumphant for a moment as Kenneth led her through the door, then disappointed that there was no mystery within, no soul of the building present like a phantom. The church felt barren, its walls whitewashed and bare, the cold confines of its stone keeping the hot day out. A tuneless organ played as the congregation entered. Depending on how you looked at it, attendance was either exceptional or dire: every uncomfortable pew was full, but there were very few pews in the church. Most of them had vanished along with its statues and gargoyles and, given the rich mahogany they'd been joined from, Elsa suspected they had all been pawned. Surrounding these few rows of worshippers spread a sea of grey flagstones, chiselled with the names and titles of the bodies interned beneath. Mosses sprouted through the cracks, and the stones were smattered with the droppings of those feathered church regulars who lived in the rafters.

Then she saw Daniel Fossiter in the front row, head bowed in piety, a conspicuous space between him and both his neighbours.

Kenneth went to sit with his choir so Elsa found a spot on the end of a back pew, as far from Daniel as possible. She'd been sitting there barely a minute when a diminutive nun wearing enormous glasses sat down beside her.

'New here?' she asked Elsa, in an ancient, impish voice.

'Quite, yes.'

The nun unfolded her hands in her lap. When she spoke her teeth showed, each one whittled away until it was set apart from the next. 'I'm *old* here,' she said. She unfolded her ancient fingers to indicate she was not only old in this church but old in the streets outside, the uplands and the mountains beyond.

'Dot,' she said, and pinched Elsa mischievously on the arm.

'Elsa.'

'And you're staying with Mr Olivier.'

'Yes,' Elsa replied, surprised at what this old lady knew. 'Kenneth, yes.'

Dot tapped the side of her crooked nose with an even more crooked finger. 'Kenneth told me to look out for you. Said you'd sit at the back. So I stuck my bones down here. I won't hear much of the sermon this far away from the lectern, but there's no harm in that, is there?'

Elsa laughed, a little too loudly, and her laughter rippled off the vault of the roof, where wings thrashed in response.

'And how was your journey?' Dot asked.

'We just walked. Kenneth doesn't live so far away.'

'No. Your journey to Thunderstown.'

'Oh,' she said absent-mindedly, 'Beautiful. You know, when the clouds are like a landscape and you want to run across them? And everybody else has their head in a book or their eyes closed and you feel like you're the only one in the world who still thinks there's magic in flying.'

'Look here,' said the nun, reaching into her crisp grey habit to pull out a little pouch. After trying unsuccessfully to remove its contents with her bent fingers, she reached across and took one of Elsa's hands, turned the palm upwards into a cup, and tipped the contents into it. On to her palm fell a fresh red flower like a baby tulip, a big yellow button, a canine tooth and a passport-sized photograph. This last item Dot picked up and showed to Elsa.

'I haven't got a husband to carry in my purse with me,' grinned Dot, 'unless of course you count the good Lord himself, who doesn't pose for photographs. But this is the next best thing.'

The photo didn't show a face but a dark mass of clouds with the sun bursting behind them, so that the cloud edges were lined with a brilliant light.

'It's a silver lining,' Elsa said.

'I've got more, many more.' She began to repack the things into their pouch. 'You should come and visit me sometime.'

Before Elsa could answer, the organ ceased playing and the priest stood and cleared his throat. He was all jowls, and had no hair on his spotted head except for a pair of eyebrows that were thick and black like rat fur. 'That priest,' Dot whispered, leaning so close that Elsa could smell her (and she smelled heady and sweet like pudding wine), 'was young here when this church was glorious. When the windowpanes were still full of stained glass.'

After an opening address and prayer, the priest informed the congregation that it was time for the choir to sing. Elsa recognized one or two of its members from around town, but she now knew all of them by name and vocal range, thanks to Kenneth's enthusiastic descriptions.

That man with the tufty moustache and greased, combed hair was Hamel Rhys, who claimed he had been suckled on bottles of beer instead of breast milk. Behind him stood Hettie Moses, wife of the town busybody Sidney, and alongside her a pair of austere old sisters, identical twins who still lived together. These Hettie had befriended, and she had done all she could to curl her hair and dress as if she were their triplet. The final member of the choir was little Abe Cosser, who kept a flock of sheep on the fields of Drum Head. It was said in Thunderstown that just as a dog resembles its owner, so too a shepherd resembles his flock, and true to form, little Abe Cosser possessed spread eyes and the slanted, reaching teeth of a ewe. Yet he also had a beautiful falsetto, and when Kenneth raised his hands (Elsa could see the nerves jittering in his left leg) and the choir began to sing, Abe's voice fluted mournfully over the amateur tones of the other members, lifting their plain song into a melancholy harmony made almost supernatural by the lofty echoes of the church. Dot closed her eyes and exhaled with pleasure, and when the singing stopped Elsa had a momentary pang of something almost like grief at its ending.

Then came the priest's sermon, addressed to the gathered faithful in his reedy voice. It was a losing battle with the acoustics of the building. The congregation cupped hands to ears to try to make out the words above echoing interruptions from sneezes, cleared throats, dropped hymn sheets and the constant commotion of pigeons up above.

Unable to follow the sermon, Elsa settled as comfortably as she could into the pew and watched the light playing across the plain frosted glass of the windows. Outside, the clouds were passing across the sun, sifting shadows down on to the town.

She remembered waking before first light on a Saturday, the door to her bedroom creaking open, and her dad appearing with a finger to his lips. Slipping out of bed, she'd padded after him and shadowed him down the stairs. There in the hallway he'd dressed her in her coat, and together they'd tiptoed out of the door with him carrying her shoes by the laces. She couldn't risk putting them on inside, in case her footsteps echoed on the floorboards. Dark mornings were different from night-times, especially when you were still brimming with sleep. She'd crept along, hand in hand with her father, obeying the only rule he imposed whenever they did this: this stays our secret, you don't breathe a word about it when we return to the house. But that would happen long after absorbing fleets of altocumulus in the dim morning glow, or the eerie disc of a lenticular cloud, floating like a spaceship above the distant Ouachita Mountains.

She kept their rule. Never told her mother she'd been up and outside long before the day had started. Told her instead that her dad had taken her to dance classes while her mum had snored through her weekend lie-in. She had to learn a few moves now and again to feign a performance, but she didn't feel bad in deceiving her. She knew her mum would go berserk if she found out what they were really doing, and besides, these trips were just as important to Elsa as they were to her dad.

Now, thinking back to it, she wondered why her dad had never come to church with them on Sundays? If he'd done that it could have been a pact: storms on a Saturday and services the day after. She knew right away why he hadn't: he was addicted. On Sunday mornings, too, he'd head out cloud-watching before dawn broke. But to Elsa those Saturday mornings felt more spiritual than the Sunday ones. It was no surprise to her that, once upon a time, people had equated storms with gods. The first time she saw a town that had been sucked up and spat out by a tornado, it broke her heart and made her question the immense indifference of the universe, just as others might question the indifference of a deity. That was what storms were: they behaved with all the splendour and barbarity of ancient deities. Clouds were not just an ornament of godly imagery, clouds were the inspiration for pantheons, awesomely real and intangible at the same time. There were thousands of them swarming across the planet at any given moment, and yet under the shelters of roofs and ceilings it was so easy to forget their existence.

The church of the sky was something she'd so often dreamed of while the hoo-ha of the Sunday service carried on around her. There seemed to her infinitely more God to be found by staring up at the never-ending universe than by looking glumly around a building of bricks and stone.

Her father's holy books were written by meteorologists. His preferred prophet was the lightning: he was on a one-man crusade to explain the inner workings of a lightning bolt to anyone he could, as if they held some revelatory value. Cab drivers, waiters, shop assistants: no one was safe. 'The lightning doesn't strike,' he would tell them, and if they made the mistake of asking him to elaborate he would do so until they managed to excuse themselves. 'It's a connection, you see. The storm reaches for the ground with an electrical feeler, invisible to the naked eye. The ground does the same, and it's like two arms trying to grasp each other in the dark. Then, if they manage to find one another, their connection is so strong it catches on fire, and is hotter than the surface of the sun.'

Not long after Elsa moved to New York, her dad received his first prison sentence. She had been hosting her flat-warming party on the night he phoned her to say he was in trouble again with the police. It was not the first time he had been caught stealing. On previous occasions he had escaped with fines and community service, but this time the judge had ruled that his repeat offences warranted something more severe.

It had been a surreal revelation. She knew he had been broke for years, but he had hidden the extent of it from her. It was because he was a storm junkie. When she was a kid he had worked at a big weather centre in Norman, but his employers had noticed the peculiar pattern of his sick days. Every time he got news of some big hurricane forming off the coast, or some mega-tornado predicted in the prairie, he'd set off in his truck to be in its company. After they fired him he got other, crappier jobs, but these exerted even less of a hold on him and his absenteeism only increased. Eventually he had no money left and stole a bag of candy bars from a mart.

She had wanted to support him at the hearing. She'd been able to see what he'd done in perspective: it was only a damned packet of candy bars, whereas he was her precious father. But he had lied to her about the court location and only subsequently did she learn of his later, escalating crimes, which had culminated in the theft of the purse of a single mother of three.

She was the only one who visited him in jail. Not her mother, not her father's side of the family, not even the storm-chaser friends who – she had always felt – had never been on his wavelength anyway. They were thrill-seekers, whereas her dad had no interest in storms as a joyride. His reasons for following them were more spiritual than that. He was the high priest of the hurricane, the liturgist of the lightning, and this image was the one she clung to, even if she knew it was only a part of the picture that was her father.

Before he was interned, Elsa had hoped that prison would knock sense back into him. Then, on her first visit, when he'd mumbled, 'I'm weather-powered, see,' she'd had a kind of premonition of how he would go to pieces behind bars.

One time, after she'd drunk a little too much bourbon, her mum said she was calling his weather-powered bluff. He was not fuelled by the energies of storms and tornadoes. He was fuelled by the company of his only child, and he had stopped functioning because she had left him for the bright lights of the city. Perhaps she had drunkenly exaggerated, but even so the idea sent Elsa's mind reeling in horror. Could she have destroyed her father through the inevitable act of growing up? She tried to ask him about it, once, in the space between that first jail term and his second, but he was too prickly to speak on the topic.

Remembering this forced her to dry her eyes. She sniffed conspicuously, but there was only the priest's mumbled sermon to distract her from her thoughts, and it had no power to do so. Then, to her comfort, Dot's tiny, buckled hand reached sideways and squeezed hers. She breathed out, bit back her tears, and got a grip. Dot turned her head and gave her a long, studied look. Elsa met it, and the two women regarded each other for a minute before the nun smiled and returned her attention to the rambling priest.

Eventually the sermon was over and the priest was leading a prayer of grace Elsa did not recognize. It was murmured by everyone who was not her, addressed equally to everyone who was not her (save for Dot who turned to her to recite it) and then the service had ended. Spines clicked and creaked as the worshippers rose to their feet, making their way back towards the closed front doors, around which an outline of daylight glowed. Elsa looked over at

Daniel Fossiter at the front of the church. He rose slowly from his seat, stretched out his spine, then glanced back across the pews and caught Elsa's eye. She looked at the ground immediately.

The priest had opened the doors, but had backed up into a slice of shadow, and she shook his frail hand on the way out and wished him well for the week before stepping out hurriedly into the late morning. She wanted to get away from the church doors before Daniel Fossiter strode out of them. The sky had filled with a sheet of grey cloud, binding the town and the surrounding mountains together.

'Altostratus,' she thought, then realized somebody else had said it out loud. It was Dot, emerging behind her.

Dot winked at her. 'You look like you've other places to be. Don't worry, I won't keep you. But we fellow cloud-watchers should never abandon each other. You must come up to see me at the nunnery. Kenneth can give you directions. And don't wait too long about it. I could show you things. More pictures. I have a great many pictures up there.'

'Thank you,' said Elsa, meaning it. 'I'm sure I will.'

Dot nodded, and turned back up the church steps, just as Daniel Fossiter emerged, stuffing his hat on to his head and scanning the assembled crowd until he saw Elsa. He moved towards her as if he intended to speak to her, but then found his path blocked by the little old nun, who cooed about how good it was to see him and pinched his elbow and asked after his health. Meanwhile Elsa seized her chance, and slipped away towards Prospect Street.

# 10

# BETTY AND THE LIGHTNING

In the late afternoon Elsa headed for a little teahouse she had happened upon whilst exploring the town. The Wallflower was reached via a snaking alleyway with walls overgrown with vegetation. Flies and moths buzzed in and out of the leaves, or hovered over gutters whose cracked covers revealed plunging shafts. Overhead, a green roof of creepers stretched from one wall to the other, some of its stems as thick as children's arms. Further along the alley she passed an electric lamp, twinkling in a prison of foliage, and this lit up a sudden memory of a hedge maze her mum and dad had taken her to once, for a birthday treat. She alone had found the centre of that maze, and had waited for a fruitless hour for either of her parents to discover her there.

Eventually the passage opened on to a courtyard enclosed by similarly verdant walls, with trellises dotted with trumpet-headed flowers. Hidden water gurgled somewhere nearby and made the air humid.

There were six small tables and a kiosk, where she ordered the same syrupy honey drink she'd enjoyed when she first found this place. The only other patron was a shrunken old man in his waxy rain cap. She recognized him as Abe Cosser, from Kenneth's choir, but he did not appear to have noticed her. He was smoking a pipe with his eyes in upturned reverie, sedentary save for the puffing of his mouth at the pipe's lip.

She chose a seat and watched an orange butterfly, whose wrinkled appearance suggested it was as old in butterfly years as Abe was in human ones, fly jerkily from flower to flower along the trellis. After a while it swept down to her table, where its wings sagged like damp cloth over its carapace. She used her teaspoon to drop a bead of her drink beside it. The butterfly approached and uncurled its doddery proboscis. It seemed to relish the taste of the liquid, for it took off rejuvenated, swerving drunkenly through the air.

She settled back into her seat and enjoyed a sip of the sticky drink. Then a movement out of the corner of her eye made her look up.

Abe Cosser had come to life. He was suddenly full of action, like those buskers who used to annoy her in subway stations by pretending to be statues, only to burst alive at the drop of a coin. He raised his hand to his head and doffed his rain cap. At first Elsa thought he had doffed it to her, but then she heard a heavy footfall behind her and looked over her shoulder.

She gasped when she saw Daniel Fossiter, then screwed up her fists under the table for being so impressionable. He stood tall in his creased old shirt, his britches, and his boots that were hobnailed and scuffed. 'Miss Beletti,' he declared in a gruff voice, then nodded to Abe, 'and Mr Cosser. A pleasure as always.'

Abe Cosser sprung to his feet. 'All mine, Mr Fossiter. But I was just on my way.' He doffed his cap again and scurried out of the courtyard.

*Keep cool*, Elsa thought to herself. She didn't feel it.

Daniel motioned to the spare seat attached to her table. 'May I?'

She shrugged.

He eased himself into the chair; it was difficult for him to squeeze his big body between its arms and to find a space for his legs beneath the table. 'I had hoped for the chance to discuss a certain matter with you, Miss Beletti.'

She swallowed. 'And what's that?'

He placed his fists down on the table. He sat rigidly – in contrast to Elsa who suddenly could not sit still – but inside he was shaking. His thoughts had been fully occupied these last few days with how best to intervene. He had prayed on his knees for the right words to persuade her, until the unrelenting church flagstones made the pain in his bones too overwhelming to pray any more. If he got this wrong, if he failed to persuade her to steer clear of Finn, then he was not sure he could cope with the guilt the inevitable disaster would bring.

'I had hoped to discuss,' he said tremulously, 'Finn Munro.'

She was agitated. 'What is there to discuss? You're going to tell me I shouldn't see him any more, and I'm going to tell you that we'll do as we please.'

He sighed and looked down into the broth he had bought at the kiosk. They were kindly to him here, keeping a sour, fermenting vegetable stock in a special jar, even though nobody but him would buy it. 'It is more complicated than you think. It isn't safe.'

'Perhaps it's less complicated than *you* think.'

Elsa wondered whether he had any genuine hold over Finn, whether if she let her anger loose and made an enemy of him he could really make their lives difficult.

For his part, he watched her and observed that she was capable of a hundred thinkings at a time, and in this he could not help but be reminded of Betty, who had been the one to teach him that human hearts were never alike. He had known that to be true between species – the mountain shrew's heart, for example, pounded ten times faster than a human being's – but Betty's had operated at ten times the speed of his own, and he had felt like a glacier around her.

He sipped his broth. Its warmth was reassuring and gave him courage. He cleared his throat and spread out his fingers on the table. He stared at his nails as he spoke. They were grubby with mountain dirt. 'You will think me a tyrant, with no right to make demands on the boy.'

She didn't disagree.

'But, Miss Beletti, you should understand that I am not asking you to stop seeing Finn because of any wrongdoing on your part. On the contrary, I am asking you because I fear for your safety.'

She gave him one of her best sarcastic smiles. 'How very selfless of you, Mr Fossiter, but I've already had this conversation with Finn. He kept insisting he was dangerous. Because of the weather in him, he said. I told him I would be the judge of that.'

Daniel slumped back in his chair, too stunned at first to digest what she'd just said, for Finn had looked him in the eye and promised him he'd told her nothing. 'You mean to say you know what's inside of him?'

'I saw and heard what's inside of him.'

He suddenly felt very cold. The sunlight on his neck and the hot broth in his mouth were icy. Finn had deceived him. 'Do you mean to say,' he asked as steadily as he could, 'that you have seen and listened to the weather in him, and that you *still* wish to befriend him?'

'Yes. Why is that so hard to believe?'

Daniel chewed his thumbnail. It was a moment before he could speak again, and even then it was hard to regulate the anxiety in his voice. 'Have you told anybody else?'

'Of course not. It's far too … personal for that.'

He breathed out. 'Thank heaven for that. At least in that matter you are not so reckless.'

'Reckless? I think you ought to know that just because I haven't told anyone, it doesn't mean I think he should be ashamed of what's inside of him. You know what? I actually think it's wonderful.'

'I am telling you this for your benefit, not his.'

'I don't think he's dangerous. I don't think he could hurt a fly.'

Daniel rubbed his eyes. 'If by that you mean that he couldn't hurt a fly *on purpose*, then we are in agreement. What I am fearful of, Miss Beletti, is what he might do by accident.'

'Both he and I are grown-ups. We can deal with it. You've got to stop treating Finn like he's still a kid.'

Daniel could not see why she was so predisposed to find him patronizing, but as a consequence he was eager to be as straight with her as possible. It did not matter, he supposed, what she thought of him. Only that she stayed away from Finn after this conversation. 'I do not treat him like a child. I treat him as I would a wild beast.'

'Jesus, that's even worse.'

He frowned. 'I find you strange, Miss Beletti. A mystery, if you will let me use the word. I cannot pretend I understand what brings you to Thunderstown, nor why you risk so much by seeing this boy.'

'I don't think I'm risking anything. On the contrary, I think *this boy* and I have everything to gain.'

'Are you quite sure of that?'

'Of course I'm sure.'

'You have not seen what Finn is capable of.'

'Yes, I have. He's capable of sweetness and softness and silence.'

He sighed. 'Perhaps it is because you are young. Only the young put their lives at risk so brazenly.'

She was about to retort but stopped herself. 'Excuse me? What do you mean?'

He narrowed his eyes. ' He has not told you, has he?'

'Told me what?'

'What he did to Bett—' he paused, exhaled; 'to his mother.'

'Please,' Elsa asked quietly, 'tell me what happened.'

Daniel closed his eyes for a second. It was painful to remember and Elsa could see that too. 'I don't know,' he began, 'how much he has described of his childhood, but it was by necessity a sheltered one. To begin with, Betty tried to pretend he was a normal little boy, but not long after he started school the other children began to pick on him. One afternoon in the playground a stone was thrown. It hit him here –' Daniel pointed to his cheekbone, '– and a swelling came up. He ran to the teachers to show them the bruise, but when they looked more closely, they discovered it was not a bruise at all. It was more like a patch of dark cloud emerging from his very skin. They were horror-struck – they had no idea what they were seeing. They hurried him out of sight, thank goodness, and eventually the school nurse gathered herself together enough to try to wipe away, whatever it was. But it was useless; more cloud just seeped through the bruise, marking out again the place where he was wounded.'

Daniel shuddered and sipped his broth.

'There was no way Finn could return to school after such an incident, and it took all of my powers to persuade the staff to stay silent. From then on, Betty taught him at home. She kept him safe from other children, and that was for the best. He was happier because he was safe and she was happier because she saw more of him. Yet it did not take away the fact that his body was full of foul weather. I sometimes wonder … if she had not kept him so safely hidden … might there have been warning signs that would have shown just what he was capable of? Might we have been more alert to the dangers? As it was, when it happened, we saw it at full force. One night, when he was sixteen and we were at supper in Betty's house, he revealed that he had met a girl. He said she was staying in Thunderstown for the summer and that she had approached him while he lay in the sun in Betty's garden. He said he did not understand why, but that he had found it hard to talk to her. He said that in her presence he had felt things twisting inside of him, and he did not know whether he had enjoyed the feeling. Betty told him not to worry, and then she looked at me to help explain to him something of what a young man goes through when he grows up.'

He leaned back in his chair with a puff.

'Well,' asked Elsa, 'what did you tell him?'

'I told him that friendship with this girl was not for him, because he and the girl were made out of different stuffs. And I told him that his twisting feeling was like a serpent he should fight. At this advice he became lost in himself. Betty was furious – I knew she would be – but I had only said what he needed to hear.' He stared down into his drink, as if its surface were a screen replaying the past. 'Then our knives and forks began to vibrate, and I could feel every follicle of my body stiffening. I watched the hairs on Betty's head lift. Finn thumped the table and at once the knives and forks flew together and locked as if they were magnets. The very air felt like pins and needles. And then it came out, as if he'd been keeping it all bottled up and something had released inside him. He demanded to know why he had been kept so isolated. Why hadn't he been able to have friends, to talk to girls and keep their company? Why had Betty kept him hostage at home, like some freak in a sideshow? Well, I took exception to this. He'd gone too far. I told him to fasten his mouth. And then ...'

Daniel frowned. 'Things happened so fast. Betty stood up in a rage. Her chair fell over behind her. I thought she was angry at Finn, but she leaned across the table and she struck me across the cheek.' He grimaced and downed the dregs of his broth. 'She turned to Finn, she reached out to him, she tried to embrace him ... he tried to hold her at bay, and then something flashed across his face. I am not talking about an expression, I am talking about a *light*. I just sat there like a damned fool, pitying myself, while Betty tried to embrace Finn again. Then all of a sudden came more flashes of light, but this time coursing through him. Elsa, it was as if he had electricity in his veins instead of blood – I could see every one of them like a branch of forked lightning!' He swallowed. 'There was a wicked, crackling sound, and then the lightning jumped into Betty's outstretched arms. The shock threw her across the room so hard that the impact broke a rib.' He stuffed his wrists into his eyes and gritted his teeth for a moment. 'If only you had smelled her burned skin ... Elsa, please. I tell you this for your own safety. You are being too reckless – Finn was not born to live among people. He should not have been born at all.'

He waited for Elsa to take it in, grimly satisfied at her white face and wide eyes. It was right that she should be appalled. He had no desire to see her this way – it gave him no satisfaction. But what his father had told him was true – the most important lessons are the ones that hurt the most.

She drained her honey drink, which had now gone tepid, in one quick motion. 'My dad died last year.'

Daniel scratched his beard uneasily. He had not expected her to say that, nor to look so suddenly composed. 'I ... I'm sorry for you.'

She shrugged. 'Thanks, I suppose. It was hard. Until then I thought he was invincible, because he had spent his life walking through storms unharmed. Once he was even struck by lightning.'

'And was he hurt very badly?'

'He was completely fine. He had a blackout, and then was back on his feet. He was storm-chasing again the very next day. So you see, sometimes when it happens, it doesn't always end in hurt.'

Daniel's spirit sunk. He closed his eyes and tried to imagine what her father would have been like. Cavalier, that much was for certain. 'He sounds,' he said, 'either very lucky or very foolish.'

'No!' She jabbed a pointing finger at him. '*You're* the foolish one. If you hadn't made matters worse for Finn, it might never have become as bad as it did!'

He gasped. It had been many decades since anyone had dared to call him foolish, and then only his grandfather, cackling at him from his deathbed as Daniel tried to pray for his eternal soul.

'When I was with Finn yesterday,' she continued, tearful all of a sudden, 'I felt like we were aligned somehow. But you couldn't possibly understand.'

'No,' he said; 'on that we agree.' He shook his head and pushed back his chair. When he got to his feet his legs felt old and weak. He could not find the strength to fully straighten his spine. He was trying not to picture Elsa with the same burns he had nursed Betty through, or worse. 'I have appreciated your time this afternoon, Miss Beletti.' He punched his hat into shape and looked at it wearily. 'I am not a man who needs to have the last word, so this will be the final thing I say. You can have the last word after I have spoken it.' He cleared his throat. 'Everybody thinks that they will be spared. Betty was lucky to survive. Your father was lucky to survive. Not everybody is lucky.' He put his hat on his head, tucked his thumbs into his britches, and waited for her to speak.

She stewed in her chair for a minute, pissed off that she couldn't think of anything cutting to say. In the end she settled for 'Whatever' and wished she had simply kept her mouth shut.

He nodded and stalked away.

She exhaled.

Only once he had gone did she let herself tremble. She wanted to be sick.

The worst was that, even when she'd lowered her head to listen at his chest then pressed her lips to his, even then Finn hadn't seen fit to tell her about this.

The butterfly she had fed earlier flittered back to her table and fanned its wings there. It took off again and circled in the air until, with a sharp slap, she knocked it down. It flapped about on its side on the floor. She stood, carefully lifted her chair and brought one of its legs down hard, screwing the bug into the ground. She spat out the taste of her honey drink, and made her way back towards Prospect Street.

# 11

# THE GORGEOUS PALACES

Bad weather ran wild through Thunderstown overnight, rattling latches and tapping on windowpanes. Elsa slept fitfully, woken every so often by the noises of the wind.

Come dawn, she was too tired to be angry. When she had gone to bed she had felt as if she were lying down in her own fury, sinking into it and tucking it up around her. She had been angry at Finn, angry at Daniel for telling her about Betty and the lightning, angry at herself for letting her defences down, angry with the world for always adding one more complication.

But in the morning she felt neither anger nor anything else. While she slept her heart had curled up into a ball.

She was not one of those people Daniel had accused her of being. She *did* believe that a person should learn from the lessons of others. All she had done was refuse to let him see it, because she didn't want to offer him the satisfaction.

She remembered visiting her dad's storm-chasing friend Luca in hospital. His wife Ana-Maria had been there too, sitting wordlessly at his bedside and picking at the stems of the flowers Elsa's dad had bought her. Her father had been just a stone's throw from Luca when the lightning bolt hit, and he was acutely aware that it could have been him, not Luca, lying in the hospital bed. Ana-Maria had clearly been thinking just that, and wishing it too.

The lighting that had taken the sight from Luca's right eye had left a sickle-shaped burn that ran from his eyebrow to his jaw. Likewise it had removed the pupil and the iris from the eyeball, leaving only a startlingly pink globe which the doctors had covered with a bandage.

It had been the kind of strike every storm-chaser feared. The one against which no precautions could be taken. Dry lightning. That meant a bolt from the blue or, more technically, a bolt from a storm some ten miles away and perhaps even out of sight, which could fork in an instant across the distance. The sky above Luca's car had been clear and summery, for they were some miles yet from the storm they were chasing, which here was but a grey fringe for the horizon. He had sat on the bonnet, humming along to his stereo, while Elsa's dad took a leak among nearby bushes.

Had she been offered the choice, Ana-Maria would have accepted Luca's partial blindness as a lucky escape; compared to the real damage, his blown-out eye was inconsequential.

The doctors explained that no human mind was built to withstand such electricity, and that the lightning had scrambled the natural circuitry of Luca's brain like a power surge frying a computer chip. Dreams, memories and learned behaviours had all been carried out of place on the currents, and had settled in new configurations. They warned that, when he came to, Luca might not be Luca any more. He might be a new man, born again with no grip on his reality. Dreams might have turned to memories and memories to dreams forgotten upon waking. All Ana-Maria could do was wait and pray. Even she might have become just a dream figure to him, an image fading from the waking day.

Yes, Elsa was well aware of the perils of lightning.

The overnight rain had made all the difference to Thunderstown's convoluted streets, making the cobbles in Tallow Row shine like a haul of fresh oysters. She did not mind the drizzle as she walked, nor that her jeans stuck to her thighs and her hair turned slowly bedraggled with the water.

Avoiding the pull of Saint Erasmus, she headed instead for Old Colp. Her route took her west through Tinacre Square, where a charm-seller stood all alone amid the drizzle, her red hair dark and damp against her neck. From Tinacre Square a quiet passageway led towards Feave Street, a shortcut where the raindrops landed lightly on the walls.

At the end of the passage, before the next began, lay a modest courtyard enclosed by the windowless backs of town houses. It was brighter than the passageway and smelled of new rain on slate. The drizzle consolidated into heavy drops, each a vertical flicker through the air.

Something landed on her hand. She looked down expecting rain but saw instead a bug, which she swatted instinctively. She made contact, but when she drew her hand away there was no squashed insect on her knuckles. There was only water. Another bug droned through the rainy air, and she realized that the walls were thick with them. They were the size and shape of ladybirds, but had dull grey shells without markings. They dotted the bricks and mortar like drops of mercury.

She froze. Something here was amiss. Her stomach had clenched because of it, but her mind took a moment to work out what was wrong. Then she realized that she had left wet footprints across the courtyard floor, which was bone dry, despite the falling rain.

A transformation was happening at knee-height. She watched a raindrop break there prematurely, shattering against the thin air. Then the shape of its suspended splash became that of spread insect wings, and then the wings flickered into life and the raindrop flew upwards. Through the wing-blur appeared a bug's miniscule antennae and dangling legs. It whizzed away to join its fellows on the courtyard walls.

With timid steps she approached the nearest wall, where she held her breath and leaned in close to inspect one of the bugs. Its body was like murky water, and similarly translucent. Through it she could see the grit of the bricks. Likewise she could find her own reflection, warped across the insect's concave back.

She reached out to touch it. It came off the wall and welled into a raindrop on her skin. Its little legs, hairs-breadth eyes and crystalline shell all vanished, and it became only a wavering drop on the tip of her finger. She laughed with wonder. Then straight away she was unnerved, and stepped back sharply.

'Finn,' she said aloud. He had invited her into the world of these insects and the world of his own strange body, and on the threshold she had faltered because he had not been straight with her about its dangers. She wanted to enter, dearly she did, but she couldn't ignore the memory of Ana-Maria's face as she sat at Luca's bedside.

She hurried on towards Old Colp.

The rain ceased as she climbed, leaving the sky smeared with so many clouds of so many shapes and shades that it looked like a painter's palette. On the lower slopes, a wind blew cotton tufts out of the grass. She paused as they floated around her, half-expecting them to transform into insects or birds, but they were just seeds wrapped in fluff. Further up the mountain she came to a gurgling little brook, its surface glimmering with crescents of sunlight that, for an astonished moment, she believed were carp swimming in the water. They were just reflections, but she had to splash her arm through the brook to be sure of it. She felt as if all appearances here were but masks, and nothing could be trusted.

When she reached the bothy, a cloud shadow swept across her and she shivered, although she could not tell whether it was from fright or excitement or simply the cold of the shade it cast. A wind hummed against the rocky bluff the cottage backed against, coaxing deep, eerie music out of the stone.

She knocked fast on the door and folded her arms. 'Hi,' she said when Finn answered.

'You look tired.'

'So do you.'

'I didn't sleep well,' he said.

'Me neither.'

He wore a jersey of black wool, frayed and unravelling at the cuffs. He looked just as troubled as her. 'Daniel told me he'd spoken to you.'

She took a deep breath. 'And is it true? What he had to say?'

'Yes. I promise you I never meant to do it. Until that moment I didn't even know I had lightning inside of me.'

'I *know* it was an accident. That doesn't matter. What's difficult is … why didn't you warn me?'

'I … I tried to tell you I was dangerous.'

'But you didn't say how.'

'I didn't want you to hate me.'

'I *wouldn't have*. But I might have been more cautious about putting my ear to your chest! Or about kissing you. Now I don't even know whether I can trust you. What if I'd found out in the same way your mother did?'

Another cloud shadow fell across them. In its shade his skin looked foggy grey. 'It wouldn't be like that,' he said. 'Lightning isn't predictable.'

'Is that supposed to reassure me? Is there anything else you've kept from me? Anybody else you've hurt?' She didn't want to make him suffer, but she had to have this out with him.

He hung his head. The cloud shadow lifted, but the soft sunlight that followed could not brighten him and he remained overcast.

'I've only ever hurt one person, and that was my mother, whom I loved very much. But there have been other moments of lightning. In the months after she left, when I missed her so badly, it kept taking me by surprise. It would come out of me while I ate, or walked in the mountains, or even while I slept. Each time it felt like my spine had been ripped out, but each time it earthed in the ground. I made sure it could never hurt anyone again, by hiding away up here. I should have told you, Elsa, I should have and I can't believe I didn't. But somehow you made it impossible.'

'You're saying it's *my fault?*'

'No. I was going to say something else.' He bit his lip and looked away up the mountain.

'Well? Whatever it was, you'd better say it now.'

'I didn't tell you because you made me feel like my hair was standing on end, even though I don't have a single hair on my body.'

She was taken aback. She glanced around at the slate and the brown mountain grass, anywhere but at Finn.

'You ...' She struggled for the words. Eventually she found some of her old resolve, but was not sure she liked the hard way it made her feel when she said, 'You still haven't answered my question. Is there anything else you've kept from me?'

He closed his eyes. 'Yes,' he said in a faint voice. 'There's something else.'

'Then now's the time to tell me.'

'I can't. Not here. I'd have to show you.'

'Where?'

'Further up the mountain. You'd have to come with me.'

She hesitated. 'Is it far?'

'Not far.'

Given what she had learned, she knew it was unsafe to be near him, although to her frustration she still wanted to see whatever it was he had to show her. As so often seemed the case in her life, what made sense and what she wanted were opposed. She nodded briskly and they set off, over slopes of whisky-hued soil, banks of black pebbles and spry grass. She hated that the silence between them, which previously she had so treasured, had turned so quickly into a gulf. On their way uphill he sprang tensely over the new mud and slicked thickets while she stumbled here and there, her feet slipping in the soil or tripping over roots that seemed to have been washed free of the earth. Then at last they reached the entrance to a tunnel, as tall as her. It looked like an old entryway to one of Thunderstown's mines, over which the timber boarding had cracked apart long ago. From its dark mouth she felt a changed air blowing against her cheeks, as if she were standing in front of an open freezer. He led the way inside and immediately something crunched under his foot: one shattered half of a miner's lantern, with a cobweb ball where a candle would once have burned.

'My torch is inside,' said Finn. 'I usually go down there without it. I can feel the way from the air currents. So to start with it will be dark for you.'

'What's in there? What if I hit my head on something? What if there are pits or sudden drops?'

'There aren't. And the ceiling is high. You'll have to trust me, although I suppose that will be harder for you now.'

She looked back at the blue sky framed by the lip of the tunnel mouth. 'Go slowly. I'll say if it gets too much.'

Further in, the smell of grass and heather that clung to Old Colp's slopes gave way to lungfuls of cold, mineral air. They quickly reached the edge of vision, where it became too black for even mosses and moulds to sprout on the walls. Here there was only smooth, blasted rock. A few steps further and the tunnel turned a corner into utter darkness. Each pace became harder than the last, for no sooner had she imagined an impending underground cliff than she had convinced herself that she was about to plunge over it. She came to a halt. 'Finn,' she said, and a long echo repeated off the F.

'Here.' He sounded only an arm's length away.

She wanted to reach out for him, but she battled back that desire. She would rather show anger than fear. 'Finn, what the hell is going on? I can't see a thing in here!' A powder of rock dust showered on to her face and tongue.

'Shh!' he hissed. 'Don't shout! Shouting,' he whispered, 'could bring the mountain down on us.'

Elsa bunched her fists. 'What can be so important that we have to go to all this effort to reach it? Can't I just wait here while you fetch it for me?'

'No. It can't be moved. You have to see it to understand. I can guide you, if you like. But to do that you'd have to take my hand.'

'I'll be fine, thank you. Carry on.'

It took great effort to follow him as slowly as she did. Her legs objected with every straining muscle. If he found it difficult to progress at such a nervy speed he said nothing. He was as silent as he was invisible.

Then a light burst on like a supernova. Elsa slapped her hands to her eyes and shrieked, thinking *lightning*. Rock dust shook in the lit-up air, but there was no thunderbolt. It was only the glow of a hand torch and she relaxed her guard, although after the total darkness it pained her retinas.

'We're here,' he said.

She blinked and blinked until eventually she saw the expanses of a cavern around them, and Finn offering her the torch by the handle. She snatched it and held it tight. Her eyes slowly accustomed to the underground and the reluctant colours locked in the rock walls. Stalactites broke the high cave roof into countless archways and winked, milky pink and orange, in the torch beam. From the ground, stalagmites pushed up to meet them, and in places the two had met and fused into palatial columns. In one instance, a frail stalactite hung like a photo of a lightning bolt, while out of the ground its nubby counterpart rose, its pearly head stopping only a millimetre beneath. She had once read an article about stalactites, and she knew it could be a century before they at last fused.

She swung the beam around the cavern. The far wall stretched upwards in a gradual curve. The flinty rock face shimmered green and peach like the skin of a trout.

Finn pointed in that direction, where in the dark a body of water oozed. 'Shine the torch over there.'

The light hit the water's surface and diffracted up the wall on the far side.

'Shine it higher.'

Beyond the water, the rock was coloured with seams of mineral. 'Higher still.'

Elsa raised the light and it revealed a cave painting.

It was a pattern of shapes painted in dark and sanguinary substances. All the cave paintings she had ever seen in books depicted bison, hounds, huntsmen or mammoths, but this was a painting of broken triangles and abstract nothings. She tried to imagine Palaeolithic painters reaching at full stretch to daub pigment on the stone. If this water had flowed here then, they would surely have risked their lives to do so.

She ventured as close as she could without losing her balance and pitching into the arc of the water. The torch trembled in her hand, making the cave painting appear to dance. Then she swung the light away and shone it at Finn, who screwed up his eyes and raised a hand to shield his face.

She lowered the light a fraction. The painting was not a pattern but a sequence. It progressed from left to right like the frames of a cinema reel. 'It's a story,' she declared. 'Each of these shapes follows on from the last.'

As far as she could tell, the story in the cave painting went something like: Once upon a time, there were cottony shapes, indistinct things with indefinable boundaries. Then, for reasons unknown, the shapes became definite. They morphed from smudges into triangles. None of the triangles were perfect: one had cracks running down it; one had a corner so smoothed away that it was now almost a half-circle; one had a dent taken out of its top.

'This one,' she said, focusing the torch and wishing she could keep her voice as steady as its clean line of light, 'is the Devil's Diadem. This one is Old Colp.'

Finn stared into the tar-black water. 'Yes, and there's more. Shine it higher.'

She did so eagerly, and discovered a painted ceiling. All the animals of prehistory were there, horses and hounds and horned goats. Yet no beast was complete. Part of each dissolved into the stone. A rearing horse had hindquarters that vanished into a craggy overhang. The forepaw of a dog stretched out and became a stalactite.

In the corner of the ceiling were the humans. They too broke down in places into blank nothingness and shadows. And some – these had been painted curled up, or bowed in despair – had white lines flying out of their hearts.

'Who are these people?' she asked. 'What does this mean?'

'I don't know for certain.'

Again she turned the torch on him. 'What do you mean, you don't know? I asked if there were any more secrets and you led me here.'

'I brought you here because I thought the paintings might help you understand.'

'Understand *what*?'

'Me. That maybe I'm not so unusual.'

She stepped away, confused. Part of her wanted to shine the

torchlight into his every pore. Part of her thought she had already risked enough.

Then she heard a faint noise like the leftover tremble after a cymbal is struck. 'Finn? What was that?'

'It was me,' he said. 'It's the thunder I have for a heartbeat, the same sound you listened to when we caught the canaries in the woods. It's just that, in these caves, it's quiet enough to hear it without putting an ear to my chest.'

Elsa felt suddenly claustrophobic. When the thunder whispered out of Finn again, it felt as though all of the weight of the mountain was about to crash down on her. She gripped the torch tightly, and flashed the light back towards the tunnel they had come from. Stalagmites and stalactites swung shadows through the beam.

'I can't stay here, Finn.'

'Elsa, please ... is there no way we can get past this?'

'It's like you said – I just don't know. For now I need some space.' She shrugged and struck out towards the lightest part of what was before her, trusting the hard rock of the tunnel wall to lead out of the cave.

Behind her the thunder sounded louder, slow and melancholy, like a lament. She took a few more faltering steps, then could not help but turn to shine the torch back.

'Elsa, a week or so after I struck my mother, she tried to tell me that she still loved me. She stood before me one sunny afternoon, and I could see her lips trying to form the words. But she had become so frightened of me that she couldn't get them out. That was the worst thing I have ever seen, and I would never risk seeing it again. Soon after that she left Thunderstown. But when you placed your ear to my chest, I felt like we were safe. I felt like we were too attuned for there to be lightning.'

His body was as still as the stalactites, but he was crying. The beam of light glittered. The air had filled with diamond dust, icy particles dancing in and out of the light. Each of Finn's tears, as it emerged from the duct, crystallized at once into a glittering speck that flew forth. The tears swirled and shimmered in the space between Elsa and Finn, and some caught the light like prisms, filling the cold cave air with rainbow colours.

Elsa stood, enchanted, in the tunnel. She wanted to stride back to Finn and melt through his wintry sorrow with the heat of a kiss. But she had always known not to toy with lightning. She turned back through an excruciating half-circle, then left him behind her in the darkness.

# 12

# GUNSHOT

At the humid close of the afternoon, Daniel walked Mole into Thunderstown. The old dog waddled slowly, pausing every few minutes to regain her wheezing breath, her good eye shut tight and her blind one fixed on the middle distance. In this stop-start fashion they made their way under the cold shadow of the Church of Saint Erasmus and eventually to the door of the Thunderstown Miners' Club. It stood in the mouth of Widdershin Road, where the leaning eaves kept it in constant shade. These days its concave door was hard to budge, and the wood strained when Daniel held it open for Mole to enter.

Inside, an old lamp hung its broken bulb over an unstaffed desk. Through a door lay the common room, which would smell forever of the generations of pipe smoke that had turned its wallpaper yellow. Bolted to its walls were pickaxes and rusty hand drills, and black-and-white photos of stiffly posed workmen or of the mines themselves, dark squares charred into the rock face.

Now that there were no miners left in Thunderstown, their club had a ragtag bunch of patrons: tradesmen and clerks and gossiping men like Sidney Moses, Hamel Rhys and Abe Cosser, who sometimes met in the common room to play chequers or sip broth and who always wore their rain caps, even indoors. Daniel never attended such gatherings, although he was counted among the club's members. The head man of the Fossiter family (although none had ever been miners) had always been given a seat at the club.

A ring of hand-me-down armchairs stood in the common room, and Mole curled up at the foot of one of these and tucked her nose into the crook of her foreleg. Daniel watched her for a minute, thinking how pitiful she was, to have changed from a huntress as lethal as a bullet to a stiff sleeper like a taxidermist's masterpiece.

He crossed to a smaller adjoining room, where shafts of light slanted down from high windows and bookshelves spanned the walls. He ran his forefinger over the spines of the tomes there. These were Thunderstown's family trees, most of which had finished branching decades ago, or else had been left incomplete by the present generation. Only the ten-volume sequence marked *Fossiter* remained dust-free, and it was the final book in this collection that Daniel now selected and took down from the shelf.

The binding still showed the stretched scars of the goat whose skin it had come from, as did the leather clasp he now popped open. The yellowed pages were all unnumbered and scrawled with handwritten notes. Connections forked down and interconnected from the top of each page to the bottom. Cousins had married second cousins; widows had been passed on to unmarried brothers. The name Daniel itself was repeated over and over: there had been a time when it occurred once in every generation. Now it was the only remnant of that grand family, a reverse Adam who would leave the final pages blank.

He returned to the common room and took a seat. Mole whimpered in her sleep, which he was glad to hear since it reassured him that she was still alive. He mimicked her stillness, sitting with his fists on the arms of the chair and the family tree open on his lap.

The names of his forefathers had all been written in the same scratchy script, in the same ink turned brown by age. His father had completed the final page at the time of Daniel's birth, drawing a straight line down from his own name to that of his son. When Daniel had discovered it he had not known whether to hate or pity the old man, for as far as this family tree recorded it, Daniel had originated out of the body of the Reverend Fossiter himself. To rectify this untruth, he had borrowed one of Sally Nairn's antique writing pens and a pot of ink that was like a jarful of tropical ocean, then returned to the family tree to slowly scratch his mother's name and the line that bound her to him. Only when he had finished writing did he wonder whether he had made a mistake. He had written Maryam Fossiter, because she was his mother and he had come from her and he was Fossiter in every cell of his body. But she had not been a Fossiter. She had not even married his father, let alone taken his name, and that had been his father's pretext for driving her away. 'It's as the Lord told us,' he had said. 'Those who are not with us are against us.'

Daniel closed his eyes and let his memories of her take centre stage. He could not picture her face (he had not been able to in decades), only her black hair dangling down to her waist. He could picture her forearms and hands and hips because he had been so small when she left that those had been the parts of her he saw the most of. He knew he had been in pain when she left Thunderstown, but it was a different kind of pain to the one that came when Betty went away. He had been too young to understand it. It had been an ocean on which he had drifted.

In his memory his mother hummed and leafed absent-mindedly through his father's theology books, chuckling now and then as if all those essays by all those learned men were but the amusing mistakes of little children. His father watched her, incensed by her unbelief but silent nevertheless. That was one of only a handful of memories, which Daniel tended to as diligently in his thinkings as he did to these family trees.

He had, however, one stranger memory of her, one which did not comfort him but rather left him cold. In it, she sat in a rocking chair, on the porch of the vicarage. He – a little older than a toddler – had been digging about in the garden and had returned to the house to show her something he had unearthed. To his dismay he'd seen two wild dogs sitting with her, their muzzles resting on her lap. Their eyes were half-closed while she stroked their heads. He'd shouted, and ran towards her, screaming and waving his arms, and the dogs had sprung up and fled into the mountains.

He harrumphed. He sometimes wished that that particular memory of his mother would recede into the past, and not present itself every time he recalled the happier ones. He got up and returned the family tree to the shelf.

Once, long ago, he had brought Betty to the Miners' Club to show her his mother's name here, along with all those hundreds from his father's side. Back then, old Mr Nairn had cooked in the club kitchen every Sunday afternoon. Mr Nairn had been a man who found vegetarianism a hard thing to comprehend, and Daniel had known that his sloppy potato patties and brown cabbage would be fried in the gloopy white fat of a swine. Although that risked turning Betty's stomach, he'd needed to bring her here to help her understand who he was and from what stock he'd come, and she had seen that and accompanied him with good grace. So many hours of so many Fossiter lives had been idled away in this common room that he could almost see the ghosts of his forebears holding forth in the armchairs that still bore the imprints of their bodies. He had brought Betty here not to taste Mr Nairn's cooking, but to introduce her to the impressions made in the furniture. He had felt so proud to have her at his side. He had always been a big man – even as a child he had towered over his classmates – but with Betty beside him he had felt weightless, as if he were floating a foot off the ground.

There was a gunshot. He blinked and for a moment did not know what year of his life he was living in. Mole had heard it too and was struggling to her feet, her ears straining and her bad eye weeping. It had come from out in the street, and Daniel headed straight for the exit from the club, Mole puffing along behind him.

They went a little further down Widdershin Road, where a junction led into tree-lined Foremans Avenue, and from there onwards to Drum Head. Thirty yards along this avenue lived Sidney Moses, who now stood outside his house with his rifle in his hands. He did not notice Daniel when he approached, for he was too fascinated by the goat that was sitting in the shade of one of the avenue's trees. Fragments of bark and lichen were stuck to its panting tongue, and a bullet wound in its neck was flushing blood into its beard. It knelt reposefully, as if dying were a state as ordinary as basking in an afternoon's hot sun.

'You fool!' yelled Daniel, snatching the rifle from Sidney's hands. Sidney offered no resistance. Daniel readied the gun, steadied his aim against the anger rushing up from inside of him, and shot the goat between the eyes. Mole barked painfully as the shot rang out. The goat's horned head dropped down to the pavement.

The gunshot brought Sidney to his senses, and he looked at his rifle in Daniel's hands as if he did not remember how it had got there. 'Mr Fossiter, I ...'

'What were you thinking?'

'I shot a goat. It had been eating the trees.'

'But you didn't shoot to kill.'

'No, I—'

'I know full well that you can fire a rifle, Mr Moses, and I declare that you did not shoot to kill!'

Sidney lifted his rain cap to wipe a line of sweat from his forehead. 'Of course I shot to kill!' He puffed out his cheeks. 'I damned well shouldn't have been forced to! This town employs a culler to keep these vermin from its streets. Have you seen him today, Mr Fossiter? He's a big man with a beard – hard to miss. He would have been useful here earlier, while this beast was munching its way along the trees of Foremans Avenue!'

'I was in the Miners' Club. You know I'm often there. You could've at least *tried* to find me.'

Sidney stole another glance at the goat, and there was that same grim fascination. He licked his lips. 'We never know where we can find you, Mr Fossiter, because you do not tell us where you are going to be.'

'Yes you do, Sidney, you all do – you know I am going to be culling the goats.'

'In the Thunderstown Miners' Club? I don't believe there are many goats in there, except for the heads of some your great-grandfather shot. And I see you have even brought that terrifying bloodhound with you!'

As if on cue, Mole sneezed and shook her head.

'I don't need a dog to catch goats.'

'And just as well – that sorry creature wouldn't say boo to a goose,' said Sidney, flourishing his arm towards the animal beneath the tree.

'Mr Moses. What do you plan to do, now, with your kill? Do you know how to skin the hide and chop the meat, or do you plan to leave it to fester here in Foremans Avenue?'

Sidney shrugged. 'I own plenty of shirts, coats and jerseys, Mr Fossiter. I have radiators in my house and I have a freezer full of chicken, lamb and fish from the market. So I need neither fleece, leather or goat mutton. What's more, I own a motor car and a trailer, with which I intend to drive this carcass out of town and dump it in the ample wilderness surrounding us, where I fully expect the crows to finish the job.'

Daniel was about to retort, but managed instead to bite his tongue. He knew full well he could not best Sidney at words. Mole sneezed again and shivered as it moved through her. Daniel stepped briskly past Sidney, grabbed the goat by the horns and made to drag it after him. 'Do not trouble yourself with your trailer and your motor car, Mr Moses. I will make leather out of it.'

He began to plod away towards his homestead, with Mole labouring behind.

'And then what?' called Sidney after him.

'I will return to my duties.'

'Must we be rivals, Mr Fossiter?'

Daniel stopped walking and turned back to him. 'I have no wish to oppose myself to anyone. You, on the other hand, seem to delight in it.'

Sidney spread his arms and looked hurt. 'You misunderstand me.' He put his hands in his pockets and sauntered closer.

'You would modernize,' said Daniel. 'You have talked about helicopters and satellite … satellite—'

'Satellite tracking,' said Sidney gently.

Daniel snorted. 'Have the goats changed in the last hundred years? Have the wild dogs begun to use helicopters? The methods of my family have always been sufficient. And always will be.'

Sidney sighed. 'We've talked about this. I don't want you forever catching goats and wild dogs. I want you to get to the root of the problem.'

Daniel scoffed. 'I would have to kill every goat within a hundred miles of Thunderstown to get to the root of the problem. I would need an army to do that.'

'I'm not talking about goats, as well you know.'

Daniel looked away shiftily down the length of the street. A wind blew and ruffled the fur of the goat he was pulling, puffing its dusty smell up into his nostrils.

'And I have told you before – Old Man Thunder's just a story. Come on, Mr Moses, there are so many tales here, why must you persist in believing this one? I'm telling you: not I, nor anyone else, will ever catch Old Man Thunder because *he does not exist* – he never did.'

Sidney smiled, but Daniel did not trust it. He was being tested, he knew, but on what subject he could not guess.

'People say they have seen him.'

'People say a lot of things. Words mean nothing, Mr Moses.'

Sidney studied him for a moment, then shrugged and licked his lips. 'Imagine for a moment that he does! Just pretend, just humour me. Let's say I did things my way, with all the new equipment I can lay my hands on, and I found him and brought him to you tomorrow. I dragged him down here to town and presented him to our culler for his judgement. What would you do?'

'You would need to prove he was Old Man Thunder.'

'And if I could? If he was stood here before you, riddled with weather, confessing *I am he*. Then what?'

Daniel snorted. 'Then nothing. This is idle speculation.'

'Would you do your duty then, Mr Fossiter? If the thing that eluded all of your forefathers was there for the taking?'

Daniel cleared his throat. 'Mr Moses, I am not sure what more I can say. I do not believe in Old Man Thunder. I have endeavoured to make that clear to you.'

'No, Mr Fossiter,' said Sidney sweetly, 'you have endeavoured to avoid the question. I do not think you could do it. The townsfolk are concerned, and think you have gone soft. That Munro woman, that one who came from overseas, she took something from you that you have struggled to get back. She left you confused and without ruthlessness, doting over your blind old dog.'

He bristled at the insult, and his shoulders squared and as they did so the fur of the goat bristled in the wind. 'Listen very carefully, Mr Moses. Were you to bring me Old Man Thunder, and were he to exist and be proven to be all that people say he is, I would slit his throat without hesitation. So that's said, and you can tell the townsfolk to forget their concerns. One more thing: Betty Munro took nothing from me, and gave me things that you could never understand. If I seem weak-willed to you, it is because I always was, not because of her.'

With that he headed for the homestead, and left Sidney Moses behind him.

# 13

# OLD WIVES' TALES

After the ceremony they held for her father, Elsa stood in the crematorium garden, drawing in deep breaths of the whipping wind. The flowers were in full bloom in their beds, bobbing in the blustering air. Elsa wondered whether the owners of the crematorium had planted bird of paradise as a joke, since its orange petals looked like flames wavering in the wind. Then again, everything became symbolic after a death. She had argued with her mother about the shape and colour of the urn, until both of them, in tears, ceded that it didn't matter and chose the least ostentatious one. She had seen a sun dog the other night, a blue and orange half-halo shining to the right of the sun, and had believed it to be a sign from her father, even though she had no faith in an afterlife and knew that sun dogs were just refraction. Only when she could not decide what the sign meant did she give in to her rational mind, and her rational mind left her to sob the evening away.

The other mourners remained near the door to the crematorium, chatting and occasionally shooting a concerned glance in her direction. The sharp-tipped evergreens that overlooked the cemetery sowed their needles on the grass, scenting the air with their aroma of pine. She took a deep breath.

Her mother came up beside her and squeezed her hand, and

Elsa turned to her teary-eyed and said, 'Can I ask you a kinda awkward question?'

'Anything you want, Elsa.'

'Well ... you're a religious person. What do you think happens to Dad now?'

Her mother didn't look Elsa in the eye, but squeezed her hand all the firmer between both of her own. The wind tore through the high branches. Green needles rained on the path. She wiped her eyes with her sleeve and said, 'The thing is ... the thing is, Elsa, that your father didn't live a good life.'

The wind that had been hurrying through the pine trees paused. There was a heartbeat's silence. Then it flew on, whooping and howling.

Elsa tugged her hand away and shoved it as a fist into her coat pocket.

'You did ask,' her mother said in a small voice.

Elsa stamped away up the path. She didn't think about the direction she was taking and the path led to a dead end where wasps hummed above the crematorium's trash cans. Her anger changed to embarrassment. She had to turn back the way she'd come and pass her mother (who was now in tears) to get back to her car.

'This little car,' said Kenneth Olivier, slapping the vehicle's white bonnet fondly, 'was Michael's. It's small, but it's good enough to take you up the Devil's Diadem.'

Elsa was setting off to make good on her promise to Sister Dot at the nunnery. I am old here, Dot had said, and Elsa hoped that age could offer her some perspective. All night she had lain awake, thinking about the way she'd left Finn crying diamond dust in the heart of the mountain.

She climbed into the car and felt the seat beneath her depress comfortably. It must have been a long time since Michael had driven it, but it still smelled faintly of a young man's fragrance: allspice and moss and bonfire toffee. Kenneth sat down on the passenger seat beside her, ostensibly to demonstrate what buttons operated what, but she could tell from the heavy way his ribcage swelled with each intake of breath that he had got in to absorb just a little of his boy's scent.

'Kenneth,' she said, 'can I ask you a kinda awkward question?'

He folded his hands on his lap. 'Anything you like.'

'What, um, what do you think happens?'

He looked at her patiently. 'I'm sorry, Elsa, I'm not sure I follow you.'

She cleared her throat. 'Well ... you're a religious person, aren't you?'

She waited in silence.

'Ah!' he declared suddenly. '*Ahh*, I think I understand.'

She stared at the car keys in her hand.

'I don't know,' he said.

She closed her eyes.

'Does that disappoint you?' he said.

'No ... it's just ... I thought ... my mum's religious, too, and she told me ...' She wished she had a bottle of water, because her tongue was so dry.

'Is this about your father?'

Elsa nodded.

'Well, let me tell you, I thought long and hard about this after Michael died. He didn't believe in anything, you see.'

'So ... so ... Does that mean you think he's ...'

Kenneth began to chuckle, then tried to hide it and failed so spectacularly that his laughter escaped in great splutters. 'If you are trying to ask whether I believe my son is in *hell* simply because he was not a religious man when he died, then no!' He wheezed, and mopped his eyes with the sleeve of his jumper. 'No, Elsa, dear me, no. To believe in hell would be to compromise who I am.' *But*, if you were to ask me where else I think he might be, then my answer would depend on when you asked me. Sitting in his car right now, how can I believe he has simply vanished? I am surrounded by him. I can smell him here, for goodness' sake! Then again, ask me in the winter, when the rain is beating down on the windows, and nobody's ringing the telephone and nobody's at the door. Then I suppose I might say that a person stops existing when their body stops breathing.' He began to chuckle again. 'Am I allowed this kind of answer, Elsa? One in which Kenneth Olivier has no damned clue? Am I allowed to say I change my mind depending on how miserable I'm feeling?'

'No!' she said with a smile, wiping her eyes. 'You were meant to have an answer! Isn't that the whole point of believing in something?'

Then, quick as clicked fingers, he was serious again. 'I would love to have an answer. But what I believe is that I *can't* have one. Which is a good deal healthier than believing that I can, and then only accepting the worst answer I can think of.'

She rubbed her face. 'Sorry,' she said. 'I miss my dad, that's all. And I'm not good at being stoic like you are.'

'It takes time,' he said sagely, 'and a great many cricket matches. You do know you'll never stop missing him, right?'

They watched a leaf fall on to the windscreen. It was pink, with scarlet edges. There were no trees nearby; the leaf had been placed there delicately by the breeze.

'Right,' Elsa said.

Kenneth cleared his throat and jingled the car keys at her. 'You will need these. And you have the map there on the dashboard, although there is only one road.'

She nodded. 'Thank you.'

He got out of the car. 'Safe journey,' he said. He closed the door behind him and slapped the bonnet to wish her on her way.

The slopes of the Devil's Diadem were pitted and potholed. Streambeds scored the earth, long since abandoned by water and filled now only with briars and the bones of those unfortunate animals who had slipped into them and become trapped.

As she left Thunderstown it felt good to be driving again. She'd not driven often in New York, but back in Oklahoma she'd loved to race an old truck flat out over the long roads even when it made her mother freak out. Now, as she relaxed into the sensation, the command of wheels gave her a liberating buzz, like she'd had in that truck. Then she started driving up the mountain's steeper road and the winds came out to meet her. She had to slow right down, fearful that a gust might flip the car on its back, so powerfully did they howl at its chassis.

Driving higher and closer, the many peaks of the mountain seemed to her like the altars of a pantheon, summoning winds to the slopes below. She felt the gusts throwing themselves at the windscreen. Then one hit the boot and threw her forwards. The seatbelt jerked her shoulder and her teeth came together with an enamel crack.

She was glad, then, when she neared the base of one of those peaks and saw, in the shadow between it and the next, the dark cube of a solitary building. As she drove closer it gradually enlarged into a walled complex, containing a small tower on which a crucifix was mounted. The outer walls were pebble-coated stone and had eroded until none of their buttresses or edges were defined, so that the whole place had the crumbling appearance of a sandcastle. Even the crucifix had weathered. Wind wrapped around it like the tremor of a heatwave.

This was the nunnery of Saint Catherine, and there was no need for a car park, given the hard, blow-dried dirt on which it was built. Elsa parked on a patch of it, took a deep breath and stepped out of the car. At once the wind grabbed a handful of her hair and yanked her back towards Thunderstown. Shocked by its ferocity, she grabbed the car for balance. Dust rushed into her eyes and she had to turn her back on the nunnery to rub the grains away. The wind did everything it could to shove her off course as she approached a tall white door in the nunnery wall. It had a large brass handle and – she was surprised to see – a lucky horseshoe nailed into the wood. She twisted the handle and to her relief found the door to be unlocked. With the wind buffeting her she half-stepped, half-tumbled inside, where she had to grit her teeth and shove with all her might to close the door again. It slammed back into its frame and the wind roared and pounded against it.

She had entered a small antechamber, a kind of airlock against the elements. Straight ahead was another large door, which she supposed led into the convent's cloister. She tied back her hair, which had become weather-tangled, and bracing herself for another assault from the wind, she opened the door.

A deep lawn coloured the cloister a lush green. Delicate plants grew in various flowerbeds, with brown bees hovering above their still petals, patiently exploring them for nectar before returning to a hive box fixed to a wall. Some of the plants boasted orange flowers as big and wafer-thin as paper crowns, and stalks so slender she supposed a single breath could snap them. Yet all was motionless, without a breath of an air current. The wind still flared high above (looking up she saw the blue sky shimmering with its disturbance), but not a flutter blew down to this sanctum.

Then she noticed that all over the walls, numbering into their many hundreds, were charms such as the one that had hung from the sill of her bedroom that she had destroyed on her first night in Thunderstown. They were made from feathers, coins in pairs, scraps of fur and canine teeth. There were so many of them it was as if they, and not the mortar, propped up the nunnery.

In another wall stood a dovecot from which drifted the smell of bird droppings and down. Opposite this, above a turquoise double door and two stained-glass windows, stood the parapet of the chapel. She wandered across to it and heard high-pitched, wavering voices singing within. The nuns were finishing prayers. She turned around to look for somewhere to sit, and then noticed an elderly man sitting on the ground with his back against one wall and his hands folded over his knees. Although he was clean-shaven, one or two white hairs spiralled perfectly amiss on his olive-skinned face, wrinkles as dark and deep as his nostrils. His eyes were pearly white, without even a fleck of a pupil or an iris. A bee buzzed unnoticed across one of his ancient cheeks, examining one of those rogue white hairs as if it were the stamen of a flower.

At that moment an old lady emerged from the dovecot with a dove perched calmly on her shoulder. She wasn't a nun, but all the same was dressed entirely in grey. She walked in a doddery zigzag to the place where the old man sat, and joined him on the ground.

Elsa copied them by sitting down, choosing a spot of soft grass where she too could rest her shoulders against the sturdy stone of the courtyard wall.

She kept thinking about Finn. In her few minutes of sleep last night she had dreamed a nightmare in which she swept around and around a whirlpool as dark as her sleep. In the water with her were the bones of lost miners, all loose and mingling in the gyre. Through lap after lap she span, until in a final dizzying plunge she dropped into the whirlpool's dark heart.

The doors of the chapel opened, interrupting her thoughts, and the nuns filed out, chattering. Elsa sprung to her feet, worried she might not recognize Dot amongst the identical habits and diminutive bodies, but no sooner had she thought it than one of the nuns hooted and hobbled over to her: Dot, her face crinkling up with excitement. 'Ah!' she croaked, 'My young cloud-spotter!' She reached out and pinched Elsa's bare arm with her buckled fingertips.

'I hope I'm not disturbing you.'

'Not at all,' said Dot, eyes a-twinkle, 'In fact, I have been expecting you. This way!' She took hold of Elsa's hand and pulled her busily towards a door in the wall. Bees droned around them as they walked, and buzzed among the tall flowers and the elderly pair sitting on the bench.

'That man over there,' whispered Elsa, 'and that old lady with the dove on her shoulder – neither of them are nuns.'

'Well, obviously,' laughed Dot. 'William and Beatrice are two of our patients. We've several folk up here who medicine can't mend.'

'What's wrong with them?'

They had reached the door. It opened on to a cool, bare corridor, and only once they were inside and Dot had closed it behind them did she explain in a low voice, 'They were struck by lightning. It's a small wonder they survived, and in some ways you might say they did not. William lost his sight when the lightning struck him. But now he says he can see things that others cannot: angels and suchlike. As for Beatrice … she can no longer maintain a conversation, unless it is with the birds. She says she has forgotten English and learned to speak Doveish only.'

Elsa thought of the lightning that had hit Luca, and Betty, and her father.

'That's awful,' she said in an unintended whisper.

They proceeded along a plain corridor and up to the second floor. Here they entered Dot's own room, a cell simply decorated with a reed mat, a reed cross on the wall, a small window and an electric lamp. Dot reached happily under the bed and struggled to lift out a pile of huge, thick books, each the size and weight of an atlas. Elsa couldn't help but take a sharp, thrilled breath. These weren't atlases of the earth, but of the sky. Books like the one her dad had given her, which had been her pride and joy until she had hurled it out into the rain after him on the day he left. Her mother had thought that good riddance, but Elsa had done it not to be rid of him, but to try to show him how desperate she was for him to stay.

'I used to have one of these,' she said, staring sadly at the cloud atlases as Dot laid them out on the bed.

The nun smiled and laid her fingertips on the cover of the largest and oldest, which was leather-bound and Bible-thick. Stuck to its cover was a sepia photo of stacked storm clouds blocking off the sun's rays.

She opened it to the first page. The spine creaked like a hinge and set free the aroma of dried ink and paper. She turned the pages through more sepia shots: single puffy cumuli or mackerel skies. Then she came to a photograph of a giant cloud made from black mist. It was like a rook from a chess set, a black tower with blistering battlements. Lines of rain tethered it to the ground. At its heart it was so black that Elsa could see Dot's reflection in the page.

'A storm,' said Elsa.

'Cumulonimbus,' whispered Dot, and the word was like the hiss of snaking winds between grasses, or the dry creep of a thunder fly. Cumulonimbus, the storm cloud. Elsa had read the name so many times in books, lumped in with cirrus, altocumulus and the rest. Yet rolling over Dot's tongue the word sounded like it had when her dad had pronounced it. Like the name of an archangel.

'This one,' Dot said, tapping the picture, 'was larger than Mount Everest. He had as much energy charged up inside of him as in five of the bombs that blew up Hiroshima. The lightning in him burned ten times hotter than the surface of the sun. And all this is commonplace in Cumulonimbus.'

Elsa stared at the picture.

'There are some,' said Dot slowly, 'who see Cumulonimbus and think he is the power of God himself, or else of witches or devils, for surely something this powerful must come from more than water and dust.'

Elsa closed her eyes and saw her father in the visiting room, on the last of her visits to the jail, at the point when he'd taken to staring at the ceiling, convincing himself he could see clouds moving across it. When she had stood up to say goodbye for what would prove to be the final time, he had looked at her with a dumb grin and pronounced, 'It's raining, Elsa.' 'Dad,' she'd said, 'we're inside.' He'd pointed at her cheek and she'd touched it with a finger. She'd withdrawn her finger with a teardrop glinting on its tip. Then he'd turned again to the ceiling and whispered, 'See? Raining.'

Now Dot reached across and took her hand. 'Let me show you something else.'

She opened another, smaller atlas, and began to flick through its pages. When she found the one she wanted she laid it side by side with the sepia cumulonimbus. The page she had selected showed a frame full of fog. In the fog floated the dark silhouette of a figure, with inhumanly long limbs and a head made of shadows. Dot turned the page and there were more snapshots of the same phenomenon: a towering shade with black tapering arms and legs.

'This ...' said Elsa under her breath, 'I've seen pictures of this before.'

'It's a cloud spectre,' whispered Dot reverentially. 'A very rare thing. The first recorded sighting was in Brocken, in Germany. A shepherd on a mountain got lost in the fog and was trying to find his way out when he saw something that looked like this. Imagine it! One minute you're miles from anyone, the next there's a figure stalking you through the clouds. The shepherd was so haunted by the sight of it that for the rest of his life he only ventured out on fair weather days.'

'But it's a trick, isn't it? A trick of the light.'

'Yes, of course. His shadow projected on to the cloud. But do you know,' Dot's tone lowered, and her old eyes sharpened through the giant lenses of her glasses, and the atmosphere of the room seemed suddenly electric, as if before a storm, 'that Betty Munro once saw a Brocken spectre?'

Elsa felt her skin tingle. For a moment she could hear the wind outside walloping the masonry. 'I think I have heard bits of this story. Can you tell me anything about her?'

Dot's eyes crinkled up behind her glasses. 'Where to begin? The first time she came to visit me here, it was because she'd heard of an old folk-cure for childlessness. Climb a mountain in a storm and drink rainwater until you're sick from it. Yes, I told her I'd heard it said. Should she try it, she asked me, and did I think it would work?' Dot sat down slowly on the bed, amid the cloud atlases. 'I told her it might work and it might not, and it might do both at the same time in ways she couldn't predict.' She sighed. 'I should have been more to the point, but I underestimated how hard it was for her, knowing she couldn't have a baby. I gave up on that urge long ago, and I suppose I had forgotten how strongly it can call to you. Sometimes someone else's life can be the only thing that makes sense of your own.'

'She tried it, then?'

'Yes. She went up into the mountains, hoping for storms. There her hopelessness turned slowly into anguish, and her anguish made her scream at the sky, and stick her head underwater and yell into empty mountain lakes. *Anything,* she promised, to anybody above or below who could hear her. *Anything anybody asks. Just give me a child.'*

Perched on the edge of the bed, Dot looked like a storyteller poised around a hearth. Elsa sat down cross-legged on the hard floor.

'One day,' continued Dot, 'up in the mist on the mountain, what did Betty see but a figure! A silhouette standing in the fog. No doubt it was a trick, a Brocken spectre, her own lonely shadow projected on to the clouds. But to her, in that moment, it was someone who had heard her! The next day she came to see me again. She wanted me to explain what she had seen.'

'What did you tell her?' ventured Elsa.

Dot pointed to a glass of water on the window sill. Elsa got up and fetched it for her, and the old nun sipped from it and smacked her lips. 'What would you have told her?'

'I don't know. I guess I would have tried to show her it was just the weather.'

Dot frowned. 'Well, I would never do anything like *that*. No. It was something to believe in, was what I said.'

Elsa frowned. 'And that was enough for her?'

'That was enough. That kept her sneaking up to look for her spectre. I don't think Betty ever did see it again, but she imagined signs of it in every rock and landslide. Then, one day,' Dot lifted up the first cloud atlas, still showing the black tower of the storm, 'Cumulonimbus came to Thunderstown. Betty was convinced that he was the one she'd seen in the mists. She said she knew it in her belly. So she climbed Drum Head in the pouring rain and tried to drink the raindrops until nausea overcame her.'

'And? What happened?'

'Have you ever tried to catch rain in your mouth? Enough to make you sick?'

'No.'

'It's as near impossible as you'd imagine. And Betty never managed it. Maybe, if she had, the legend would have been proved true. But no. Instead, Betty was struck by lightning. Bang! A million volts of electricity, aimed right at her belly. And then the storm cleared and it was a fine evening.'

Dot put down the book, and closed it so the balmier skies of the cover hid the cumulonimbus within.

'What had happened to her?' asked Elsa.

Dot's eyes twinkled. 'This much you already know, Elsa. She had become pregnant. She told it to the search party when they found her sleeping peacefully on the mountain, though they thought she was raving. Pregnant! Only, it wasn't quite what she'd wanted. It wasn't her baby, just as it wasn't anybody else's baby. It was Cumulonimbus.'

Elsa was too lost in the story to notice at first that Dot had removed her glasses and plugged up her eyes with her bent palms. She joined her on the bed, placing a gentle hand on her shoulders. 'What's wrong, Dot? Why are you crying?'

Dot found a handkerchief from under the pillow and dabbed her eyes. Then she reinstated her spectacles and patted Elsa's knee. 'I'm sorry, it's just that I didn't want to stop her. She was so happy to have him that I couldn't bear to remind her *he's not yours*. Because she thought he was, you see? And I wasn't ever sure if it mattered.'

'No. I don't get it. Who else did he belong to?'

'Himself! He was Cumulonimbus. Elsa, in these mountains the weather can take many forms, but never a person, or so I always thought. A person would be too complicated. But that night, Cumulonimbus did it! He made himself into a speck of baby, even though it took all of his power to do so.'

'Wait … wait.'

Dot reached for her hand and squeezed it with all her small might. 'You have fallen in love with a storm cloud, my dear.'

'*Wait*! Nobody said anything about love.'

'Oh. Forgive me. I thought that was why you came up here.'

'I … I …' She swallowed. She had kissed him. She had touched her ear to his chest. She had chatted with him and he had been nervous and embarrassed and pleased to be with her. 'I …' she said.

Dot retained her grip on Elsa's hand. 'When Finn – Cumulonimbus – was sixteen, he struck his mother with a bolt of lightning. Daniel Fossiter brought Betty here to be treated, but I did not get to talk to Cumulonimbus, as I would have liked. I must confess, I am somewhat jealous of you for getting that chance. But you deserve it. And I think you do love him, don't you?'

'How could I *love* him? We only just met. I can't even work out how – if – I can I ever get close to him.'

Dot's eyes were half-closed. 'Put it this way: one of the terrifying things about my life is that it belongs to me. It has never been lived before, nor will it ever be again. Every second is a brand-new possession.'

'You're talking in riddles again.'

'And *you* still haven't answered my question.'

'What question?'

'Do you love him?'

'You can prove that love is just chemicals and electricity in the brain.'

'Of course you can, but that doesn't help you deal with it. Do you love him?'

'What if I can't answer?'

Dot shrugged. 'Be lost, Elsa. That is the best advice anyone can give you, and I get the feeling your father would have approved of it. And now be on your way.'

# 14

# BIRTHDAYS

On the day when Finn had shown her the sunbeam birds, she had
made a secret plan to throw him a birthday party. The idea had
come to her when they'd returned to the bothy. He'd kicked off his
shoes and left them in the doorway, where they'd looked so tatty
and busted open that she'd wanted to bury them. She had sneaked
a look at the inside heels and seen his shoe size in faded ink, then
remembered he'd said he had not celebrated his birthday since his
mother left Thunderstown. Her plan had formulated in that instant,
then been forgotten amid the distractions of the subsequent days.

Now she stood outside a cobbler's workshop on Welcan Row,
admiring the overstatement of its tradesman's sign, which read,
*Bryn Cobbler: Cobbler.* She pushed open the door and took a deep
sniff of the polished air. Whatever in the shop wasn't leather was
fashioned from wood just as brown, and Bryn Cobbler himself
was a tanned man in a buff shirt and hide apron. She'd envisaged
buying Finn a pair of colourful sneakers such as she might choose
for herself, but she quickly realized that was out of the question.
From moccasins to boots, everything on sale was made from a
leather as brown as caramel. 'It gives you lucky feet,' explained
Bryn, 'and makes you tread as safely as the goats it's made from.'

She bought two pairs of shoes, since the prices were reasonable
and she wasn't sure which would fit Finn better. Then she headed

back to Prospect Street, where Kenneth had promised to help her with the second part of her plan.

Kenneth was chuckling with enthusiasm when she reached him. He had all of the ingredients lined up on the kitchen counter, and when the electric whisk purred too hard and threw mix all over the two of them he guffawed and she thought, *At least I have made his day, which is a good start.*

Then, when the cake came out of the oven, he provided her with the *pièce de résistance*: a set of fine, tall candles, each with a crisp new wick and a scarlet thread twisting through the white wax. She paused for a moment, staring at them.

'Everything all right, Elsa?'

'Yes. Yes. Perfect, thank you.'

She had been remembering a cake that her mum had once baked her: a sloppy chocolate mound with candles drowning in the icing. Nevertheless it had been delicious and she had been happy sitting at the table with her parents, eating and eating until their bellies could take no more and their chins and cheeks were sticky. Then, after they had cleaned themselves up, her Mum and Dad had given her a present in a long thin package. She had caught them glancing conspiratorially at each other as she unwrapped it: they knew they'd found her something perfect. It was a parasol, an artwork of stunning lace, with silky white clouds sewn into its canopy.

She helped Kenneth plug the candles into the cake, and was soon on her way.

En route to Old Colp, in a yard in Auger Lane made green by weeds uprising against the flagstones, a pair of old women had set up spinning wheels. They talked in a hushed pitch as they spun, only their consonants carrying over the click and whirr of their machines. Elsa slowed to watch them for an engrossed moment, and as she watched the spokes turn and the thread cycle through the wheels, she remembered the afternoon of that chocolate cake birthday, when they had gone to the hedgerow maze in which she had run off ahead, trying to find the centre on her own. She remembered trotting along one leafy route and hearing familiar voices from the path parallel to hers. The hedge grew too tight to see through, but she knew the voices were those of her parents, laughing and teasing each other about who knew best which turn to take. There was no question about it, they would not take different paths, and Elsa eavesdropped with pleasure until at last they headed along the one chosen by her mother, jibing each other as they went.

When she shook off that memory and left the women to their spinning, she was too distracted to remember where she was going and ended up back at Saint Erasmus. Still, she was pleased to find that her memory had left her resolute. If she were to be lost, she would be lost along with Finn.

The first thing Elsa noticed when Finn opened the bothy door were the blisters on his cheeks. Each was a cauterized pink and teardrop-sized, such as a case of frostbite might leave. His eyelids were red and lacerated around the ducts. He looked abject, but cheered up when he saw her. 'I didn't think I'd see you again.'

'Finn! What happened to you?'

'I'm okay,' he said. 'I suppose I just can't hide the things I feel.'

'Finn, I was angry at you.'

'You were within your rights to be.'

She plunged her face forwards and seized his lips with her own. She reached up her hands to hold his bald head. She realized when he whimpered that she was holding him as tightly as a treasure, almost biting to hold his lips between hers. She pulled back and loosened her grip.

He looked astonished. 'I thought—' he said, but she silenced him with a finger over his lips. With her other hand she traced lines between the sores on his cheeks. At her touch they gave up little whispers of steam that followed her fingers.

They kissed again, and once more she couldn't help but cling hard to him, locking her arms around his back and shoulders. When they stopped he gave a bewildered gasp. She savoured his breath against her face, breathing it in. It smelled like dew at the crack of dawn. It made her lungs feel fresh and full of him. Then she noticed a diffuse glow across the side of his scalp. It was a fine haze of cloud picked out by the sunlight, and then it was gone in the blink of an eye.

'Finn …'

'What's wrong?'

'There was… a kind of haze across your head. It's gone now.'

He rubbed his head cautiously.

It had been such a fine, ethereal substance that she could not find it frightening. 'Never mind,' she said, and kissed him again. Then she squeezed his hand and said, 'Happy birthday.'

'Um … it's not my birthday.'

'It is now.' She opened the cake tin to show him. 'I just need a plate and a knife.'

In the bothy, all of the paper birds had gone, although the bin overflowed with white litter. In place of them Finn had been making paper people. With these he seemed to have been having difficulty, and had only managed a dozen.

He cleared his throat with embarrassment when she saw them, then hastily began to scoop them up to press them into the bin. She grabbed his arm to stop him, and took the damaged models from his hands to admire. Half of them were paper women and half paper men, and she knew without asking that they were meant to be the two of them.

'Yesterday I visited the convent on the Devil's Diadem.'

'That old place? What were you doing up there?'

She took a deep breath. 'Asking an old nun some questions. She made me realize that I'd treated you badly.'

'No, Elsa, you were right. I should have told you about what was inside of me.'

'But you were right too. I might have freaked out and we'd never have got to where we are now. And anyway, it's not *what's inside of you*, is it? It's what you are.'

He hung his head. 'Yes, I suppose so.'

'See, I think it's wrong to be upset by that. It's what makes you who you are, and it's the reason that I, you know ...' She gulped. 'Like you. I mean ... the reason why I more than like you.'

He blushed gratefully. 'I more than like you, too.'

'You know, Finn, I think we can work. I'll trust you as long as you trust yourself. Then you'll know, I reckon, and be able to warn me if things become too much.'

They kissed to broker the deal.

'And now,' she asked, 'have you got any matches?'

'Matches?'

'For your birthday candles.'

After she had pulled the curtains and brought the cake through with its tiny flames wavering in time with the tune of her happy birthday song, he blew them all out in one great big puff. She thought of the blowing cloud faces carved into the wardrobe in her room in Thunderstown, and about huffing out the sinking candles of that sloppy chocolate birthday cake, and about being blown loose from her old life and drifting into this one.

'There's a present, too. Two presents, actually, but they're both the same. I just hope one pair fits.'

The larger ones were just right for him. He walked around the bothy with a grin on his face, and the new leather creaked luxuriantly with each step. As he walked, she saw again a momentary gleaming brushstroke of cloud across the top of his head, such as she had seen after kissing him earlier, and then it was gone. She sat back and reckoned she would be happy just to watch him walk in circles, around and around forever.

# 15

# PAPER BIRDS

On the morning of Betty's departure, Daniel had paid an unexpected visit to her house on Candle Street. It was a chill day, a premonition of autumn adrift in summer, and over the rooftops the sky was pressed white by clouds as fine as swan feathers.

He was surprised to discover her car parked on the curb, its boot open. Two bags had already been packed inside it, and now Betty hurried from the house carrying a third. She jumped when she saw him, then collected herself and put down the luggage.

She looked cold there in her threadbare jumper. Her blonde hair was a damp mess and her makeup had been applied in a hurry. 'Hello, Daniel,' she said. 'I was just on my way to see you.'

He looked suspiciously from Betty to her car. He disliked the distance a vehicle put between a person and the ground, which was a damned deal more than its foot or two of suspension. 'You've a lot of luggage for a trip across town.'

'Daniel, listen, I'm … going away for a bit.'

He frowned. 'Where to?'

'Just somewhere I can find some perspective.'

He panicked, although he didn't show it. He wanted to dismantle the car's engine and run his knife through its tyres. He licked his lips. 'Can I come with you?'

'I'm so sorry, Daniel. No, you can't come with me. Nobody can.

I need space. Everything that's happened … it's just too much.'

He had to look away for a moment, up the street towards Old Colp's ebony dome. 'What about Finn? Are you taking him?'

'No, and he doesn't know about this just yet. He's gone up into the mountains today.' She gestured to the open front door. 'Come in out of the cold for a minute.'

He had forgotten the temperature, but he followed her gratefully into the house. The rooms were the cleanest he had ever seen them. Everything had been put away, unless it had been packed into the final bag lying in the hall. The house was as tidy as a show home.

He held a hand to his forehead. All of a sudden his knees and ankles felt like nuts and bolts worked loose. 'Betty,' he managed to ask, 'how long are you going for?'

She shrugged.

*Commit every detail of her to your memory,* he thought to himself. He stared into her face, at the green hue of her irises, the diamond-shaped space where her lips parted.

'Daniel?'

The mole on the underside of her chin, the patterns of her earlobes, the drift of freckles over her narrow nose and the tops of her cheeks.

'Daniel.' She stepped forwards and wrapped her arms around him. She pressed the side of her face against his throat, her head fitting neatly between his beard and collarbone. His back was too broad for her arms to wrap tightly around it, so her hands held to the knobs of his shoulder blades. Her thighs touched his, her hips his, her breasts his ribcage. She was warm and skinny and smelled of fresh soap and water. He looked down into her hair and refused to blink, knowing there was no second worth losing, and no hope of committing this to memory in all its fullness.

'Betty.' Her name came out of him like the groan of a beast bleeding in a trap. 'Don't go.'

She stepped apart from him. Very carefully, he reached out to support himself against the wall.

'I have to. I'm sorry.'

He could barely feel his legs. His belly was in free fall. He knew if he were to let go of the wall he would collapse into a heap on the floorboards.

She emptied a smile at him. 'Please do something for me. While I'm gone.'

He managed to nod.

'Take care of Finn for me.'

He would do anything she asked.

'Okay, then,' she said.

She stepped up on tiptoes to kiss him, then backed away and picked up her final suitcase. 'All right,' she said. 'I think that's everything. Will you lock the house for me?'

He nodded.

Then, as if a leash she had been straining against had suddenly snapped, she sprang out of the door and down the path and quickly climbed into her car. He staggered out into the yard to watch her disappear along Candle Street. When the car turned out of sight he let himself drop. He hit the paving like a stack of stones. He stayed there for a long time, staring down the length of the road. Then at last he dragged himself back into the house and moved slowly through it, sitting on every chair, inhaling the air of every cupboard, pressing his face into Betty's pillow. Eventually he came to Finn's room and noticed on top of a pile of his things an envelope, crisp and newly sealed, with *Finn* written on it in Betty's beautiful handwriting. When he picked it up it weighed as much as all the jealousy and confusion that accompanied the discovery. Why had she left no envelope addressed to *Daniel*?

He slipped the letter into his shirt pocket, and when he returned to the Fossiter homestead, that was where it remained.

*Take care of Finn for me.*

He realized he did not know how he would do as she asked. He could keep a roof over the boy's head and keep him well stocked with groceries, but there was another duty implicit in Betty's request, one that required more than practical measures. How to shepherd the weather in the boy? He turned to the memories of his father and grandfather for guidance, but they were cowering away from him and telling him to do the thing the darkest part of his heart instructed, the thing he would not do because the love of his life had requested that he *take care of Finn for me.* He reflected that during his own formative years his father and grandfather had abandoned him to deal with the turmoil inside of himself alone. There had been times in his youth when his emotions had risen up from the depths of him as implacably as floodwater, and he had felt as if he were drowning. He had cast around for help then and found neither his father nor his grandfather present. All he could do was try to tread water until the flood receded.

He had ignored the damage those waters left in their wake. For just as a flood in a house leaves an aftermath of warped timbers and weakened foundations, he recognized there was a rotting and ruined layer inside of him too.

He knew by these criteria that he could not look after Finn, and within an hour of Betty's departure he had already failed in the task, when he told Finn the news and the boy asked, disbelieving, 'Did she not leave anything for me? Not even a note?'

'No,' he replied, 'not a thing.'

With those few words he had made it impossible to ever hand over Betty's letter. So he clung on to the envelope, and never told Finn of its existence. Eventually he become too fond of it to think of it as belonging to the boy in the first place. For that single specimen of her handwriting was the freshest piece of Betty he had left. To begin with he kept it tucked in his shirt pocket. For days and restless nights it remained there, on his person at all times like a locket. When finally he had to wash that shirt, that her fingers had brushed against and her chest had pressed to, he transferred the now crumpled letter to the pocket of his new shirt, and continued to carry it with him everywhere he went.

Eventually it had grown so dog-eared that the seal had started – tantalizingly – to peel open. This at last made it too much for him to carry around, so he locked it in his trunk with his father's Bible and his grandfather's violin and still did not tell Finn it existed.

Time passed. No call, no mail or message from Betty. And as the long months congested into the first half-year of her absence, the letter in his trunk took on a new significance. Secreted in its envelope were words of hers, words he had not heard before. Not only did he long for the sight of her handwriting, but he hoped that to read it would prompt the sound of her voice in his head. He began to want badly to unseal the letter and read it for himself. She would be disappointed in him, of course, and the threat of that guilt kept the letter locked up and safe.

Further months passed. Betty neither returned nor made the slightest contact. He tried fruitlessly to track her down. He sought out the telephone numbers of old friends and relatives, but they knew nothing of her whereabouts and were as anxious about her as he was. Still he resisted reading the letter, although as time slouched by his motives for doing so shifted. Now fear stayed his hand instead of guilt. Were he to read it, there would be nothing new of her left to experience. He did not know whether he could cope with that. So he kept the letter sealed, even though every so often he took it from the trunk for his fingers to play at its corners, teasing him of their own accord.

He began to dream about the lifeline of her handwriting, but he could no longer imagine her voice with clear diction. When he tried to replay things she had said she sounded suppressed, as if she were talking on the other side of a wall. He strode the mountains with his thoughts bent on the envelope in his trunk, hoping that to read her words might return her voice to him.

Back in the homestead he would sit turning the envelope between his fore and index fingers, hypnotizing himself with its revolutions, just as his grandfather had so often with a playing card. He would think about Betty's request – *take care of Finn for me* – and he would ask his thinking whether there was something he could give the boy to replace the stolen letter.

A year after Betty's departure his thinkings gave him the answer. He and Finn sat in garden chairs in the sunshine behind the bothy, with the rock walls of the bluff dashed golden and the sky full of blue, and he cleared his throat and said, 'I would like to teach you something that my mother taught me.'

His mother had shown him this thing not long before her own departure from Thunderstown. That departure had not been a shock like Betty's had been, although it had plagued him as sickeningly as an infection. He had always known she was going to leave. He had known it even when he learned to crawl, even when he learned to tug her little finger and call her Mama. More specifically, he had known it since he first watched his father berate her.

She did not leave without teaching him the trick which had delighted him since infancy: paper birds. She had kept their creation a closely guarded secret. He would find one waiting for him on his pillow at night, or tucked into his school bag, and he would immediately set upon it and take it apart, trying to understand how the folds built beak and wing. But he couldn't comprehend their designs, and his mother kept her silence. She seemed to possess innate understanding of the design of a bird, so that she could fold without instruction any species from a flat expanse of paper.

Then, in her final week in Thunderstown, when her bags were already packed, she had sat him down in front of her with a stack of crisp sheets and helped his fingers through the folds.

He did his best to teach Finn, well aware that his own blunt attempts retained little of the magic of his mother's. Still he tried his hardest, meticulous with concentration, poking his tongue out beneath his moustache. He held the result up to the sunlight. A paper dove with outstretched wings.

Finn took the model from Daniel's hands and turned it around and around in awe. He tugged at its wings as if there were a danger of wounding it.

'I thought you'd like it,' said Daniel, and offered Finn a sheet of paper. 'Could you tell how it was made?'

Finn nodded and hungrily set to work. If the boy made a mistake, Daniel would silently reach out and reposition his fingers, motioning them through the line a fold should take.

'Pretty good,' he whistled when Finn had finished. The boy's dove was easily as accomplished as his own, with a wonky wing its only imperfection. They looked at each other, and for a moment, were unguardedly amazed. Daniel marvelled that this skill had passed from his own self into Finn, just as once it had passed from his mother into him. He felt as if the three of them were layered together, as closely as the closed pages of a book.

Finn was eager to try again. Daniel sat back and observed, without interruption, the best dove so far take form. Finn laid it delicately between his first attempt and Daniel's, so that the three birds perched side by side. Then for a while they just stared at them, remembering the missing third member of their company, the one more perfect than the two that remained.

For a while after that, Finn would make Daniel a paper bird every time he paid a visit. Daniel would come to the bothy after church and find one waiting for him on the table. He kept them all, placing each carefully into his trunk beside his father's Bible and his grandfather's violin. Sometimes he would test their flight before storing them, and the birds would always soar true, and this would excite Mole into yapping and pouncing after them as if they were butterflies, at which they proved just as elusive and dinked at the last minute away from her biting jaws, and this in turn reminded him of Betty and Mole chasing one another around the lawn beside the homestead, which was like Betty dancing, which was like the marvellous night of Mr Nairn's one-hundredth birthday, when he and Betty had stamped and flicked their legs in time with each other until the last note sounded from the fiddles of the band.

Then one day Finn did not give him a bird when they met. They ate together at the bothy, and afterwards Daniel left. Only once he had reached the bottom of the mountain did he realize that his hands were empty. He did not comment, presuming the boy had forgotten. Likewise he left it unmentioned when the same happened after their next meeting. Reluctantly he supposed that Finn had grown tired of giving presents, and each time they parted thereafter he would look down at the creases of his palms and still be surprised to find himself wishing they held a paper bird.


A mile outside Thunderstown a gorge with grizzled rock walls severed the foothills of the Devil's Diadem. The gorge's base was a dark road of sharp stones, but its sides were as rugged as any canyon's and hewn with dangerously narrow tracks that only goats could tread. On inaccessible ledges eagles had built their eyries, but the eagles here were tatty-feathered birds and they flew without majesty. Above them, rough cirrus clouds hung in the sky, each like the scratched claw marks of some wild beast.

Elsa had followed Finn up here with her hand held in his, except for in one steep stretch of the trail where hands were needed to help climb. They made up for that moment's parting with a kiss, and as they kissed they pressed their bodies in a close embrace and Elsa delighted in the smoothness of Finn's shape.

She had carried a rug with her from Thunderstown, while he had brought a long cardboard tube, tucked under his arm. They were making their way along the top of the gorge, where the path squeezed between the sheer drop on their left and a screen of jutting boulders on their right. Elsa held on to their knobbly surfaces as she walked, feeling the height of the cliff as a tingle in the nerves of her toes. She was glad when they found a place to sit down, a U-shaped cleave among the boulders, sheltered on all sides bar the cliff's. A lizard who had been basking on the rock walls watched them for a moment, then begrudgingly vacated the spot, his legs peddling away over the tawny stone.

'This is the best place for it?'

Finn nodded enthusiastically and she threw down the rug. He opened his cardboard tube and sat down beside her on the fabric. The rocks enclosed their spot so dependably that when he took out and unrolled the sheets of paper they lay still on the floor.

'Time to teach you,' he said.

'I'm pretty bad at this kind of stuff. I can barely fold a letter into an envelope.'

'This is different.'

He folded a sheet in half, turned its corners into flaps, bent it in on itself again, and then she lost track. Folds, twists, turnings in on turnings, and then all of a sudden a paper dove, nestling in the palm of his hand.

'May I?' She took the dove and began to unfold it, trying to understand how it had been constructed. She could see that the angle of one fold allowed its wings to take shape, and that the halving of the paper defined its back, but beyond that the folds bent mystically into folds. When she had unfolded it entirely, only the creases were left. Nothing bird-like about it.

'Your turn,' he said.

'Honestly, Finn, I won't be able to.'

He began to instruct her. Even at dummy's pace she found it impossible to follow, but when she erred he led her hands back into position, setting right each finger as carefully as if it were the needle of a record player. His touch was cool, refreshing in the heat, and his instructions precise. He seemed to understand the workings of her hands as instinctively as he did the making of the bird.

She quickly gave up trying to comprehend what she was doing. Under his tutelage she simply took each stage as it came. At last the finished article lay upside down on the rug.

She laughed. 'It looks more like a scraggy old pigeon than a dove.'

He scratched his head. 'I don't understand what went wrong.'

'It's me, stupid.' She shrugged. 'Don't worry, I came to terms with my lack of creativity a long time ago. But I'm afraid I wouldn't back this thing to fly.'

He took it from her, opened it up and tinkered with its folds. Then he handed it back to her, beautified slightly. 'Try it.'

She tossed it into the gorge.

It dipped to begin with. She thought it was going to drop like a stone, but it swooped unexpectedly at the last, out along a flat trajectory then up in a half-circle against the yawning air. She grinned and threw his bird after hers. His soared instantly, catching the updrafts, wind making its paper wings flutter. The two birds drifted at different altitudes, his gliding gracefully, hers with a laboured bent, until with a croak an eagle flapped up from the gorge's depths to investigate. It chased Finn's bird, caught it and stabbed it hard with its beak. The paper buckled and lost its buoyancy. The broken dove dropped quickly into the shadows.

Elsa cackled and clapped her hands. 'Does that make mine the winner?'

He offered her another sheet, but she raised her hands.

'I'll quit while I'm ahead. I'm happy just to sit back and watch you. Do something complicated, something difficult.'

He squinted up at the eagle, pursed his lips, then began to fold swiftly until he had built an eagle of his own, with a hook in its beak and wings with saw-toothed edges. He threw it into the air and watched it ascend majestically. The first eagle, the blood-and-feather one who was still patrolling the thermals, shrieked as its paper counterpart whooshed past. It fled the scene and left Finn's bird circling.

Elsa gave him a round of applause. 'That's perfect! How did you do that? You're amazing, Finn!'

He blushed, and even though they had been kissing on the way up here she felt goofy for gushing that out in such awestruck tones. She was still unused to the openness that had so readily fallen into place between them. Her relationship with Peter had been a sort of cautious dance, a series of suggestions and cool flirtations. If what she had found with Finn was any kind of dance at all, it was the unconscious ballet of two sleeping lovers who wake throughout the night to find their limbs in new tangles.

'Well,' he said, 'I can't take the credit because I don't really think about it. It's just something I've had a knack for since I first tried it.'

She watched his eagle flutter and roll, and bank to the side through the hot air. 'I think it's wonderful.'

Finn stared out across the cleft of the gorge.

She shuffled conspicuously closer, so that their bodies were touching.

'Elsa,' he asked, 'did you ever lie on your back as a kid, and watch the clouds go by?'

'Yeah, of course. I loved doing that.'

'And did you ever get the feeling that that was the right way up to be? With your back against the planet, looking straight out at the universe?'

'I used to lie like that until I no longer felt like the sky was up. The sky was forwards, and up was whichever direction my head happened to be pointing in. That way the clouds were in front of me, on a level with me, and it felt like they could be reached. I used to love that. The world felt, I don't know, like it had always meant to be that way up. As if it had been knocked over, and to lie like that was to put it right again.'

'That,' he said, 'is exactly how I feel when I'm with you. You've put me the right way up. You've fixed me. For the first time since I was tiny I feel like I fit together.'

'Finn?'

'I don't have to choose between being a man and being the weather. You've helped me see that. I can be both at once.'

'Finn, hang on, there's something stuck to your cheek ...'

She reached across for what looked like a bit of cotton or fluff, but it broke apart at her touch. It was a wisp of cloud. She brushed it away and beneath it his skin was smooth. Then she saw another strand on the crown of his scalp, as white and curled as a pillow feather. She stroked her palm through it and it dispersed.

'What is it?' he asked, trying in vain to look up at his own head.

She left her hand caressing his cheek and temples. Another lock of mist emerged along the curve of his ear and masked the detail of the lobe. 'I don't know,' she said. 'It's like a tiny cloud.'

He touched his fingers to his head, confused. Another ribbon of cloud shimmered across his scalp, as bubbly a vapour as the gas that floats free of opened champagne. 'This has never happened before.'

She reached out for his hand as delicately as she might for a floating bubble. Cloud clung to his fingers where he had touched his head.

'What do you think we should do about it?' he asked worriedly.

A longer drift of cloud had appeared along the inside of his collar, and now another thickened out of a haze along his brow.

'Nothing,' she said. 'This isn't like storm cloud. This is like those clouds we used to watch as kids. You're still in one piece, aren't you?

Perhaps this is exactly what you were just talking about. Perhaps this is being a man and being the weather at the same time.'

It was not long before so much of the strange soft mist had emerged that it outlined his body. It kept coming, fuming gently out of his pores and reaching ethereally into the air. At its thickest it was white as snow, but its edge began to catch the light and the sun outlined it in yellow.

'You've got a silver lining,' she whispered, and kissed him.

While their lips moved the cloud grew, and filled their little boulder-backed enclave with mist. The gorge vanished, the sky vanished. It was just the two of them in a cottony world. Then he tensed and she stopped kissing him and backed off slightly. 'What's wrong?'

'Nothing.'

She knew there was something. The cloud had made him blurred, like an unfocused photograph, so it took her a moment to notice the bulge in his jeans.

For a moment everything was quiet. She heard his tiny groan of embarrassment. Then she roared with laughter that something so earthly had overcome him. 'Finn!' she exclaimed, and threw her arms around him. The mist shimmered. 'It's okay!'

'Then why are you laughing?'

She pushed him on to his back and the cloud swirled around them. She reached down lightly to touch him and he made a dumb contented noise.

'Are you okay with this?'

He nodded. She undid the popper at the top of his fly.

They undressed in a nervous flurry of clothes. At first he didn't know what to do. He just sat there naked and hazy with the sunlight diffusing through the vapour and framing him in a corona. They locked lips again and then she climbed on top of him. When his confidence grew she moved on to her back.

Then, as he lost himself in her, she gasped because the sunlight dropped a blanket of rainbow through the cloud. It settled over their two skins with a prismatic shudder and they were bound together in seven colours.

# 16

# BROOK HORSE

On the stroke of midday, when the sun was directly overhead and its rays could find no route through the windows, the Church of Saint Erasmus was at its darkest, and a congregation of shadows occupied the pews and aisles. Here, in the murk, Daniel sometimes sat from mid-morning, enjoying the failing of the light. A private eclipse, with all the lonely silence of the church to share it with.

Today's gloom was just such an exquisite affair. He reclined in it as other men might in a hot bath. There was a darkness such as this inside of him too, which this one helped appease. It made him feel undone out of his skin, so that it was hard to tell where Daniel Fossiter ended and the world began. In this way he felt released, an uncorked genie floating for a few precious moments beyond his lamp.

He heard someone whisper his name. 'Daniel.'

Startled, he looked around him. The church was too dim to be sure, but all of the pews were empty and when he sprung to his feet and searched behind the pillars he found nobody hiding there.

'Daniel.' There it was again. 'Daniel Fossiter.'

He covered his ears with his hands to test whether the voice was inside his mind, but there were only the silent flowings of his thinkings, and no sooner did he let his hands drop to his sides than he heard it again, louder this time. 'Daniel Fossiter!'

'You fool, Daniel,' he scolded himself, as he realized it was not a whisper but a yell, coming from outside.

When he threw open the doors and screwed up his face against the sunlight, his name was shouted enthusiastically. Some fifteen townspeople were approaching the church steps. They had with them a pony, a bedraggled-looking thing that walked with a limp. Sidney Moses held a rope tied around its neck and by this he had evidently forced it to Saint Erasmus Square. 'Mr Fossiter!' he cried up the steps. 'Look what Abe Cosser found up on Drum Head. A brook horse!'

Sidney clapped Abe across the shoulders, knocking the scrawny shepherd two steps forwards, and urging, 'Tell him! Tell him, Abe! Tell Mr Fossiter what happened!'

'Well, sir,' mumbled Abe, 'it was like this. I was up on Drum Head, you see, to check how the sheep had done in that rain we had, and maybe to move them down a pasture, if they were up to their necks in boggy ground. And, well—'

Sidney clapped his hands. 'Cut to it, Abe!'

The pony snorted and flapped an ear at an interested fly. Daniel folded his arms.

'Well, sir, it was like this. Up there the rain must have been a damn sight heavier because the tarn at Gravel Point had filled up so much that she'd burst her banks and all the earth around her had turned to mush and puddles.' Sidney Moses cleared his throat as a warning, but Daniel raised a finger. 'Let him finish, Mr Moses. In your own time, Abe.'

Sidney rolled his eyes.

'*Well*, sir, what should I see stood dumbly in the mud but this brook horse? Since I meant to spend the better part of the day up there with the flock, I had some provisions on me. Nothing a brook horse likes more than a fishy sandwich, my old man used to say, and it just so happened I had, well …' He waved a nibbled sardine sandwich through the air and the pony whinnied eagerly.

Daniel plodded down the steps. 'Why do you think it is a brook horse?'

'You've only got to look at its tail,' chipped in Sidney. He stepped right up alongside Daniel to demonstrate how he should do just that.

Daniel laid both hands on the pony's back and made a deep noise in the back of his throat. The pony puffed algae-smelling air from its nostrils and lowered its head as if it were in need of sleep. Daniel rubbed the coarse hair of its flank and moved along its side to examine its tail.

Instead of the long, swishing appendage common to other wild horses and hill ponies, this beast had a tapering stub, bald and calloused at its end. It did not look diseased, more likely that the pony had been born with it deformed in this way. At the very tip of the tail Daniel discovered three hard plates of skin, each the size and shape of a fingernail. He pondered these for a moment, the only noise that of a rook croaking as it settled on one of the church's eaves. The crowd's excitement was palpable, but they knew well enough to stay silent while Daniel conducted his examination.

He crouched down to inspect the back leg, for he had seen how lamely the pony had limped after Sidney Moses. This too did not look diseased or injured. Instead, its muscles were thin and its hoof was too small to support its share of weight. Around the ankle were a dozen more scaly callouses like those on the tip of its tail, and between these drooped a thin inch of transparent skin which Daniel ran lightly between his forefinger and thumb. It had a wrinkled, slimy texture that reminded him of the fin of a fish.

He sighed. He was feeling soft today. He could sense the bulk of the church behind him frowning like the ghost of the Reverend Fossiter. Just like his father, who had deserted his role as culler because he opposed what the crowd now expected from it, Daniel had no wish to execute this brook horse. A goat was one thing because a goat was full of greed, but this poor being would have shied away from Thunderstown had it not been led down here. Abe Cosser was a fool for capturing it and bringing it to a man as bloodthirsty as Sidney Moses.

'Be hard like an anvil,' his grandfather used to say, 'and then the hammer blows stop hurting.' Daniel looked from face to anxious face, until doing so returned him to the sorry brook horse. He wondered how many times his grandfathers had stood in this plaza surrounded by men with names like Cosser or Moses, and with them some deviant creature of the weather brought forth for Mr Fossiter's judgement. This thought gave him comfort. His own feelings meant little in the torrent of history. What he was about to do was in his very flesh and bones. It was the only way he knew.

Then he remembered out of nowhere his first encounter with Miss Beletti. In this square, against the walls of this church, he had broken the neck of a wild dog and she had confronted him afterwards, with her anger as brilliant as a sunrise.

'It is a brook horse,' he sighed, and every member of the crowd took a satisfied breath. 'But I have no knife. Mr Moses, hand me that rope leash. I will lead the devil back to my homestead and do right by it there.'

Sidney licked his lips. 'It's all right, Daniel. I didn't expect you to take your knife with you to church, so as luck would have it I stopped by my house and grabbed hold of mine.'

Without breaking eye contact, he reached down to his belt and retrieved a long steel blade with a plastic handle, which he offered to Daniel.

*Betty,* thought Daniel out of nowhere. How she had so hated this sort of thing. He took the knife and considered it with disgust. A good culling knife should have a handle of bone. It showed its purpose. A plastic handle was Sidney through and through, and Daniel longed to return it to him with the blade sheathed in his stomach.

He shook himself. His father; Betty; Elsa: none of them would agree with this. Only his hateful grandfather, who had once axed the head from a chicken just to laugh at its body racing around the yard. So why did it trouble him what a contemptible man like Sidney Moses thought? Again he scanned the earnest faces of the crowd, asking himself who he cared for among these people. There was Hamel Rhys, a pervert and a snake. There was Bryn Cobbler, a drunken shoemaker. There was Sally Nairn, whom he did care for, who had helped him once choose the right flowers to present to Betty, but who now would not meet his eye. She was as subscribed to this as the rest of them. All of them had come here for a killing, for a sacrifice to their own good fortunes.

'Mr Fossiter,' prompted Sidney, 'we are waiting.'

It's in your bones, whispered the voice of his DNA, it *is* your bones. Without it you would have no shape.

'I fear,' said Sidney, sideways to the crowd, 'that Mr Fossiter is not himself.'

Daniel wanted to return to the church's dark. There, in the shadows where everything was without limit, he could cope better with the mess of his thinkings.

'I fear that Mr Fossiter has not been himself in a very long time. Not since Betty Munro took the heart out of him.'

Daniel patted the pony's grey neck, scratched its mane, felt the warmth of its throat. 'You have made a very big show, of late,' he said, turning back to Sidney, 'of being the one who tells me who I am and who I am not.'

Sidney looked affronted. 'Well, it's as I've always said. Everybody must be accountable. Nobody is bigger than the town.'

'Except you, Mr Moses, isn't that right? You with your fingers soft from paperwork and your lips gone crooked from too much politicking.'

Sidney bristled. '*Mr Fossiter!*' His eyes goggled and his chin retracted into his jowls. He looked as ridiculous as a turkey. 'All I have ever asked of you is that you be more ambitious in the way you conduct your business. That you help us find Old Man Thunder!'

At that name the crowd murmured their assent.

'What if conducting my business has taught me when and where it is needed? I have no desire to kill this animal.'

Sidney was flabbergasted. He spread his hands theatrically. 'Since when has desire come into anything? You are employed to carry out a duty! If your *desires* have so confused you of your purpose, perhaps it is time for somebody else to take the lead. We will never catch Old Man Thunder if we dither over cases such as this.'

One or two more impressionable townsfolk drew in a sharp breath at this flagrant opposition to their culler. Several pairs of pleading eyes fixed on Daniel, and he fancied that they carried no more love for Sidney than he did. They wanted him to break whatever spell had enchanted him and turn the knife on the brook horse.

He looked down at the blade and tested it with the side of his thumb. To Sidney's credit it was sharp enough to draw a trace of blood. He gripped the handle hard.

'Who on earth is going to take that lead, Sidney? Who knows the ways of the mountains like I do? You? You would trip over your own pot belly and fall to your death on the Merrow Wold. If you think that all there is to culling is taking potshots at goats while you lean on your garden fence, then you are greatly mistaken.' He snorted and tossed the knife at Sidney's feet, where the steel clattered against the paving. 'I will not kill this brook horse. Abe, lead it back up to the place where you found it, and set it free.'

With that he turned and began to plod away towards his homestead. He tried to carry himself steadily, but the thrill of what he had just done made him want to dance. Dance a jig, like he and Betty had danced at Mr Nairn's one-hundredth birthday party. Waltz and whirl, because he had disobeyed not only Sidney, but all of them, back through history.

Then he heard a brief whinny and a horrible pop followed by a tearing noise.

He turned in time to see Sidney pull the knife from the brook horse's jugular.

If they had judged wrongly and it were a true pony, Sidney and the crowd might have been kicked and thrown about as the animal struggled against death, but it was a brook horse so it only collapsed to its knees. From the wound in its neck, water frothed where blood should have flowed, spattering on to the paving and Sidney's polished shoes.

The frame of the animal sagged and its back rippled. It flopped on to its side, still gushing water. The crowd retreated a few paces as the last of the liquid bubbled out of its throat. Its hide wrinkled and drooped into the puddle it had made. There was a smell of stale water and sediment, for where one might have expected bones and muscles to have filled the brook horse's skin there was only dirty flood water, seeping outwards from a shrivelled coat.

Sidney was doing all he could to hold on to the knife with trembling hands. His shirt was soaked and stuck to his skin, showing his pink belly through the cotton. Some of the crowd had covered their mouths with their hands, but others were staring angrily at Daniel. Sally Nairn looked betrayed. Abe Cosser looked like a kicked dog. Others regarded the man holding the plastic-handled knife with a newfound respect.

'Th-that,' declared Sidney before clearing his throat and trying again, 'that is what we'll do to Old Man Thunder.'

Daniel stared at the hide in the puddle. The crowd whispered to each other, and then someone said, 'Hear hear,' albeit cautiously. Daniel felt as if he had woken from a blissful dream to find himself in the dock of a courtroom.

'Let's not get carried away,' said Sidney, regaining confidence enough to raise one commanding finger. 'Mr Fossiter evidently needs rest. He needs time off. Should, after that, he decide to honour the wishes of his employers and return to work, well, then I'm sure we shall be very glad to consider it.'

Somebody at the back of the crowd hit a few claps of applause. Somebody else crossed themselves and stared at Daniel as if he had been unmasked as a witch. Daniel looked at the dead brook horse and the last liquid flowing out of it and searched himself for the feeling of a minute earlier. Where before he had felt free and liberated, now he only felt lost.

When he arrived, shaken and pensive, back at the homestead, Mole was dead beneath the table. He crouched and rubbed her back, but there was no warmth in her. He lifted her and carried her outside and laid her gently on the grass. Thirty yards from the homestead a lifeless, slanting tree made a circle of shade over a row of small gravestones. He found his shovel and plodded over to this tiny cemetery, reading the names of all of the hounds who had been buried there. Flint, Hunter, Sharpeye, the list went on in this fashion. Then Esme and Prosper, his father's housedogs. Then the patch of green grass he had been keeping watered and soft so it would be ready to dig on this day.

He looked back over his shoulder at the small black shape lying by the homestead. 'Get up,' he urged, beneath his breath, and tried with all his might to will it into happening. The grass shifted in the breeze. A speckling of cloud blew across the sky. He put his shovel down. 'Don't worry, Mole, I won't make you rest with these.'

He went to the workshop and collected his axe. Then he returned to the dead cemetery tree and began to chop at the parched lower branches. When he had severed a good many, he split them into lengths and carried them in armfuls to a good flat place to pile them.

Once he had got the fire going around Mole, he crouched at a distance with his sleeve across his mouth and nose. The black fumes came up from the flames, dancing and leaping. A plaited column of smoke rose high into the air. He thought about the days when Mole and Betty had chased each other across this very spot, and rolled in it laughing and barking, and he wished he could go back, and fall about with them in the green grass.

# 17

# KITE

A dragging day of work followed, in which she filed the photocopies she had made on her prior shifts there. At lunchtime she overheard her supervisor Lily gossiping about her with another girl who worked in the offices. Lily was recounting what Elsa had said on her first day at work, about coming to Thunderstown *to find out what I wanted life to be*. At this both Lily and the other girl giggled snidely. 'She thinks this is another world,' sniffed Lily. 'And she left New York for it. Can you believe it? New York!'

She spent the day with the click of the hole punch, the snow of its emptied paper circles, the snap of the ring binder opening and closing. In the evening she ate, with Kenneth, a coal pot stew he'd cooked with so many chillies that, after her final mouthful, she slumped exhausted in her chair and could think of nothing but an early night. Her bedroom was hot and she slept without sheets. In the small hours she woke from the heat and pushed both the windows open. It did little to lower the temperature, but it brought in a dry air that smelled of heather blossom.

Just before dawn she woke to a thump above her. She propped herself up on her elbows and listened. Another thump, then another, as if something were moving on the roof of the house. A tickling breeze came in through the open windows. The sky was a navy blue, with a pale fuzz building along the outline of Drum Head.

Then, rushing through the window and welling in the dead end of her room, came a wind. Her hair fluttered and a book she had left on the bedside table opened its cover and flicked its pages. A paper goose that Finn had made her took off from the shelf where she'd decided to display it. The wardrobe door – which she had left ajar – swung open.

Suddenly, something more than blown air came in through the window. She shrieked and huddled backwards against the headboard. A pour of grey fur had landed in the shadows at the foot of her bed. It looked up at her with navy eyes and its ears pricked up. She bunched her fists against her mouth, too petrified to call for help.

The dog lost interest in her almost at once and lowered its nose to the floorboards. It sniffed along the wood until it came to the opened wardrobe. Placing its forepaws on the base, it ducked its head inside and snuffled around among her things.

When it backtracked out of the wardrobe it had the presents her mother had given her held lightly between its teeth. They were, of course, still wrapped in their sparkling red paper, but even though she had left them unopened her heart lurched at the idea that the dog might steal or damage them. It carried them across the floor and pounced up on to the window sill.

She threw herself out of bed, yelling, 'Wait!'

The dog seemed unfazed by the three-storey drop. It tensed its grey haunches and bent its knees, as if preparing to leap.

She reached out her arms. 'Give those back! Please!'

It wagged its tail. The fur thudded against the window frame. 'Please.'

It crouched. It was going to jump.

She lunged forwards to seize the packages, but at the last minute it dropped them gamely into her reaching hands. As she cuddled them to her chest, the dog flickered its tongue out across its nose and stepped casually out of the window. When she looked out after it, it was nowhere to be seen. There was only a weathervane turning south.

She closed the window and collapsed on to the bed, still cradling the presents. She did not know whether to laugh or cry or just sag with relief. Nor did her diaphragm, which made her hiccup with a mix of gratitude and fright.

After a minute she wiped her eyes on her t-shirt and placed the presents side by side on the mattress. Both were flat and square, but one was rigid where the other flexed. She realized she loved the scarlet glitter of the wrapping paper her mother had chosen, and when she slid her finger under the tape of the first present she did so with the utmost care.

When she saw what was beneath she had to look away and wait for the beaded tears to drop from her eyelash. She heard the wind hum back past the window.

It was her favourite record. Nina Simone's *Live at Town Hall*. She must have been five years old when she stole it from her dad's record collection and determined to carry it with her everywhere she went. 'Just think what good taste you have,' her dad remarked once, but she had taken it because it was his favourite too. She had loved other records since, records that had arrested her with an incisive lyric or a melody that cut straight to the heart, but it was for this LP that her affections endured. She'd grown up on its songs, turned back to them in times of need. Just the other day, in fact, she'd been missing this record, when all along it lay wrapped in her room. It was the only possession of her father's that her mother had not thrown out with the man himself, and it had been Elsa's soundtrack to becoming a young woman, her soundtrack to leaving Oklahoma. On her first nights in New York she had played it as loud as her cheap record player could bear. Played as the walls rattled when the subway passed, or when she sat in the window frame as she had had the habit of doing back then.

In the weeks before she'd left New York for Thunderstown, she had sold off or scrapped all of her possessions. Only a handful of them survived the clear-out, and these she had delivered to her mum's house in Norman, to be stowed there in her attic. Her mother must have found the record among those items, and recalled at once its importance to her daughter. With no means of playing it now, she held the record in her hands and stared at the photo on the cover, which showed Simone from a distance and from behind, on a stage in the spotlight, absorbed in her piano. Elsa thought of her mother, all alone in her living room in Norman.

There was no need for a record player: the songs struck up of their own accord in her head, made her mouth hum them and her tongue sing their lyrics on the edge of her breath. She remembered splashing about in puddles when she was younger, trying to recreate the moody chords of Simone's version of 'Fine and Mellow' by whistling through a cardboard tube. She remembered discovering with a thrill that the plinking notes of the piano sounded like falling rain, and Simone's voice like the breathy cooing of the wind itself.

Likewise she had listened to that song on the day of her dad's release from jail, when she had played it on the car stereo as she drove excitedly to meet him, taking with her his old plastic raincoat. He'd loved that watertight coat, which was as yellow as a fisherman's, because, as he liked to point out, 'Fishermen and weather-watchers are like family. Spending all of their time staring into water. Hoping for a sight of something.' She'd hoped it would bring back some of his old cheer. In her final few visits he'd been a total wreck, and all he could talk about was weather. 'The lightning doesn't strike,' he'd repeated on each occasion. 'It's a connection made in secret by the earth and the storm. Only when it's made does it catch fire, hotter than the surface of the sun.'

'Yeah,' she'd said. 'Yeah, you told me about that before.'

Then he had lied to her about the time of his release and when she enquired at the gate she discovered to her horror that he had left the jail four hours earlier and was long gone on his way into the prairie. She had held his plastic coat in her arms, sitting in disbelief in her car outside the prison gates, a copy of this album playing on loop on the stereo.

She put the record down on the bed and dried her eyes again. Just as those songs could still disturb the air, should the needle take its slow spiralling journey towards the centre of the vinyl, memories of her father could still stir up such intense feelings in her that she could barely breathe. She looked at the phone in the corner of her room and wished there was a number she could call which would lead to his voice breathing down the line. She wanted badly to tell him about Finn and what she had found in him. But there were billions of combinations of digits you could punch into a telephone and not one single string of them could connect her to her father.

She put the record aside.

When she tried to unwrap the second gift, her hands were trembling and she had to put it down again. She considered for a moment picking up the handset and miming the act of dialling her dad's old number. Then she could pretend he had answered and let him know all the things that she felt. There was so much to tell him that she would not know where to start. Perhaps she would start by telling him that … Perhaps she would …

She fanned her face because the blood had rushed to her head and tears were threatening once more.

She would tell him that he was a bastard. He should have been there on that day when she – the only one who still cared – arrived at the jail with his beloved yellow raincoat and Nina Simone playing on the stereo and money saved up to help him get back on his feet. Instead he had vanished, found himself a tornado to die in, left everything *unfinished*.

He had made her feel as if he loved storms more than he loved his daughter.

She grabbed a handkerchief and blew her nose. Then, with bleary eyes that meant she tore the paper, she opened the second present.

It was a kite.

A diamond-shaped kite made from quartz-white fabric. The tail, bunched up in polythene, was tied with silver bows. As she took it from the packet the tail fell to its full length with the grace of a waterfall. Her chest tightened and her shoulders bunched forwards. She picked up the phone and this time she did not mime but punched in the numbers. The clicks and crackles of receivers connecting across continents. Then the ringing tone that itself reminded her so much of her mother.

'Hello? Who is this?' Her mother sounded shattered, and only then did Elsa realize that it would be the middle of the night in America.

She had no idea what to say. She pressed the handset tight against her ear and cheek.

'Who's there? Do you know what time it is?'

'Mum …'

'Elsa! Oh my God!'

'Hello, Mum.'

'*Elsa!*'

'Um, thank you, Mum, for my presents.'

If her mother was cross with her for not calling, or upset that she had only just now opened her gifts, her voice didn't show it. 'You liked them? Elsa, I can't believe it's you! Have you flown the kite yet?'

'No, I … I'm going to fly it today. With someone I met here.'

'I'm so pleased, Elsa. I've got the receipt if it's no good. But I guess you're a long way from the store …'

'Yeah. Yeah, I probably am.'

Silence – apart from the rummaging static of a few thousand miles of crossed air and leapfrogged oceans – but she had learned from Finn that an unfilled silence could be worth more than a hurried word.

'And the record?' her mother asked. 'It still plays okay?'

'I don't have a record player, but that doesn't matter.'

'Ah. It was … I know it's funny to give you something that's already yours but, you know … Oh, Elsa, I can't believe it's you.'

Elsa looked down at the telephone cord twisted round her fingers. It wasn't already hers, it was and had always been her dad's. Her mum used to infuriate her with such mistakes, but not today. 'It's perfect, Mum. I mean, it's a massive surprise because it was … because it was …'

'Because it was your father's?'

'Yes.'

She could hear the breath passing over her mother's lips. She wondered whether, if she could but listen hard enough, she might hear the clock ticking on the wall above her mum's phone, or the Oklahoman wind blowing through the avenues of Norman.

Mum blew her nose. 'Sorry, Elsa, it's just so marvellous to hear your voice. I wonder, did I ever tell you what my favourite line on that album was?'

'I didn't think you cared for it, Mum.'

'"*Like a leaf clings to a tree, oh my darling cling to me. Don't you know you're life itself …*" She cleared her throat. Elsa knew it was hard for her mother to talk about her emotions, even if it was in quotation marks. 'Your father,' she continued, 'played that to me on the night we got engaged, after we got back from the beach where he proposed to me. Do you want to know what he told me after that?'

Elsa bit her lip and nodded silently. Her mother waited for a moment and continued. 'He said human beings were like a wind blowing. He said that sometimes we're loud and sometimes we're a whisper, sometimes we're warm and sometimes we're frighteningly cold. But however we blow, we blow onwards, and leave no sign of us behind.'

'Mum,' Elsa gulped, 'I think I fell in love.'

She yelped with excitement. 'What? Love? I never thought I'd hear you say that!'

'Well, I – he – changed my mind.'

'Who *is* he?'

'His name is …' she hesitated. She was tempted to say Cumulonimbus. 'His name is Finn.'

'And what does he do?'

'He, er, he makes me happy.'

'Good. Good. He sounds very mysterious. Although he'd have to be, to cut through all your opposition to falling in love.'

'Well, you know, you and Dad never really made the best case for it, Mum.'

Her mum didn't reply at once, and Elsa cringed and wished she hadn't said that. It was so easy to slip back into the old ways of talking.

'I loved your father very much, to begin with, but with all his storm-chasing he might as well have had another woman on the go. You won't believe it, but when I was pregnant with you, I was the more whimsical, the one who did things on the spur of the moment.'

'I know. I never even thanked you for all those practical things you did.'

'Don't be silly, dear, of course you did.'

'That's kind of you, but I know I didn't.'

'You don't need to say something to mean it.'

'All the same … thank you.'

Her mum blew her nose again, an explosion of snorts and gasped breath, distorted by the long-distance connection into something truly horrific.

'So,' said Elsa when they had both recovered, 'are you not going to ask me where I've gone?'

'I'm not allowed to, am I?'

'Oh, Mum, I'm so sorry. I just … I needed …'

'I know. You don't have to explain.'

'Well, you can call me whenever you like.' And she gave her mother her telephone number and address and she told her about Thunderstown and Kenneth Olivier and each of the mountains and again, eventually, about Finn, although on that subject there was very little more she could say.

By the time Elsa's phone call had finished, the sun was up and the winds were blowing above the mountains, chasing a bunch of white clouds through the high fields of the sky. She pulled on her sneakers and left the house, the kite rustling under her arm.

As soon as Finn opened the bothy door, she sprung on him and wrapped her arms around him. She leaned her head against his neck and heard the small swallowing noises of his throat and beneath that his breath, the expansion and contraction of his chest. Surprised, he returned her embrace. Their bodies fitted together like separated continents.

After a while she took a step backwards so she could look at him. 'I've got something for us,' she said, and handed him the kite.

He took it out of its packet, the bows shimmering as he shook out the tail. He ran his hand over its glittering surface.

'I want us to fly it together,' she said.

'But I don't know how to fly a kite.'

'I'll teach you.'

A wind came rushing down the mountain, throwing up leaves and dust and humming through the bothy's walls.

'It's the perfect day for it,' she said.

He leaned forwards and kissed her. 'Come on, then.'

Old Colp's higher reaches inclined gently, giving way to meadows of dark tufty grass and dried-out ferns curled up into orbs. Finn led Elsa to one such place, an expanse dotted with poppies that had – for the time being at least – dodged the attentions of the goats. Their scarlet heads bobbed in the sweeping wind, and the meadow grass keeled left and right in its currents.

'It's easy,' Elsa said, when they were standing side by side and the wind was eagerly flapping her hair. 'We each take one end of it, and I hold the guide strings. Then we run. As fast as we can, and when I shout to let go we throw the kite into the air. Got it?'

He nodded, concentrating, and took his side of the kite. She looked at him, laughed at how seriously he was taking it, then shouted, 'Run!'

And off they shot, over the springy grass with the wind racing along with them and surging up their backs. The fabric of the kite crackled like a firework about to go off. They ran at breakneck speed – she hadn't run this fast in years – and then she yelled, 'Throw!' and they launched the kite into the air. It took off with a hungry crackle and ripped upwards on the currents. They skidded to a halt, and Elsa turned to guide its flight with the strings, although all she really needed to do was to anchor it. It looped high above them in a dazzle, the sunlight making the colour glitter in its fabric.

'How do you control it?' he puffed.

'Like this,' she said, demonstrating. 'It's easy, especially in this wind. Here, have a go.'

He took the guide handles from her as cautiously as if they were eggshells, but he quickly grew in confidence. He tugged experimentally at one handle and the kite dinked to the side. He grinned and made it reverse the other way. He had mastered it in no time, just as he had mastered the art of folding paper birds. Now he made it dance a figure of eight, now zigzag across the deep sky. Its tail coursed in its wake.

Elsa watched Finn's face. It would not be possible for his grin to be any larger. 'I wonder if ...' he mused as he experimented with the strings. 'Watch this!'

He made the kite move at a blur through an arc and another arc, so that it traced an E in the sky. After that it shot vertically in a straight line, then shimmied back down on itself. Finally it zipped through a circle, signing off with a dash.

'You wrote my name!'

He nodded happily, and offered her the strings. 'Your turn.'

She got through a loosely defined F, then sent the kite crashing down to the ground where its fabric ruffled indignantly, caught in the grass. They picked it up together and dusted it off.

'Try again?' he asked.

'Damn right!'

She began to run. Finn chased along beside her and the kite crackled between them, already straining to ride the wind. They raced across the flowery earth and she was about to shout, 'Now!' when she tripped and flew forwards, losing her grip. The sheer surprise of it made him trip too. He yelped and clutched in vain at the kite's tail as he fell along with her on to the grass. They rolled on to their backs just in time to watch the kite shoot free, wriggling away like a snake swimming through water.

Elsa laughed.

'You aren't cross that it's gone?'

'No. It was fun while it lasted.'

He nodded.

She moved across to lay her head down on his chest. There was a noise in there of distant thunder. She lay against him, looking up at the kite until it diminished into a white dot, a star in the daytime.

'We should go too,' he said.

'What? We only just got up here.'

He became serious. 'No. I mean, you and I should go away. We should have an adventure together.'

She stared outwards at the great blue atmosphere and wondered how far their kite had flown. There was infinity beyond that cerulean expanse. 'Where would we go?'

'I don't know. That's the exciting thing about it.'

'I've only just started my job. I might not be able to book the holiday.'

'Elsa, that's not what I meant. I meant we should leave Thunderstown.'

'Oh. Wow. That's a big step.'

'Yes. That's the whole point of it.'

'Finn, I've only just got here. It was only this morning that I told my mum where I'd gone.'

'You don't have to lose touch with her again; I'm not suggesting that. But think how exciting it would be to pick a horizon and head off for it.'

What if, she wondered, Thunderstown had never been her destination, but only the starting post for an important journey that was to come? She tested herself to see if she had grown too attached to leave. She had not fled New York in search of a change of bricks and mortar. She had left it in search of a different life. Kenneth would be disappointed, and she realized just how much it would hurt to leave him; but they could always stay in touch.

The wind gushed above them, playing the air like a saw. She remembered the dog that had intruded into her room that morning and taken the kite in its teeth. Already now that kite was far away, lost over undiscovered country.

'Deal,' she said.

'What? Are you serious?'

She yanked his arm so that he followed and lay across her, looking down at her with only an inch of air between them. 'Deadly. But for the moment let's just stay here.'

He grinned. Then, once again, that champagne-cloud began to show around the outline of his head, catching the light and giving him a silver lining. A gaseous halo, this time stretched and snatched at by the wind. She stroked her hand up over the bald dome of his head and the cloud parted at the motion.

'This is your happiness,' she whispered, 'and I am so glad that I helped you to discover it.'

# 18

# THE LETTER FROM BETTY

In the morning Daniel trekked up Drum Head, to check the traps he had set there. He could taste moisture on the air – a change of weather was due. The sky was rugged with altocumulus, apart from in the north where the pointed peaks of the Devil's Diadem had torn strips out of the clouds. Above him, the sun looked perched on the peak of the mountain, as if it were considering turning back down the far slopes. Below, in Thunderstown, somebody was having a bonfire: a thin helix of smoke drifted up from somewhere in the vicinity of Corris Street.

He huffed, and turned his back on the town. He was still hurting from his treatment at the hands of Sidney Moses and his followers. He should have done his duty and killed that brook horse, not indulged a weak-hearted mood that must have made him seem like a silly, bleating little lamb.

He came to a part of the mountain where bristling spears of slate jutted out of the earth. To progress uphill he had to wind his way between them – the slate spears were as regular as trees in a tight forest. This was a good place to kill goats, for the routes between the stones were narrow and could be laid with traps until the place was like a minefield. He trod carefully, watching the pebbly ground to ensure he didn't fall victim to one of his own concealed devices. 'Hah!' he cried, the noise ricocheting between the trunks of rock, Sidney Moses would not last five minutes up here. He would no doubt chop his own hands off when he tried to prime his first trap. Likewise, Hamel Rhys would be done for within moments, and Sally Nairn too, and even a man such as Abe Cosser, who knew something of the mountains, wouldn't survive.

The first and second traps he came upon were empty, but in the third he found a young nanny who had died overnight in a vice of steel. He unhinged the metal jaws and slumped her body against a rock, where it would make quick crow fodder. He reset the trap, winching back the lever that helped open wide the jaws and lock them in their deadly circle, then he stood for a while with his hands in his pockets, looking at the saw-toothed metal.

If you judged it rationally then of course it was futile. Even his grandfather had admitted that. One man with a rifle and a collection of snares could never hope to keep in check the population of an entire species. What mattered was the trying. A culler's real work was not done up on the mountains but in the perception of the townsfolk, where it affirmed that somebody was out there in the wild, keeping Thunderstown safe.

With a snort he crouched down and picked up a chunk of slate. He tossed it up and down a few times, then hurled it as hard as he could at the trap. With a crack and a clang the rock hit the pressure plate and the jaws slammed closed. He picked his way along the winding paths until he came upon his next trap, and this too he disarmed, and so on up the mountain until, come late afternoon, he had neutralized them all.

When he got back to the homestead in the afternoon, he washed in cold water, sieving handfuls of cool fluid over his hair and face. Then he regarded himself in the mirror for a time, droplets occasionally falling from his beard. He tried to count all of the new wrinkles and grey hairs that Betty would not recognize if she ever came back, but there were too many.

When he had dried himself he plodded down to the kitchen, tore a hunk of bread and sliced tomatoes across it. He took this through to the main hall and living space of the homestead. Stout wooden columns propped up the ceiling, and in a wall at the far end an impressive fireplace (lit as rarely as Daniel felt the cold) was surrounded by soft chairs that he never lounged in. The walls of the hall were crammed with portraits of Fossiters past, each sporting the same furrowed eyebrows and clipped black beard that Daniel wore. Previous generations had raised large families in this place, but there were no pictures of children or their mothers on these walls. His ancestors had had little time for either.

He sat at the sturdy wooden table at which the Fossiters had eaten for centuries. He picked at the food, but no sooner had he sat down to eat it than he lost his appetite.

He had always known that he was of two minds. His first was the slow-paced, sombre mind that the townsfolk recognized as Daniel Fossiter's. This mind was the one he used to think and plan and reason, but with his other mind he could not manipulate or second-guess. It surged in the depths of himself, just as an ocean surges beneath the boat bobbing on its surface. It had its own thinkings, to which he was not privy, but which sometimes, looking down, he would glimpse for a second like the shape of a whale moving underwater. At other times it rocked him with such intense waves of feeling that all he could do was cling to some solid and rational thought until it stilled. It always did, eventually, or at least it always had done until now.

He got up and crossed to his trunk, gently lifting the wooden lid. Inside were the paper birds Finn used to make him, which he parted carefully so as not to dent their wings. Beneath them lay his father's Bible and his grandfather's violin and, tucked between those, the letter Betty had written long ago for Finn.

He returned to the table and placed the letter squarely on its surface, making sure it lined up perpendicular to the edges of the table. He wondered whether he could wait any more.

He summoned his most treasured memories of her. A birthday of his on which, as with all prior birthdays, he had let the occasion go unacknowledged. He remembered that he had returned to the homestead after an afternoon's labour to find it springing all over with flowers. A cake on the table, a russet-coloured sponge with fruit pieces as dark as ink blots. Betty, its baker, waiting for him in the doorway, wearing a silly pointed party hat and holding something wrapped in bright paper that was a present for him.

Another memory, this time in the dead of night, when he heard a noise at his bedroom window. He sat up startled in bed, fists raised like a boxer's. There Betty was, scrambling in through the open window in a dress pale as the moonlight. It made marble sculpture from her bare shoulders, but instead of sitting gobsmacked and admiring her, he protested that there was a front door downstairs designed for entering the premises. She cut back that life was better like this, if you let yourself be carried on it.

He needed her wise words now more than ever, so he started to pick at the seal of the envelope. Then he paused and thought that to open it with his thick fingers would be like opening a jewellery box with a battering ram. He rushed to the sideboard and found the thin silver letter opener of his father's. This he sliced precisely through the space between the sealed gum and the corner of the envelope.

He raised the paper to his face and pressed his nose against the seal. It did not smell of Betty, as he had hoped, so he tried to imagine her favourite perfume. He found that he could not.

No matter. The words were what would count. After eight

patient years he would at last receive some sentiment of hers. The sheer shape of her handwriting would be enough.

He opened the envelope. He had speculated, fantasized, dreamed about this moment so many times that to begin with he could hardly look.

Inside were two sheets of paper which he unfolded. He stared into the grid of her handwriting and at first didn't let himself read the words. He savoured instead the moment, absorbed the arrangement of her sentences, treated them like a dance he could imagine her hand and her pen fox-trotting through. Then he wiped his face on his sleeve and began to read.

Finn,

There have been so many different versions of this letter. I have spent all day trying to write it. And if there's only one thing you take from these words, it should be this: I have not left you. Please don't think it even for a minute.

Things have changed in these last few months and I need room to set my thoughts in order. You should know, though, that I don't blame you for the burns I received from the lightning. It wasn't your fault, and nor is it your fault that I'm going away for a bit.

I've always known that you had lightning in you, and I've always accepted it. Daniel warned me again and again that you might be dangerous, but I couldn't make him see that perhaps each of us is a danger, if we don't know what's inside of us. Now you understand about it too, and I feel like I should have given you some warning long ago. At your last birthday I tried to explain it. Sixteen years old seemed like a fitting time to tell you, but I could not find the words. Do you remember your birthday picnic on Drum Head, when I sat in silence and you asked me what was wrong? I was trying to tell you then. Trying to tell you that you were a thundercloud once, but that I love you just the same.

And yet, I am frightened. I'm writing this and not speaking it because I could never say such a thing in person.

How can I explain this fear? It's like this … The greatest joy of parenthood is passing things on. It's what I always dreamed about doing – giving away all the things I thought were good in my own life and holding back all the bad. And I have wondered whether all we ever are is this: a filter of the good and the bad, trying to work out which is which, which we should withhold and which we should pass on. So before I digress and restart this letter for the hundredth time, here's the start of the point I'm trying to make: I loved Daniel Fossiter for a little while. He was so absorbed in his fears, but sometimes I could prize them open and let out a part of him that was like a little boy, able to lose itself in life again, and that was the thing I loved. Yet all along, at the same time, he was trying to pass something on to me. Those fears he had grown up with and surrounded himself with, he wanted me to feel them too. They were, ultimately, all fears of things unexplainable. Fears of things like you, Finn.

When the lightning came out of you he said it was proof. That there was something terribly wrong with you and that it needed righting. I said it only proved you were a miracle. Then a kind of zeal came over him and it made me sick to look him in the eye. He was so eager for us all to be doomed. And then I went to you, and as I have said I held nothing against you because of what happened, but no sooner did I see you than my body froze up with fear.

I grew up in a rational world, Finn. A place far, far away from here. I am used to reason: if I know I am not frightened of you, then it follows that I am not frightened. But my body doesn't think in the same way. I had worked everything through in my mind, and I intended for nothing to be different between us. Then I saw you for the first time after you struck me, and you looked so small and sheepish, and I was nearly paralyzed by fear. I am so, so sorry for how that must have made you feel.

I ran back to Daniel after that. At last I understood him, for it was his fear that I now had inside of me. It had been passed on, just as he always hoped to pass it on by persuasion. No sooner did I understand him than I did not love him any more, and I realized I needed to be away from him and from Thunderstown.

You are my salvation: a child when before I could have none. But now I feel like I am suffocating whenever Daniel is near. It's like his words are smoke in the air. I flinch every time he opens his mouth. So I am going away, and by the time you read this I will have left Thunderstown. I have asked him to look after you. Please do your best to look after him in return. He is shrill with fear, and he does not know the first thing about it.

Don't worry, I will be back soon, I just need to breathe some fresh air and be in the company of strangers. You're perhaps too young to feel the need for such a change, but I've learned that sometimes the things we don't understand are the things that compel us most profoundly, and we have to decide whether to suffocate them or let them carry us. There's no middle way.

One more thing to say: you are a man. Now that you know what's inside of you, you've grown up. You couldn't be a child again even if you wanted to be. And the bleak and wonderful thing about growing up is that you have to work everything out on your own. You will do a fine job, I am sure, and before long we will be together again.

Your loving mother,

Betty

For a time Daniel did not move. The second hand on the old clock made its slow struggle around the face, and only after it had turned a full circuit did he give a great bellow and batter his fists against his knees. He tore at his beard. She could not mean these things she had written. She could never have been so affected by the things he had felt about Finn.

'Because I was wrong, Betty!' he wailed. 'Wrong!'

Had he – with his constant haranguing – *had he* been the one who had changed her thinkings and strangled her feelings for him out of her? Man, his father had said, is cursed to love. To feel it as powerfully as he does. Man, his grandfather had said with a grin, dreamed up love because he was weak-willed, for a lover is a man who lets his guard down, and after that the killing blow comes in.

'Except,' he growled in reply to the voices of his ancestors, 'you don't say what is to be *done* about it.' It seemed ridiculous to sit and speculate, when love was a thing that grabbed you by the guts and not the head and you did not know how to ride it out. He did not give a damn about whether love was a weakness or a curse, since trying not to fall in love was as doomed to failure as trying to murder yourself only by holding your breath. If the whole of Drum Head had been torn out of the earth and placed down on his chest, it would not have weighed as much as did the realization that he had put his own wretched fear into Betty, even though he had loved her with every atom of his body.

Worse still, she had intended to leave only briefly. At times during these last eight years he had hoped that when she'd said as much, on the day that she'd left Thunderstown, she had lied to him. If it were a lie and a lack of caring it was possible to imagine her forging a new life in a new landscape, and although that was painful at least it meant she was alive to live it. What if, by accident or design, she had taken that journey from which there was no possible return?

From the walls of their homestead the Fossiter portraits watched in silence. 'Damn you,' he growled at them, including himself among their countenances. 'Damn you all.'

He could not bear to be in their company so he charged outside, into the climbing sunlight of the morning. In the yard he paused and bit hard on his tongue. He wondered what he might have done for her or said, had he known what he did now.

He blundered across to the workshop. In here hung the corpse of the last goat he had hung, beheaded and drip-dried now of the blood that had filled it. He unknotted the cords that kept it dangling from its hooves and thumped it on to his butchering table, a wood-topped counter stained by the blood of generations of goats, spilled by generations of Fossiters. Its surface was notched like a prison wall by the tally blows of their cleavers.

He had often wondered what differentiated the goats' burly, braying existences from a man's. A goat lived its life like every goat in every generation before it. It chewed on anything it could, polished its horns against tree bark, moulted in the autumn, rutted in the spring. All this it did with dull stony eyes and a placid expression, as if its life were a routine played out a million times, a chore lived with duty and not wonder.

But a man … a man had a fire, a spark in his eye. His life seemed to him an exquisite flame, and he would tend it greedily. What was that fire, wondered Daniel, and where did it come from?

'Betty!' he gasped without planning to do so, croaking up at the ceiling.

And why did he address the ceiling? Because he thought God lay up there? God in the heavens? God in the workshop's loft? The goats did not croak at the sky when they died their slow deaths with their legs bent in metal jaws. All that was up in the sky was water and dust on the wind, and then a nothingness beyond human imagination, so everlasting that it could not even be measured in light years. He closed his eyes and pictured God the Father seated on His throne, and God the Father had a serious brow, a long nose and a black beard. God the Father was a Fossiter.

He took up his flaying knife and returned to the carcass on the butchering table. Parting the dirty hair around the goat's crotch, he worked the knife into its groin and cut out an exit for the slop of its innards, which he dragged out in his fist and plopped into a bowl. Then he set to work with the knife, drawing with its blade the practised patterns of cuts and slices that gave him a grip on the animal's skin. With tugs and pulls he undressed the body of its coat, as easy as if it had been a cardigan on a human being.

He rubbed salt into the newly removed goat skin and hung it up to cure. He chose another cleaver and chopped briskly through the meat and bones, separating out the body into joints and chops. Then he could go on no more.

He twisted around and flung the cleaver through the air. It whistled as it flew, then slammed into the woodwork of the door frame. He kicked over the bleed trough so that its liquid mix of innards and viscera sprayed out across the workshop wall. His hands were shaking and he screwed up his eyes and yelled into the darkness of his thinkings. After yanking free the cleaver he headed back into the homestead. The first thing to hand was his father's bookshelf, which he broke from the wall with one powerful blow, so that all of the books fell in a mess to the floor. He dropped after them on to his knees and one by one slammed the cleaver through their covers until the floor was snowy with paper. Then he sprung up and swung the cleaver at his grandfather's favourite armchair, hacking through the arm and ripping open the cushions until he spluttered on the dust and the feathers flying forth. He kicked over the table, and butted his head against a painting of his great-great-grandfather so that the canvas smashed in. He slashed and scored his way along the wall of portraits, until he came to his old trunk in the corner. Greedily he threw it back open – and then stopped.

The paper birds turned his rage into a ceremonial fury.

He lifted from the trunk his grandfather's violin and his father's weighty Bible. He righted the table and placed both objects on it, the instrument on top of the book. He regarded them for a moment, then raised the cleaver over his head with both hands and slammed it down with all of his might. It carved cleanly through the violin, sending frayed strings thrumming to both sides. It split the Bible in half like an apple and wedged into the wood of the table.

He crashed back on to his rump and sat there panting. After some time had passed he began to realize the wreck he had made of the homestead. Filled with sudden doubt and superstition, he reached out and touched the nearer half of the violin. To his surprise he saw that there was a folded piece of card taped inside it. His grandfather must have secreted it there by sticking it into the bole of the instrument. Daniel removed it and unfolded it cautiously.

A photograph of his mother and father.

His mother, Maryam. It was the first time he had seen her since he was seven years old.

He gasped at the sight of her. 'Look at you!' he said, pawing at her. He had always considered his looks to be yet one more product of the Fossiter lineage, but he marvelled to see that he also looked like her. She had his severe brow and dark eyes, and hair as black as his, although hers was long enough to reach down to her elbows. And there was something in her eyes he could not quite place, a cold kind of knowledge. She looked as if she were withholding some immense secret. 'Look at you,' he whispered, tracing her outline with his finger.

Her gauzy dress was tailored from a translucent cloth, and at the moment the photograph had been taken a wind had puffed and the dress had billowed and flapped out along with her long black locks and she looked half woman and half mist. For a while he didn't blink, in case this image of her would prove as fleeting as the ones in his dreams and vanish under other memories. Eventually his eyes were swimming and he had to refresh them, but to his delight the photo remained when they reopened. He slid on to the floorboards and lay on his back, gripping the photograph tight. He felt cut off from the man he had been yesterday, even from the man he had been one hour ago. Cut off and stranded, lost in a chill dark. He began to shiver. It was a hot day and the sunlight flaring in through the homestead's windows lit him directly. Even so he felt icy cold.

Then he realized that he could see his breath hanging in the air.

He got up and retreated on all fours, but his next exhalation, and the next too, hung where he had breathed it. A trilogy of sparkling clouds, as if the warm air of the homestead were freezing. Terrified, he dared not breathe further. He clasped his hands over his mouth until he turned red-faced and his veins began to throb in his neck and forehead. Still the clouds of breath hung there glittering, until reluctantly he gasped and his heart fluttered with relief because his next breath was invisible again.

The three clouds dispersed gradually in the air. He puffed out several times, just to be sure. Nothing. He pinched his cheeks, wiped his palms across his shirt to remove the cold sweat that had formed on them, then pressed a hand to his chest and felt for his heartbeat. To his relief it did not boom with thunder, but with the powerful pump of ventricles.

He did not know what to make of what had just happened, so he turned again to the photograph of his parents. He collected the cleaver with which he had destroyed his house, and carefully scored a line between the couple. His father he left amid the destruction of the homestead. His mother he regarded for a long minute, then slipped into his shirt pocket, to walk out with her into what promised to become a fine summer evening.

He stood for a long while in the yard, leaning on the fence, staring upwards at the azure heavens and feeling as groundless as the clouds that passed above.

When he looked down he was surprised to see a man approaching from the west. He moved with such zip that it took Daniel a moment to realize it was Finn. Even when he reached the homestead, Daniel did not know what to say.

Eventually Finn said, 'You look different.'

Daniel looked down at his hands, dried in places with blood from his earlier butchery, and stuck here and there with bits of debris from the chaos he had made of the hall. He cleared his throat. 'I feel different.'

'We need to talk. Can I … I mean, are you going to invite me in?'

Daniel nodded sideways at the front door. 'Lead the way.'

Finn took a few steps inside, then stopped to gape at the damage. 'Daniel … what have you done?'

Daniel rubbed his beard. 'I don't know why I did it, but I think … it was the right thing to do.'

Finn approached the ruined portraits. The top half of one sitter's face remained in the frame, but a sweep of the cleaver had slit the canvas beneath the nose and the bottom half of the painting had flapped away. 'This was your grandfather!'

'Yes.' He stood beside Finn to look into the oil of the old man's eyes.

'You … you have nothing but respect for your grandfather.'

Daniel reached up and tore out the top half of the canvas, which he discarded on the floor.

Finn was astonished. 'Daniel, what's happened?'

'The past,' he said, sweeping an arm through the air to indicate the entire contents of the room, 'became the past. And you,' he raised a commanding finger, which to his dismay Finn flinched from, 'are owed a thousand apologies.'

'What for?'

'I let my fear get the better of me.'

'Daniel, this is all … really unexpected. And … and …' He smiled nervously. 'If it will make you feel better, then apology accepted.'

*If only,* thought Daniel, *the two of us could start anew from here.* He relished, for a moment, the way the destruction had made the two of them unguarded, then he turned away from Finn and with a sigh took the letter from Betty off the table. 'Here. It was meant for you. Back on the day she left us. I hoarded it because … I loved your mother deeply. I know I had the wrong ways of showing it, I … I do not acknowledge your acceptance of my apology. Not until you have read this letter, when I suspect you shall be glad of the chance to retract it.'

Finn received the two sheets as if they were halves of a treasure map.

When he had finished reading he folded the letter but continued to stare at its ageing paper. Daniel steadied his ankles and locked his knees, as if bracing to be crashed into by a great wave. *At least,* he thought, *I deserve this.* He wrung his fingers, and waited.

Finn threw his arms around him and embraced him. He squeezed his shoulders tightly, while Daniel could do nothing but gawp.

'All my life,' said Finn, stepping away, 'you have seemed so invincible. When I was a child you were terrifying. I thought I might wake one night with your hands around my throat.'

Daniel looked down and screwed up his eyes. 'Is there anything I can do to make amends?'

'I think you have done it. And if there's anything I should know it's this: people can change, just like the clouds. I forgive you.'

'I do not deserve it.'

'If you didn't deserve it, I wouldn't need to forgive you.'

'I will be better to you, Finn, I swear. For the rest of my days.'

Finn looked away. ' I thought coming here would be difficult, but not because of this. It was because I've got something to tell you and now I don't know how, but... I'm leaving, Daniel. I'm leaving Thunderstown.'

Daniel stared at him blankly, expecting a punchline. When none came he swallowed and asked, 'Is that the truth?'

'Yes. Elsa and I, we're going away. Together. It feels like we're meant to.'

Daniel righted a chair he had thrown over in his earlier fury, and slumped into it with his hands between his knees. 'I had hoped for the chance to make amends to you.'

'Yes. I can see.'

'Where will you go?'

'Somewhere. Anywhere. Not having a destination is sort of the whole point.'

For a moment he pictured Finn wracked with lightning in some busy street of the bustling world, and he opened his mouth to forewarn him, but then stopped himself to let the fear go. To his delight he was able to do so. Unanchored, it drifted away from him.

'You must do as you see fit,' he said, 'although still there are practicalities. There are things you will need.'

Finn shrugged. 'We'll muddle through.'

'I had hoped to make up for lost time.'

Finn puffed out his cheeks. 'I never thought we would have a conversation like this.'

Daniel got up and paced over to his trunk, untouched amid the debris. 'As you know, I have never been a spendthrift.' He removed from the trunk a clasped wooden box. 'So I have saved up some money, as well as the sums that I inherited from my father and grandfather.'

He popped open the box and inside were squeezed wads of bank notes, tied together by string.

'Take these with you, and all practicality is dealt with.'

'Daniel, it's too much; you might need it.'

He held up a hand. 'On the contrary it is too little. Besides, I like the thought that my forefathers' savings will be turned to the purposes of romance. It will be a kind of revenge for me.'

Finn sighed and accepted the box. 'We'll come and see you before we leave.'

'I would be grateful for that. I will try to get the place in better shape before then. I have some mess to clear up, and a bonfire to make.'

Finn laughed, hesitated, then hugged Daniel again. Daniel could not remember ever having being clasped with such affection.

'Finn,' he said when they stepped apart, 'there's something caught on your ear.'

Finn reached up and retracted his hand with a scrap of mist looped round his fingers. More of it formed out of the side of his head, blowing in clumps as light as blossom.

'This keeps happening,' he said. 'I think it means I'm happy.'

Daniel pointed to himself. 'Because of what we just said?'

He nodded. Daniel's mouth opened and closed, but since it seemed their earlier words had been such marvellous things, he chose not to risk muddying them with any more.

'For now,' said Finn, 'I'd best be on my way. Elsa is telling Kenneth Olivier that we're leaving, and then we're going to meet each other in the square. We're going to take a goodbye tour of Thunderstown.'

Daniel walked out with him and stood in the road. He waved to him as he walked off towards town, and marvelled at the faint haze of happiness that glimmered in Finn's wake.

# 19

# THINGS SPIRAL

Elsa took a deep breath. 'I'm leaving Thunderstown.'

They were in Kenneth's front yard, where she had found him sitting in a polo shirt of many clashing colours, and rereading one of his well-thumbed almanacs. At her news he slumped back with a puff. 'Oh,' he said, and looked lost for words.

The day had reached an in-between hour, neither afternoon nor evening. The sun was still trying to shine, but so many pinched rows of cloud were moving from west to east that the sky looked like an upside-down sea, and the sun some great sunken orb glowing underwater.

Kenneth looked up for inspiration. 'Well,' he said eventually, 'can I ask why?'

'I met someone.'

Kenneth was too genial to let his disappointment hold back a smile, or to prevent that smile from turning to a chuckle. 'I might have known! A Thunderstown man?'

'Kind of. His name is Finn. Finn Munro.'

Kenneth frowned. 'Hmm, I can't put a face to that name.'

'That's because he, er, well …' She wanted to tell him the truth, and reckoned he had been good enough to her to deserve it. She cleared her throat. 'This is going to sound strange,' she began, and then told him everything in a hurry, every detail of all that had happened: the way she'd first caught Finn dissolving into cloud;

the sneaked visits to the bothy and the way he'd shown her air in his veins instead of blood; their trip into the cave and the paintings there; the reasons Dot had given for Finn's strange body; the way, now that he was happy, he became prone to a hazy lining. When she'd finished talking she was breathless, and waited for him to announce his disbelief.

'I have to confess, Elsa, I knew some of this already.' He looked embarrassed. 'When we made the cake it was obvious that it was for someone special. But also, well, little old nuns are such fiendish gossips. Dot said you might need my support, but I don't think you need much help from anyone except this Finn. It sounds like – if I may be so bold – you have begun to know your own heart. I think perhaps that that's what you came to Thunderstown hoping to do.' He stood up and held wide his arms. 'So,' he said, 'congratulations! I wish you all the very best.'

They hugged, then he stepped back with his hands still on her shoulders. 'And you will take Michael's car with you.'

'What? No, Kenneth. I couldn't.'

'Yes. How else will you get out of Thunderstown? Don't worry, it's not a selfless gift. I hope it will remind you to send me a postcard now and then.'

She grinned. 'Before long you'll be wishing you hadn't asked that. I'll send you heaps of them. And I'll call. I want to stay in touch. It might sound corny, but you really saved my neck when you let me stay here. I wouldn't have gotten anywhere without you.'

He bowed. 'You're too kind, Elsa. Will I get to meet this strange lucky cloud of yours, before the two of you depart?'

'Oh, of course. I'd like to see his face when he tries your chilli coal pot! Not even lightning burns like that stuff! But for now I'd better go and meet him. We're going to kiss goodbye to these old streets. I've become quite attached to them while I've been here.'

Kenneth remained on his feet to watch her walk away, and she wished somehow that she could take him with her, even though of course it was out of the question and he would never come. Before she turned down Welcan Row she looked back over her shoulder and saw him still standing there. He looked older than she had thought him, even with his shirt like a fruit salad.

She waved, then set off down the road towards Saint Erasmus, although she knew she could walk in any direction and be pulled there. She would miss these circling streets and decaying buildings when she left them, but she supposed that she and Finn were already being called elsewhere by another secret gravity.

Finn was waiting for her in the shade of the church. He looked smaller, down here in the town, and he kept shifting from foot to foot, as if the presence of so many bricks unsettled him.

'The walls can't bite you,' she said as she drew close.

'It's not that.'

Elsa embraced Finn, pressing her forehead against the underside of his jaw while he held her for a quiet moment. While they stood there, a haze again emerged from him, beginning as a white band like a cloud tiara, then spilling out across his skin until it was a patina of mist. Above them a wind moved, and whistled under the church's arches.

'I went to see Daniel,' he said, while she stroked her hand across his cheek, 'and he was … so nice to me.'

Elsa could barely even picture it. 'You sure he'd not been drinking?'

'No … he was in a strange mood. He'd smashed up his house, for one thing. But I genuinely think that he meant it – the kindness, I mean. Do you know, I think this is the first time in my life that he's said a kind word to me?'

'I can believe it.'

Finn looked thoughtful. The sun was too low now to turn his haze into a silver lining, but it flushed it nevertheless with the faintest rose hue, which found out the dimples and fluctuations in the cloud. Then Finn told her about the letter from his mother and the money Daniel had offered them, and while he talked a handful of leaves blew in a circle around their feet and then skittered onwards across the square.

'I reckon you deserve all that,' she said when he'd finished.

'It certainly wasn't what I went there expecting. It left me feeling so full of energy. I was here early, because I walked so fast from Daniel's house. When I stepped out of his door I felt like everything was new. If he could change so drastically, anything might be possible. It's hard to explain.'

'You don't need to,' Elsa said. 'You're growing into yourself. You're getting used to whatever, whoever, you are. You're getting used to being Finn.'

She stroked her hand across his forehead and fragments of cloud broke around her fingers. It suited him, this faint second skin of vapour. She was about to kiss him again when she realized they were being watched. A stern woman in a shawl stood midway across the square, then scuttled away when she realized she'd been spotted, breaking into a trot as soon as she reached the entrance to Feave Street.

'Shall we take our farewell tour?' suggested Elsa.

'Let's,' Finn said, and they joined hands.

When they were a little way down Feave Street, somebody behind them shouted her name. She looked over her shoulder and saw the woman who had been watching them, along with a small bunch of townsfolk whom she must have alerted. One of them called her name like a summons, and a shiver rippled through her.

'Ignore them,' she said, 'and just keep walking.'

This was a narrow street of three-storey terraces, each with an overhanging roof like a frown. Elsa had never much liked this road, whose paving dipped and bumped so that she couldn't tell what was supposed to be flat and what was supposed to be uneven. In the distance, the Devil's Diadem and the crinkled cloud cover did nothing to help, forming a hatched backdrop of lined rock and atmosphere.

Finn looked back. 'There's nine or ten people following us. Are they friends of yours?'

'I have no idea who they are. Finn, I have a bad feeling about this. Can we just skip our tour and go back to your bothy?'

'Elsa, I don't think we need to be frightened of them.'

The small crowd was still out of earshot, but she whispered nevertheless. 'You have a coat of cloud, Finn, all over your skin. *They're* the ones who will be frightened.'

'Well, if they say anything, perhaps I can persuade them that there's nothing to be scared of.'

Elsa sighed. She looked up at the rooftops, where the weathervanes were all pointing away towards Old Colp. 'I don't know, Finn. Call me crazy, but can we just get out of here?'

She heard her name called again.

'They want to speak to you.'

'I don't care what they want.'

'Okay,' he said, and they cut back on themselves down Auger Lane.

Before they reached the next junction a man stepped out in front of them, his hands tucked in his pockets. He wore the same rain cap and coat as most men of the town, but still she recognized him from his plump neck and intrigued eyes.

'Just thought I'd head you off here,' said Sidney Moses, 'to ask you a question or two.'

Elsa glanced across at Finn. He did not appear at all troubled, even though – she bit her lip – cloud still hung against his skin like dusty cobwebs.

'We've got places to be,' she said.

The small band of townsfolk caught up with them, one or two of them out of breath from the speed at which they'd followed.

She didn't like how grave they looked, nor how they all hung back from taking the final few paces towards Finn, glancing instead to Sidney for guidance.

'Haven't you all got something better to be doing?' she asked.

Sidney licked his lips but didn't answer at once. A pair of magpies took off from further down the street and flew overhead, arguing in rasps as they went.

'The thing is,' said Sidney carefully, 'that Sally Nairn just saw something.'

'That's him, Sidney,' said the stern-faced woman in the shawl.

'Sally said she saw a kind of fog around this boyfriend of yours. And lo and behold …' He gazed with a mixture of disgust and fascination at the delicate vapour that smudged the air around Finn.

Finn folded his arms. 'I have a name, you know, which you can address me by if you can be polite enough to ask for it.'

Sidney turned his attention to Finn. 'When Miss Beletti arrived in Thunderstown, it wasn't long before we all knew her face. Yet I don't recognize yours, lest it's from a story I once heard. When did you arrive?'

'I've always been here.'

Elsa winced. 'Finn, this guy just wants trouble …'

'It's okay, Elsa. They're just confused by what they're seeing.'

Sidney nodded. 'What are we seeing, exactly?'

'I have a storm inside of me.'

The crowd wrung their hands and whispered to each other. Sidney looked as if he had unearthed buried treasure. 'Do you admit to it, just like that?'

'I am not ashamed of it any more. And I'm sick of hiding up a mountain. I'm as safe to be around as any of you.'

Sidney puffed himself up. 'You are very brazen, to come down here and say such things, after all that you have done to us.'

'This is ridiculous,' said Elsa, rolling her eyes. 'He hasn't done anything.'

Sidney didn't take his gaze off Finn. 'We know who you are.'

She tugged at Finn's hand. 'Come on, Finn. Let's get going.'

'You are Old Man Thunder.'

She bristled. 'Don't be so stupid. You know nothing about Finn. How could you possibly suggest that?'

Sidney glared at her. 'Just because Kenneth Olivier says you're welcome in Thunderstown, it doesn't mean that you are. *He* isn't much welcome here either.'

One or two of the crowd looked doubtful at that, but they didn't protest. Elsa's stomach knotted when she saw how quickly their obedience overcame their doubts. She became acutely aware of how greatly they outnumbered her and Finn. Again she tugged at Finn's arm. He didn't budge.

'Daniel told me about you, Mr Moses,' he said. 'But I thought he'd made you out to be worse than you actually are.'

While they had been talking, the strands of cloud clinging to Finn's bald head had thickened. Now they were as opaque as ash. Sidney watched them with grim interest, and turned to the crowd. 'Look at him! Look at his skin. What do you see?' One of the townsfolk whimpered, '*Weather!*' and they all started burbling like frightened hens.

Elsa remembered the fear on these same faces on her first day in Thunderstown, when Daniel killed a wild dog. A cold anticipation locked the joints of her elbows and knees. 'Finn, please,' she said, wishing she could spirit them both away like a magician.

'Prove it,' said Sidney.

'Prove what?'

'Prove that you're real.'

'What do you mean? Of course I'm real.'

'You would say that. But we don't think you are. We think you're a storm, pretending to be a man.'

*Deny it,* Elsa thought, *even though there's cloud all over you.*

'I'm not pretending. I am a storm, and a man as well. But I'm not Old Man Thunder.'

Sidney gaped at the crowd with theatrical disbelief. 'Do my ears deceive me? First he looks like a storm masquerading as a man. Then we give him a chance to deny it, and instead he pleads guilty!'

The crowd had bunched up shoulder to shoulder. Abe Cosser's left leg was jittering, his old boot rapping off the stone road.

'Come on, Finn,' said Elsa, tugging at his arm.

He resisted. 'No, Elsa. We can make them understand. What proof do you want from me, Mr Moses?'

Sidney reached down to his belt and unclipped the knife that was attached there. He offered it, still sheathed, to Finn, saying, 'They say Old Man Thunder can't bleed.'

Finn didn't take the knife. 'I'm not going to cut myself open for you. Don't be ridiculous.'

But as he spoke a wind blew down the street and tried to steal away the cloud clinging to his skin, stretching it out for a moment like silver tresses, then scattering it across the air. In the crowd, a terrified Abe Cosser commenced the Lord's Prayer.

'Does it always have to be the case,' asked Finn, and there was a rumbling edge on his voice that didn't come from his vocal cords, 'that people find devils in the things they don't understand? Believe me, I've been frightened by myself too, but doesn't that make me all the more able to explain it to you? I used to think I was a kind of monster, but all it took was a little kindness to realize – ' he squeezed Elsa's hand in recognition ' – that I'm just like any of you.'

For a moment Elsa was proud enough of him to forget her anxiety, but when she turned triumphantly to Sidney he had spread out his arms to address the townsfolk and she could see where this was headed and it was as if her heart had dropped out of her.

'He admits to it!'

'He didn't admit to anything,' said Elsa, but her voice sounded reedy.

'He *admits*,' declared Sidney with steely composure, 'and that's all we need to know.'

The crowd looked like a satisfied jury.

'He didn't admit,' objected Elsa, 'because there's nothing to admit to.' She wished they had just kept on walking. Even if the crowd had besieged them in the bothy they could have at least locked them out. She remembered suddenly a fight on the sidewalk a few years back, some alcohol-fuelled altercation between a stranger, who had said something about her, and Peter, who had drunkenly tried to stand up to him. 'Let's go, Finn. All he wants is a fight.'

Finn was about to say something more, but she pulled his arm so hard that he got the message, nodded and turned away. Together they walked down the street, but no pace was fast enough for her. She felt like she was trapped in a flinch. All of her clothes felt too small.

'Don't look back,' she whispered.

They walked fast along Auger Lane then turned off into Candle Street, which led uphill towards Old Colp's reclusive slopes. A scruffy cat, who had been sleeping on a yard wall, fixed its yellow eyes on Finn and hissed. The crowd trailed them and she hoped like hell that, when the going got steep on the mountain slopes, they would lose interest. Above Old Colp the clouds appeared to be clearing. The sun flung late light through the gap, and all of Thunderstown's shadows lengthened.

Suddenly Finn lurched forwards and clutched the back of his head. Elsa heard something rattle off the flagstones. It was a nugget of slate. Finn crouched, blinking hard with pain, one hand held to his crown. She could hear the air hissing out where the slate had cut him. At first she couldn't move because a panic filled her up as if with needles. Then she exclaimed 'Finn!' and grabbed hold of him. 'Are you okay?'

He nodded groggily. Wild-eyed, she spun around to confront the townsfolk, but Sidney Moses looked as surprised as her. Somebody else had thrown it.

Finn had still not stood upright, and now there was a deeper noise behind the hiss from his cut, a noise like a distant train passing. Layers of dark, heavy gas opened out of the cut like the petals of a flower. The cat who had hissed at them sprang down from its wall and fled as fast as its four legs could carry it.

Elsa railed at the townspeople. 'You should be ashamed of yourselves!'

They all ignored her, enraptured by the dusky cloud growing out of Finn's gashed scalp. It grew fat and puffy, a gaseous tumour expanding by the second.

Elsa crouched beside him, supporting his shoulder and whispering his name. He was staring, dazed, at the floor, with his face beaded by drops of clear water. Every now and then one of them welled big enough to fall and splash against the road. The cloud kept swelling, now the size of his head, now twice the size. Then it skewed and distended, and broke open across his back so that he was crouched under a fleecy heap. Elsa tried to think of what to do, but her heartbeat was a din in her ears. All she could think was to squeeze his arm and whisper his name. Beneath the cloud his shirt had become damp.

The townsfolk edged closer, until she snapped at them, 'Get away from him!' and all bar Sidney Moses took a step back.

'Elsa ...' whispered Finn, and when he spoke a patter of rainwater dribbled over his lips. She whimpered to see it, and clung to him tighter.

'Finn? How badly are you hurt? Do you think you can stand? Here, I'll help you.' She steadied herself to support his big frame and helped him, although she was a very shaky prop, back to his feet. The cloud spilled to either side as he stood, so that he was framed in an oval of fog. It kept coming from him, pouring out grey filaments so that he looked like a smouldering effigy.

'Who ...' he began, and more water dribbled over his chin and fell in a sheet to the road, 'threw ...' He swooned for a second and she had to throw her whole weight against him to help him regain his balance. At the same time the cloud mushroomed and a shadowy cap rose out of its highest point. A raindrop formed and plinked off the flagstones. Her own clothes were becoming speckled by them. Her breathing had become sharp, each inhalation like a slap to her lungs.

'Who did this?' Elsa hissed at the crowd. 'Show yourself.'

Heads turned to quiz one another, and then the crowd parted and left little Abe Cosser isolated, clutching another pebble of slate in his shaking fist.

'You ...' said Finn, then spat out water again, 'don't need to be frightened. The weather is just like you.'

Abe looked from Finn to Elsa to Sidney to his peers, but all seemed to have cut him loose. He looked down at the slate in his hand. 'Lord have mercy,' he muttered, and threw the stone at Finn.

Elsa shrieked when it struck Finn in the jaw and his head snapped sideways with a gargle. She had to catch him again, grabbing hold of him and leaning into him to help him steady his balance. She wished she was bigger and stronger: she had never felt so slight in all her life. He pawed at the cut the stone had made, which immediately began to fizz with gas. His jawline became bandaged with it, a second outpouring that pushed the cloud to new heights. In no time at all its dense cap had bulged some ten feet into the air, while to the left and right it unfurled like a wingspan. A chill trickle condensed on the back of her neck and raced down beneath her collar.

'Finn,' she gasped, holding him up, 'do you think you can walk? Do you think we can get out of here? I'll help you, Finn.'

She threw one of his arms over her shoulders, but she did not have the strength to pull him along with her. She looked back through the cloud that was now swirling tightly around them, and saw Abe Cosser still stranded from his fellows, trembling and clutching one more stone.

'Please, Mr Cosser,' she cried, 'please stop this!'

Abe looked at her with rabbit-in-the-headlights eyes but, before he could respond, Sidney Moses stepped up beside him and put a hand on his shoulder. 'You're a good man, Abe. Whereas this is not even a man at all.'

'Please,' Elsa implored them, '*please* leave us alone! We're going away! We're going anyway! You don't need to do this!'

Sidney shrugged. 'This does not concern you, nor your plans. This is saving our town from the weather. Best to step away from it now, Miss Beletti. It's a cloud that has duped you into thinking it's a man, but as you can see its disguise is easily removed.'

'He's *both*!' Elsa tried to get Finn to take a groggy step towards Old Colp. She did her best to guide him, but with each plod she feared they'd both tip over.

'Step away from him, Miss Beletti.'

She ignored him. It was going to be difficult to get Finn up the mountain in this state, but once they reached the bothy she would look after him and not leave his side until he had recovered. Now the cloud had become too large to see its extremities: it had filled the street from eave to eave and shut out the sky. She squeezed Finn's hand, and much to her relief, he said, 'Thank you, Elsa,' amid a patter of drooled water.

Abe Cosser threw the stone.

It scuffed off the top of Finn's head and clattered away somewhere against the wall. Finn went down, pawing at his scalp, and an instant spout of soot-black cloud gushed up into the greyer stuff that fogged the road. Elsa shrieked and knelt beside him, but the cloud wrapped them up too opaquely for her to even see her outstretched hands. People were shouting and someone grabbed her beneath the shoulders and she was dragged across the rough paving screeching and thrashing. She kicked someone but it made no difference. She could see nothing in the fog, save for gloomy outlines closing in on Finn.

But he lit up.

For a split second, lines of white fire branched through his body. It was as if his entire nervous system had turned to light. She heard Sidney screech and smelled burned meat. Then the light fizzed away into the stone and the flagstones reeked of coal and the townspeople erupted into shrieks and yells. Elsa was dropped roughly on to the floor, and she heard people fleeing in every direction, and somebody mewling like a baby while they hoisted him away.

When she stood, she was too frightened to straighten her spine. Nor could she close her mouth, since her lips were seized back in a grimace.

She staggered through the fog with her arms out in front of her, and nearly tripped over Finn when she found him lying on the road. He was on his back with his arms and legs outstretched. His eyes were open but unblinking.

'Finn!'

She grabbed his hand and clenched it between hers. His fingers felt more brittle and thinner than she remembered them being.

'What did they do to you, Finn?'

Still the cloud thickened, and now it steamed so dense that even when she bent her face down to touch his it made a veil between them. She held on tightly to his hand, but it felt light now like something he had made from paper. Through such fog it was impossible to tell how badly they had hurt him in those last moments, so all she could do was throw her other arm across him and cling to his torso. 'Hold on,' she whispered, not knowing what else to say. 'Please hold on.'

Yet the issuing cloud did not hold on. It became a blindfold. She clung to him as he became fragile and frail. His chest seemed to shrink and harden. She pushed her lips against his, hoping that to kiss him might save him, but his head felt skeletal in the murk and his lips were like the wrinkled skin of a deflating balloon. She kissed them regardless, and they were limp and rubbery between hers. She heard something barking above her, and something howling in the sky. His soaked shirt sagged over his accentuating ribs. His fingers, when she groped for them in the fog, were as thin and cold as icicles. Then for a moment she thought she felt warmth return to them and she yelped with joy, but it was just her own fingers, for his had melted away . She clawed around to try to find them again, but they had vanished and her fingernails scraped on the stone of the street. His ribcage sank and was flat. Panic filled her. She chased her lips after his, but they only kissed wet stone where his head should have been, and she was lying face down in the thickest fog of her life, with only Finn's soaked and emptied clothes between her and the cracked surface of the road.

She lay on the floor, convulsing with sobs. The cloud fumed around her until, eventually, it began to rise into the air. The rain knocked on her back, but she did not move. It pulsed across the road and rang off the walls. After a while she found the strength to roll over and feel the water scattering her face and making her clothes weigh heavy.

The cloud had lifted off the ground and formed a charcoal ceiling for the street. Because she did not know what else she could do, she groped around her until she had bundled up Finn's empty shirt, drenched jeans, underwear and the new shoes she had bought him for his impromptu birthday.

She lay there until his cloud heaved itself off the rooftops and took to the air, rising with unstoppable buoyancy. As it lifted, the sun slipped in beneath it and she remembered that it still had not set. For a minute the light turned the rain shafts to harp strings, then was put out again by the expanding cloud.

It kept ascending until it shuddered with a light of its own and gave a shout of thunder so human that she sat up and cried out to him. He did not reply, but the rain redoubled and hissed as it hit the stone.

A second sheet of lightning floodlit the street and for a moment made every drenched surface shine white. Elsa found herself praying to whatever remnant of her mother's God she still believed in, asking to have this all turned around, but still the rain fell in harder blows until an opening salvo of hail rattled off the masonry and nipped at her skin. She let it sting her. She had no desire to take shelter. If she wanted to go anywhere it was up, to follow Finn into the air.

The street was deserted now. Elsa pictured the townsfolk locking themselves indoors, terrified of what they had unleashed. She hated them and hoped Finn's storm would break down their doors and smash their lives apart.

The cloud kept growing. It was a slow black vortex coiling around itself. It swelled up like a lung inhaling. A line of lightning throbbed across it like a brilliant white artery and she could feel the electricity accumulating in the earth in response, attracted from the deep places by the magnetism of the storm.

Her eyes widened. She stood up and covered her mouth with her hands. She'd had an idea, so dangerous it might just work.

She set off at a run, racing down Candle Street with rain and hail exploding around her and lightning testing its range across the blackened sky. When she swerved into Auger Lane, a forked bolt jagged into life and whipped down to blast apart a chimney. She skidded to a halt in time to dodge the avalanche of broken bricks, then skipped over them and pelted onwards until she reached Saint Erasmus Square. There the storm cloud floated like an ark above the town. Around it the last of the evening light ducked away, and then there was only the cumulonimbus.

The entire plaza fizzled with jumping raindrops. The gutters gurgled as they tried to drain the deepening water. Behind the rain the church was a defeated giant, its dark dominance laid low by the storm. With an ear-splitting crash, lightning slammed into the church's belfry. The strike rang a warped echo out of each and every windowpane in the square. Then, in its aftermath, all seemed to fall silent and a residual tremor tingled underfoot. Elsa swallowed. That was where she was going, up there where the church bell resonated with a brassy hum.

She splashed across the square and up the church steps, heaved open the door, bundled through it and shoved it closed behind her.

Being in the church was like being inside a drum. The storm's noises boomed between the pillars and made her ears pop. The panicked pigeons in the rafters threw themselves about, flying into each other or the stone walls. One lay dead where it had collided with the pulpit. With her hands over her ears, and leaving a trail of wet footprints along the aisle, she made her way to the door that accessed the belfry. It opened on to a spiral staircase leading upwards into darkness. Up she went, her soaked sneakers slapping against the steps, round and round until the dim light from below could reach her no longer and everywhere was pitch black. The weather howling against the stone compelled her on, until she was dizzied and felt as if she were ascending a tornado.

Just when she thought her legs would take her no further she realized she could see the stairs. Light had stirred into the darkness. She could see moisture shining off the stone walls, and then – so alien after the countless steps that she had to press her body against the rough surface to be sure of it – a door.

The moment she lifted the latch, the wind flung it open for her. She staggered out on to the balcony and was nearly bowled over by it. It screamed as it flew around her, and Finn's storm heaved with thunder in reply. The sky was as black and unstable as a lake of boiling tar.

Pressing herself against the wall for support, she edged her way along a narrow balcony. Beside her in the belfry the great Thunderstown bell vibrated with a bass tone. She looked down and saw the streets and houses made miniature, the weathervanes twitching and spinning like whirligigs, and the plaza bulging with water. She looked up and saw only roiling darkness.

'Finn,' she whispered. Raising her voice would be pointless, even if she had the breath left after her rushed climb. 'Finn, can you hear me?' She felt her way further along the wall until she found what she had come up here for: the lightning conductor. She gripped it as tight as her freezing hands would allow.

'Lightning doesn't *strike*,' her dad had told her for the umpteenth time, on the last day she had seen him alive. She had looked down at her fingers in her lap and felt empty that their relationship had descended into this single repeated conversation. 'The earth and the storm make a connection, Elsa, and the lightning is that connection on fire.'

She felt the earth's deep electricity filling up the church below her, just as the floodwater filled the streets. It flushed up from ancient rocks and secret subterranean caverns, from the gyro of the great globe itself, up into the foundations and the vaults, rising through the stone walls, surging up the church's pillars, playing over buttresses and arches, adding its whine to the bell's hum. It filled every cell of her body. Billions of particles of the earth's electricity channelled into her, a mountain of energy of which she was the peak. Her jaw fell heavily open. Her mouth tasted full of lead.

'Finn,' she managed to croak. She couldn't move. She could sense the energy rising out from the top of her head, lifting her hair with it, reaching up for the storm. She closed her eyes and imagined Finn's face was only an inch away from hers.

A pillar of white. Everything in freeze-frame. Raindrops suspended like perfect pearls. And everything getting whiter and whiter until it was all so searing and bright that it was as if her eyes had been replaced with stars. She heard a scream from somewhere. She guessed it was her own.

The lightning didn't strike. It set their connection on fire.

# 20

# AS DREAMS ARE MADE ON

Elsa came to. She thought she had opened her eyes because she could see lights twinkling in their hundreds. After a moment she realized she wasn't blinking. The lights were inside her head and her eyelids were closed.

Somebody said something. Her body felt like a bottle bobbing on an ocean. She drifted back into unconsciousness.

She came to again, slower this time. She was lying on a firm but comfortable mattress. There were no lights, only the blotched darkness of her closed eyelids. With great effort, she opened them. Looking at anything felt like staring into the sun, so she quickly shut them again.

Somebody spoke, but the words were just fuzz in her ears. She tried once more to open her eyes and found the bright world a fraction more bearable. She could make out surfaces, although they all seemed aglow. A shape loomed over her. 'Try to focus, Elsa.'

Slowly the shape took on colours, hundreds of them dancing a scintillating jig. Her eyes rolled out of concert with each other.

'Elsa, it's okay.'

She took a deep breath. The colours kaleidoscoped across her vision. She choked her need to cry out. At last the colours settled into rows of diamonds, each a different shade and each sickeningly vivid. Together they made a pattern.

One of Kenneth Olivier's jumpers.

She shielded her eyes.

'Elsa!' Kenneth cried out with relief. 'Thank God! How are you feeling?'

She nodded and looked away, at anything but his clothing. This strange bare room she was lying in had grey stone walls, a grey stone floor and a grey stone ceiling, although her blurry vision added green hues to everything she saw, as if the room were lit by gaslight.

'Where am I?' Her words tasted bitter.

'Drink some water.'

She sipped from the glass he offered her, unable to look at him. The water felt like molten metal in her throat.

'You're in the nunnery of Saint Catherine. It's where we take all people who are struck by lightning.'

Of course, she remembered it now. She had been on the belfry with the wind tearing at her clothes and the rain crackling in her ears. She had looked up at the pitch black underside of the storm and whispered Finn's name.

The lightning strike had lasted under a second, but she had experienced it as if in slow motion. It started with the air constricting, pressing bluntly at her jugular and the pulses in her wrists. Then her hair had lifted as if she were underwater. She had stood very straight, her spine like a taut rope, and felt the connection her dad had described so many times. A line of electrified air that had joined her to Finn's storm. She'd stared upwards, awaiting the bolt, but it had not come down from the cloud. It had begun in *her*, her vision blazing with more light than it felt possible for her eyeballs to contain. Then white fire had ascended in time with her whisper. 'Finn.'

For a moment she'd felt so interconnected with him that it was as if they were inside each other's minds. Her thoughts had boiled with things he remembered and things he felt, carried on the lightning to the root of her imagination, so that they became as lucid as scenes of her own life flashing before her eyes. Betty turning out the light after kissing him goodnight; a canary materializing out of sunlight on to his cupped palms; a mouse creeping over the doorstep of the bothy; a broken vase; a winter's day when icicles hung as long as swords; Daniel demonstrating how to fold paper birds; Betty laying out cakes and sandwiches for a picnic; starting a campfire by rubbing two logs together and feeling immeasurably pleased at the first fizzling spark; the shockwave of lightning that had flicked Betty away from him; the self-hatred that followed; and at last *her*, on the day when he first saw her outside the ruined windmill.

Then, like a fire stamped out, all of it had been over and gone and she had tipped backwards into darkness.

Kenneth tried to stop her from sitting up. He needn't have worried because a pain in her ribcage nailed her back to the mattress. She grunted as she hit the pillow.

'Elsa, please go slowly. You need rest.'

'Kenneth …' She tried to wet her dry lips, but her tongue was like a pebble. 'He's up there! I saw him … in the lightning!'

She tried to sit up again, but hot tears of pain rolled from her eyes. She wheezed and screwed up the bed sheet in her fists. 'What's wrong with me?'

'Nothing a good rest won't heal, but all of your muscles seized up when the lightning struck. It will be a while before you can get out of bed.'

She shook her head. 'That's no good. I have to get back to him.' Again she tried to sit up and again her muscles mutinied. She flopped back in stiff pain.

'You can't go anywhere,' lulled Kenneth. 'You simply need to rest.'

She began to sob, and her strained muscles doubled her hurt. She had connected with Finn, but she did not know what it meant to have done so. Even if, as it had seemed in the lightning strike, he was up there somehow, disembodied in the chaos of the storm, how could she reach him if she were stuck in this bed?

Although the cell walls were built from thick stone, she thought she could hear a hushed rumble beyond. 'Is he still there, Kenneth?' she sniffed. 'Please look out of the window for me.'

The cell had a window that overlooked Thunderstown. With some reservation, Kenneth got up and peered out of it. After a moment he came back to her bedside. 'It's a strange thing. Up here the night is so calm, but down there the storm is still raging, yes.'

She gasped with relief. She grabbed Kenneth's hand and squeezed it fearfully. 'How long do you think he can last for?'

'Elsa, what do you mean?'

'How much longer do you think he can rain for?'

'I … I don't know what to say, Elsa. I think you should save your energy. It's a terrible thing to lose a person. Preserve your strength.'

An appeal of thunder penetrated the cell. She could feel it in the springs of the mattress beneath her.

'Don't say I've lost him. How could you say I've lost him when you've seen for yourself he's still up in the sky?'

He sighed. 'I don't know, Elsa. I just don't know.'

When once again she tried to sit up she could barely even budge an inch. The bed felt like a coffin and she grunted in frustration.

'Elsa, Elsa,' soothed Kenneth. 'Rest. Things are going to be tough for you. You need to look after yourself. You can't leave this bed until tomorrow.'

Stuck like this, any hope that she'd woken with deserted her. Back came the powerlessness that she'd felt in Candle Street, and a red-hot hatred for Sidney Moses and Abe Cosser, and a sense that love – in which she had banked her trust – had betrayed her.

Her dad, too, had let her down. His old story about the lightning's path to connection – she had been sure that would be her rescue. But what good did it do to connect with Finn for only a fraction of a second? All it did was demonstrate how helpless she was.

'Elsa,' Kenneth mopped her mouth with a handkerchief, 'you are very unwell. Perhaps you should go back to sleep.'

'How can I sleep when he's right there? When the next time I wake he might have rained himself away?'

'Just know that you are among friends and we will do all we can. Dot will be back soon. And Daniel, I expect.'

'Daniel?'

'Yes. He was here for a while after he brought you in. He waited by your bedside and fussed about you and argued with the nuns over what was best for you. Then, when you almost came to earlier, he panicked. He said he'd be the last person you'd want to see, and headed off to hide in the chapel. As for me, I'm just glad he found you. If he hadn't thought to check the church was secured against the storm … I dread to think what would have happened.'

Eventually Elsa managed to drink some more water, but that used up all her energy. After that Kenneth wished her well and said he should go and fetch Dot, who would want to check in on her now she was awake. He hesitated, then kissed her, father-like, on the forehead. He nodded after doing this, embarrassed but satisfied, and shuffled out of the room.

She exhaled, taking in the stony shade of her surroundings. Her eyes were still hypersensitive from the lightning, making her bed seem to stretch forever, a nightmare of perspective headed for her distant feet. A moth flew in silence around the ceiling, and she wished she could share in its fluttering freedom. There was a chair and a low bedside table, but there was not so much as a vase of flowers or a Bible occupying it. The room was as bereft of distractions as she was of ways to get to Finn.

The door opened and somebody cleared their throat to request entry.

'Come in.'

Not Dot but Daniel, who stopped just inside the doorway and bobbed there in an agitated manner that she wasn't used to seeing in him. 'Elsa, it is good to see you awake. Um … I'll go away again if you would prefer.'

'No, it's okay.' Anything to take her mind off itself. 'I'm just surprised to see you. Kenneth said you were holed up in the chapel.'

He looked unkempt, as if he had slept there, but he sat down urgently at her side and bent his bearded head close to hers. 'Elsa, I … I have come to apologize. I have been a fool beyond reckoning. I never should have tried to get in the way of you and Finn. I hope there is something, someday, that I can do to make it up to you.'

She sighed. His interferences seemed like years ago now. 'Unless you can turn clouds back into men, I doubt there's anything you can do.'

He ran his hands back through his hair. 'I will see to Sidney Moses.'

She grimaced. 'I don't want to know. I can't bear to think about him.'

He nodded, and bunched his fists together between his knees. After he had heard what the townsfolk had done, he had been full of the need for justice. He had considered taking his rifle to the Moses residence, but he had been needed elsewhere. He knew, from bitter experience, what unfulfilled love could do to a life, and he longed somehow to save Elsa from the agony of it.

'Is it true,' she asked, 'that you apologized to Finn?'

'Yes. Although now my promise is as good as broken. I would have made it mean something with deeds, but I never got the chance.'

'Do you ... do you think he's gone, then? Kenneth was talking as if he had.'

'I don't know. There is a storm above Thunderstown, so in a sense he is still there. Elsa ... what possessed you to go up to the belfry?'

She told him about her dad's lightning mantra, and how on its advice she had climbed the church tower. Daniel listened gloomily, and after she had finished he could see no more hope than her.

He chewed his lip. 'Elsa, you know I have never been good at letting things go. Heaven knows I have spent my whole life clinging on to things that I should have left behind me. Only lately have I learned that sometimes you have to let the past leave you. You cannot return to it, and if you cling to it life marches on without you.'

She covered her eyes. 'It's just that ... when the lightning struck me, I saw him there. I can't give up on him after that. But I don't know what I can do now.'

'You misunderstand me. I meant to say that I will not let go of him, even if every last raindrop falls out of the sky. Even if every last trace of him evaporates and the sun shines through. They will say I am mad, no doubt, and that this particular madness of mine has held me back my whole life. But that will only make me well practised.'

'Thank you. That means something to me.' Elsa stared up at the ceiling. She took a deep breath and it made a dry rasping noise like the call of a crow. Daniel steepled his big blunt fingers and pressed them to his forehead, tapping them against his brow while he thought. Far past the nunnery walls, the thunder moaned once more, but now the noise just made her hurt. There would have been a time when she would have enjoyed the hard light enforced on the world by the death of a thundercloud, when the sun knocked down the storm wall and bored a rainbow through air it had turned violet. Now she dreaded that spectacle more than anything else.

'What do you think will happen to him,' she whispered, 'after the last of the rain falls?'

He frowned. 'I hope it will not come to that.'

'But if it does?' She found she could not imagine, even though she wished she could, any alternative. She would lie here prone in a nun's cell while the man she had fallen in love with poured himself apart in the sky.

'There is some medicine if you wish for it,' he said, picking up a packet of pills left by the nuns. She took two of them with a grunt, but had to keep swallowing to drag them down her aching throat.

The moth that had been looping on the ceiling settled. It spread its wings and stilled. She followed its example, finally letting the pillow support her heavy head, finally closing her eyes and surrendering to the fact that all she could do was listen. She awaited each distant murmur of Finn's storm, each faint hiss of the lightning. How tired she was. Or perhaps that was because of the pills. She fought sleep because she needed to be awake to rescue Finn, although she did not know how she was going to do it. She closed her eyes. She thought she could hear an ocean. She thought she was flying high above a whirlpool. She had drifted off to sleep.

Daniel ran his hands through his hair and stood up. He moved to the cell's window and stared at the world without. Up on the Devil's Diadem the sky was bare and the land calm. Finn's cloud over Thunderstown was the only one in the sky, but it was grey and massive like a fifth mountain. The sun had already set beyond Old Colp, but a red sheen still coloured the western sky and bloodied the upper reaches of the storm.

When his father died, his grandfather had expressed no remorse, no softening of the enmity he had felt for his son. But when his grandfather's favourite hunting dog had died that same year, then his grandfather had wept into his glass of beer. That night he'd burst into Daniel's bedroom long past midnight, turned on the light and crashed down reeking of alcohol on to the bed beside his grandson. 'It feels as if, wherever he has gone, he has taken every other one of my ribs with him,' he'd said before passing out. At about three or four in the morning, having not slept a wink, Daniel could no longer resist the temptation to feel in the dark for his grandfather's ancient ribcage, to run his forefinger over the bones. All the ribs could be accounted for, and Daniel had stayed confused and wide awake until the sun took the night away.

He left the cell window and paced to the door, then back to the window, then so on back and forth over the stone floor. Now at last he understood what the old man had meant. If that sensation had been inflicted on his grandfather by the death of something as simple as a damned mutt, how much greater was Daniel's own hurt at the loss of Finn, this sudden feeling of multiple cavities in his torso, and the accompanying feeling that his legs and arms and even his skull had been cleaved in two, and the greater halves stolen away from him?

He became aware of the sound of his own breathing. Worrying that he might disturb Elsa's sleep, he slipped out of the door and walked the cold corridors of the nunnery.

He was as familiar with this place as he was with the vaults and aisles of the Church of Saint Erasmus. When he was a child his father used to bring him up here, even though he was more often than not a strain on his father's priestly duties. While the Reverend Fossiter conducted longwinded meetings with the abbess, Daniel had sulked in the courtyard or played hide-and-seek with himself in the cloister. On other occasions he had run madly through the laps of the corridors, or along the route of the chapel's prayer labyrinth, which was a pattern of concentrically circling red tiles embedded before the altar. Once, his father had caught him whirling along that path and right away forced him to lean over a pew while he struck him with the back of his hand. Then he made him walk in contemplation along the red line of the tiles, until he reached the centre and promptly burst into tears.

The nunnery's cloister, when Daniel emerged into it, was deserted. Overhead the first stars were peeking through. There was no wind: that was all down in Thunderstown, playing in Finn's storm.

He crossed to the chapel, which was just as empty. Inside, the only movement came from a flickering bay of prayer candles burning in an alcove. With no light in the sky to shine through them, the designs on the stained-glass windows were hard to make out, but he had been here enough times to have memorized their depictions. They showed fearful saints on their knees, praying to their god in the clouds for miracles and signs.

He slumped down on the back pew, throat dry, head sore with sorrow. He pushed aside the Bible and the prayer book on the shelf in front of him. He kicked away the cushion used for kneeling.

'I would have become something gentler,' he whispered through clenched teeth. 'I would have been like a father to Finn.'

He wiped his eyes and tried to focus. 'What might be done?' he muttered. What might be done? His thinkings drew back with no solutions.

The chapel door squeezed open.

Kenneth Olivier slipped inside, letting the evening air of the cloister into the waxy murk of the chapel. He closed the door softly, then stood in the aisle with his hands in his pockets, alongside Daniel's pew but not facing it, looking instead at the tidy altar and its cream-coloured cloth, embroidered with a cross.

'I don't know about you,' he said after a while, 'but I'm terrified for her.'

Daniel's eyes swivelled up to look at Kenneth. The two of them had shared the space of the Church of Saint Erasmus on more occasions than Daniel cared to remember, but aside from Sunday pleasantries they rarely talked. Their last meaningful exchange had been on that awful day when Kenneth's son went missing in the mountains.

'Are you aware,' asked Daniel gruffly, 'that this is entirely my fault?'

Kenneth shrugged. 'You say that, but I think it's mine. All of it.'

Daniel frowned. 'No. How could you possibly think that?'

'How could *you*?'

Daniel opened his mouth to respond, but Kenneth stopped him with a raised finger. He opened a bag he had with him and displayed, as tenderly as if they were eggs in a nest, two cans of beer.

'You and I have not really talked for a long while,' he said.

Daniel motioned to the altar, to the prayer labyrinth painted on the tiles before it, to the statue of Saint Catherine raising her face to the heavens, to Christ nailed to the cross on the far wall.

'Not here, of course,' said Kenneth, and took hold of the door handle. 'But will you join me?'

With a laboured puff, Daniel put his hands on his knees, stuck out his elbows and eased himself to his feet. 'After you,' he said, and the two of them left the chapel.

Kenneth led the way through the short antechamber that exited the nunnery. Beyond the main door the slopes of the Devil's Diadem skidded all the way down to Thunderstown, whose rooftops were nigh on invisible beneath the darkness of the rain. From this distance Finn's cloud looked like some jellyfish of the ocean, its downpour like graceful tentacles stroking the buildings beneath. The last of the coloured sunset had faded, and a ring of stars encircled the storm.

The rocks and sparse slopes of the mountains were all deathly still, and when a shudder of lightning branched across the cloud they lit up and looked as fragile and white as porcelain. The thunder sounded moments later, a rush of sound that could be felt as well as heard.

The two men rested their backs against the nunnery wall while

Kenneth cracked the ring pulls of the beers and handed one to Daniel. He proceeded to drink his while Daniel stared through the opening of the can into the dark liquid within.

'It's my fault,' said Kenneth after a sip, 'because I should have done more to warn her. I had so many chances to tell her about the ways of this town, but I never did. I thought she might laugh at me, I suppose, and I let that stop me. I let her come to this town with only me for a guide, and yet I never warned her of its true character.'

Daniel raised his eyebrows and drank deeply from the beer. 'It's not your fault. I am responsible for this. I should have stopped Sidney Moses.'

'You couldn't have done. You weren't there.'

'Precisely.'

Kenneth sighed. 'We could argue about it forever.'

There was a short silence.

'It's been a while now,' he said, 'since Michael went away.'

'Yes.'

'Did I ever tell you how grateful I was to you for everything you did?'

'Yes,' said Daniel. 'You gave me a bottle.'

He remembered the rum Kenneth had presented to him, sweet and stinging at once, like eating honeycomb along with the bees that had made it. He had shared it with Betty and they had underestimated its potency and dozed off flopped against each other.

Yet he also remembered the reason for the gift, the diving and diving into and into the tarn in which Michael was last seen. Scouring the gloom of the water for any trace of him and finding nothing. Diving again and again until long after every other rescuer had abandoned the cause, surfacing and submerging until he lost track of what was water and what was air. Only when, because of his confusion, he inhaled liquid did he stop, and only then because his body failed him. His lungs had spasmed and forced him to lie down in defeat on the banks.

'I wish,' said Kenneth, 'I could have drowned instead.' He paused to control his emotions. 'Today I realized I've come to thinking, completely without meaning to, of Elsa a little like I thought of Michael. Having her around, hearing her footsteps going up and down the stairs, catching a noise of her singing in the shower, her coming and going all hours. Just having a younger soul around the house.'

Daniel nodded.

'Now, seeing her lying in that bed, so unwell ...' He shivered. 'It's terrible.'

'She will be all right. She's healthy enough to pull through.'

'Yes, of course, when you put it like that. But that's the other thing, isn't it? She's lost someone. That doesn't heal like the body does. Now she will be like you and I. Heartbroken.'

Silence.

Kenneth, stood up, shaking his empty can. 'I had better get back inside and check on her.'

Daniel nodded and watched him go. He finished his beer, then dropped his can to the ground and screwed it medallion-flat with his boot. Maybe it was the alcohol, of which he drank so little these days, or maybe it was something Kenneth had said. Either way, he could feel some deep part of his brain carrying on with the thinkings to which his forethoughts were not privy. When he tried to focus on them they eluded him, but he sensed them all the same, as if they were the preparatory movements behind a stage curtain, before it lifts for a play. He waited impatiently for that performance to begin, then when it did not he trudged back to the chapel.

Inside, he let the door swing shut behind him with a judder, while he stood in the aisle with his rain cap rolled up tightly in his fist. While he had been talking with Kenneth, many of the prayer candles on their frail metal table had burned out. He approached them and counted fifteen exhausted rings of tallow: fifteen secret woes that had called for their burning. He dropped some coins in the collection box and replaced each candle, mesmerized by the tiny flames that duplicated on to each wick they touched. When all were alight he turned from the bay and walked into the sanctuary, not to pray at the altar but to stand on the prayer labyrinth that was marked out like a mosaic on the floor.

In his memory it was an expansive crimson spiral, but here in his present it was a faint pattern like the age rings of a tree stump. It took only a few of his big paces to circle into its centre. There he remained for a while with his eyes closed, hoping for a revelation. He wished he had a mind like his father's, which could work through any disaster with ice-cold rationality.

Only when more of the candles began to wink out did he move again. He might have been standing there for hours, but his mind had made no progress. All he could think was that he had lost Finn and that he did not know what could be done about it. He hung his head and plodded towards the chapel door, pausing with his fingers on the handle and hoping that some final inspiration would strike. Then he exited into the cloister, where the distant hum of Finn's storm was at odds with the balmy night and the glinting constellations. Starlight found the metal and enamel in the countless charms hanging from the walls.

He pulled his handkerchief – his great-grandfather's and embroidered D.F. – from his pocket and blew his nose. He had meant what he'd said to Kenneth. All of this was his fault, or at least the fault of his family, for whom he was responsible. If they had been different men they might have guided the town to peace with the weather. What might have happened if they had followed the example of his mother? She had not plied the teeth from the corpses of wild dogs to string up with paired coins and tatty feathers in the hope of driving them away. No, she had petted them and stroked them and they had growled pleasurably in her company.

He reached into his pocket for the photograph he had found of her. He admired it. Her hair was black like a dream, her dress a frost's silver. Then abruptly he remembered how his breath had crystallized in the air when he found this picture. He tucked it back into his pocket, screwing up his eyes and drumming his fists against his temples in the hope of shaking out a way to save Finn. None came, so he returned via the shadowy corridors to the cell in which Elsa slept.

Elsa found his presence reassuring when she woke next. At first he did not say anything to her, did not even nod. She preferred it that he didn't. They kept each other company, saying little. Theirs was a shared seriousness that did not require any mask of small talk and gesture. Every so often Daniel asked her something about Finn he said he hadn't understood, then would listen rapt to her answer, then fall back into frowning, contemplative silence.

'Did Finn ever tell you,' he asked eventually, 'about my mother?'

'I don't believe he did.'

'Maryam. I have a photograph of her.'

She took it when he offered it. Maryam's eyes and brow were just like Daniel's, serious and severe. But there was also something lighter than Daniel in her looks. Or perhaps that was just an impression made by the wind blowing through her dress.

Elsa held it back out to him. He did not take it.

'I would appreciate it if you kept this likeness of her.'

'Daniel, I can't …'

'I insist.'

She sighed. She could not find the strength to argue. 'I'll only accept it if you do something for me.'

'What's that?'

'Take me to the window. I want to see the storm. In case it's my last chance. I don't want him to rain away without having seen him one last time.'

He was hesitant. 'You're not supposed to leave the bed.'

'If you say no, you're having this photo back.'

He reached his arms under her shoulders and lifted her as gently as he could, but gravity tore at her muscles and she screeched through gritted teeth. At the window he propped her down on her feet and she leaned against him, one of his arms supporting her shoulders and the other her waist.

'Can you see?'

She nodded, giddy with pain.

Finn's storm was spread out over Thunderstown. He looked so still from this distance – apart from when lightning turned all his black billows white – but she knew up close there would be so much *life*. There would be arteries of arctic cold, pumping fist-sized hailstones around his body of cloud. A heart of water, keeping him alive.

A jagged white line danced across him. Then came a flutter of short flashes and a jolt of lightning the noise of which reached them two seconds later. She savoured the reverberations it made in her bones, even though they twanged at her muscles. She longed for the next stroke of thunder, so that she could feel him again.

Meanwhile, Daniel watched the lightning earth in the town and marvelled at Elsa's bravery. She had charged up to the belfry to try to reach Finn, with no thought for her own fragility. Again the storm flashed bright, and for a moment a line of light coursed out and branched down fifty paths. The sound came seconds later, a bass rumble that washed over them while they stood pressed together.

'What possessed you,' he whispered with marvel, 'to climb up there and be struck by lightning?'

She laughed bitterly. 'I told you. It was that thing my dad used to say. I remembered it and for some reason hoped it might save Finn. He used to say, over and over again, that the lightning is a connection, not a one-way strike. So I thought that maybe I could use it to connect again with Finn.'

He was about to respond, but then he shut his mouth with a *clack* and his whole body tensed. She noticed the hairs on his forearms rising.

'What's wrong, Daniel?'

For a silent minute he stared out at the storm, and she could have sworn he did not blink in all that time. Then he turned to her with a mad look in his eyes and whispered, 'It's going to be all right.'

'Daniel … I can't believe that. Now it's you who needs some rest. I'm not sure if it will ever be all right. I came to before and I thought I could get him back somehow. But now I can't see a way. All I know is that I'm going to fall apart when the last of his rain falls. Is that what you mean when you say it's going to be all right?'

She broke down again into tears, sobs that were like blows punched into her breastbone.

Daniel stared bluntly back at her.

'See? See?' she gasped, 'It's no good you saying it will be *all right!*' She wiped the tears from her cheeks but instantly they were replaced by fresh ones.

He helped her back to the bed. She let herself be carried, the pain now feeling like a natural extension of the emotions inside her. She had done all she could. She lay back on the mattress and he tucked her up like an invalid, which she supposed she was.

'You know,' she sniffed, 'when you hear people say that life is short, that you should live every last second to the full. Well, it's too hard. *Hard*, when trusting someone can let them hurt you, when you don't really know your own mind, when the things you want turn out to be the things you never wanted, when you can't connect with friends and family, when there are groceries to buy and dishes to be done, and photocopying and filing and timetables and diaries and *distractions.*'

He reached down and she felt him lift her chin, with the exact same gesture her dad used to use to raise her head and restore her confidence when she was a little girl.

And then he did something she had never seen him do before. Not once, she realized, in all her time in Thunderstown.

He smiled.

He had the largest, heartiest smile she had ever seen. His teeth were strong and white and the lines of his face that were usually so set in contemplation or a frown fell away, and new lines appeared that accentuated the depth of his beaming, heartening smile.

He has gone mad, she thought, to think he has found something to smile about.

And then he let go of her hand, and the smile dropped from his face like snow slipping off a branch. He became earnest again. He met for a long moment her eyes, then nodded and left the room.

And although she did not know it then, she would never see Daniel Fossiter again.

# 21

# WERE ALL SPIRITS, AND ARE MELTED INTO AIR

Daniel Fossiter stood on the Devil's Diadem in the windless night, with his back to the walls of the nunnery and Finn's storm still pouring over Thunderstown below.

The night had become too dark to distinguish the cumulonimbus from the black sky surrounding it. Only when a blade of lightning stabbed down at a chimney or at Saint Erasmus's belfry was its shape revealed: a citadel of fumes with towers as high as any of the mountain peaks. Sometimes the lightning revealed steep ramparts of cloud, with battlements reflecting the light as coldly as stone.

This was not the first storm he had watched from the nunnery's vantage point. He remembered being up here with his father once, as a child, not long after his mother left, watching a storm drift away into the east. It had been a red flotilla in the sunset, and Daniel had looked from it to his father and seen – for the only time in his life – the old man on the edge of tears. 'Just watch it go, son,' his father had whispered, 'and don't blink. Don't forget one beautiful second of it.'

Daniel heard his name spoken and turned around. Dot had come out to find him. When she spoke, her voice seemed able to anticipate the lulls in the storm's noises and to dart between them. 'It's getting late. Do you want to come inside for something to eat?'

He shook his head. A blue-white flicker of lightning sputtered inside the storm.

Dot regarded him for a moment: his coat buttoned up to his beard and his broad-brimmed hat wedged on his head. 'You look as if you are going somewhere.'

He shrugged. 'I believe I am. Although I am not sure where.'

Thunder passed over them like the beating of wings. Dot waited for it to boom into the distance, then asked, 'Would you like us to keep some food out for you?'

'There's no need. I hope I do not come back.'

She stayed quiet, digesting what he'd just said. 'I think,' she said eventually, 'I understand you. Are you sure you know what you're doing?'

In his childhood memories of this place, she was just as ancient as she was today. He could remember first encountering her, back when he was three or four feet tall. Then to his young eyes her age had seemed preposterous and grotesque, barely even human.

'No,' he said, 'but someone has to try it, and it should not be Elsa.'

'Perhaps I can give you something to take with you?'

He laughed. 'What more do I need, other than my own two legs?'

'How about a story? When your father used to come up here, when he'd spend long hours in conversations with the abbess ... well, sometimes I was present for those discussions.'

'Forgive me, Sister, but I'm not sure that stories of my father are what I need to hear right now.'

Dot ignored him. 'Mostly we talked shop, but on one occasion the Reverend Fossiter wanted to confide in us.'

'Confide what?'

Dot drew a deep breath. 'That your mother, when she left Thunderstown, didn't go to Paris or Delhi or Beijing, or anywhere like that. She went somewhere both nearer and further away. She went back to the place she had come from.' She placed a buckled hand on his arm. 'Upwards, Daniel. But you had guessed that already, hadn't you?'

He nodded mutely.

'Your father said he had fallen in love with a witch. That was what he wanted to confide in us. *A monster of the air*, he called her. He said that he had thought her to be an angel to begin with, but that after a time she had convinced him she was of the devil, because of the way she would defend the weather.'

Daniel clenched his fists, rueing his father's superstitions.

'Of course,' Dot continued, 'she was neither devil nor angel. She was utterly ordinary. There are three thousand of her kind present on the earth in any given moment.'

Daniel waited for this to sink in, but he discovered that his thinkings had already prepared him for it. It was as if they had known this secret all along. 'If that were true,' he scratched his head, 'shouldn't I be like them too? I assure you that when I am cut I bleed blood, not air. Only once have I ever – only a day ago, in fact – seen anything like weather come from inside of myself.'

Dot smiled sadly, her face folding up under her wrinkles. 'Perhaps some of us don't see it as often as we might. Perhaps that means we have lost touch. Or perhaps those of us who do see it need to be better at holding ourselves together.'

'What about me? Do you think I am enough like them? To do what I have to do now?'

'I don't know. I suppose it depends on whether Finn is still there to be saved. I suppose if you believe he is, it may be possible.' She patted his arm lightly. 'I think that is all I can offer you. I wish you well, Mr Fossiter, wherever you are going.'

And with that she pushed him gently in the small of the back.

He set off like a racer at the starting gunshot. When he was some distance down the slope a wind arrived to spur him on, and when on a ridge top he looked back over his shoulder at the now distant nunnery, the wind smeared his black hair across his eyes so that he could not see and be tempted to turn back.

He raced downhill, towards Thunderstown, but only when he reached its outskirts did he truly appreciate the severity of the storm. The town hid behind a curtain of rain, and he had to hold his arms up in front of his face to make his way through it. The sky smashed open again and again with lightning. Torrential rain hammered the pavements, smashing off the flagstones like sparks off an anvil. It stung his eyes and soaked his clothing, bringing with it hailstones hard enough to chip the paint from doors. He shielded his eyes as he got his bearings, then toiled in the direction of Saint Erasmus Square.

In Welcan Row, old mine shafts were overflowing. Rotten ropes, mushed mosses and scrap metal emerged and were carried away on a stream of filthy liquid that slicked the street. In Corris Street he splashed through shin-deep water, then headed south through Bradawl Alley, where the cobbles had turned to islands. In each street the floodwater was deeper than the last, but he sloshed onwards with his boots soaked through and squelching.

In Foremans Avenue, trees rattled and creaked as the storm shook them. With a noise like a record distorting, one cracked down the length of its trunk. The road beneath it popped open and roots sprang out, then the nearer half of the tree crashed down with a bending squeal and a shiver of leaves. He looked up as he passed the Moses residence, and was satisfied to see floodwater frothing under the front door, and one window blasted out of its frame by lightning. He hurried on. He had to get to the Church of Saint Erasmus.

Rain pinged off car bonnets, twanged off the pavements, flicked him with hard ice as he struggled, grabbing now and then a lamp post for support, to the end of Widdershin Road and at last into the wide church square. He could barely see a stone's throw in front of him, let alone up to the spire. Rain scratched out all visibility. The plaza was awash, gurgling with scummy white eddies.

He had to wade the final few metres before he reached the high ground of the church's steps. There he looked back for a moment across the square. Liquid rushed in from every street, bearing debris and caked scum, churning in the pattern of a whirlpool around the church. Watching it made him dizzy, as if not just the water but the entire town were turning in that gyre.

He battled into the church and slammed the doors behind him, then paused to collect his breath. How still the air was in here. The roof rang with the strikes of so many raindrops that their echoes combined into a single throbbing note. It was so dark that he was forced to squint his way along the aisle by memory, picturing the place as he had known it through the years. His memory added the details: his father at the pulpit, with his face bunched in devoted prayer; his grandfather slouched bored or tipsy in a back pew; Betty, watching him with a look he still believed had been a fond one, on that single time when he had tried to give a reading from the book of his namesake and his tongue had sunk into silence at the lectern. 'I, Daniel,' he had read, 'was troubled in spirit, and the visions that passed through my mind disturbed me.'

He walked slowly towards the altar. He paused at the front pew where he himself had sat every Sunday for years. He stroked the cold wood, removed his soaked leather hat, and laid it on the seat. Then he crossed to the side door and climbed the spiral staircase to the belfry. The stairwell was full of the din of falling water.

When he emerged on to the belfry he at once felt the electricity humming in the stones beneath him, hissing in the tumbling rain. The masonry zinged with energy. And there was the storm in an indigo expanse.

This high up, he felt almost intimately close to the thunder. He was convinced that if he reached for the cloud – which he did now, raising himself on his tiptoes – he would be able to stroke his fingers through it. He touched nothing and retracted his hand, feeling foolish, but the sky had seemed too small for such a monstrous cloud. It puzzled him that something so enormous could not be grasped. Hail rattled on the belfry like thrown dice, and stung the skin of his upturned face. Rain made the old stone sizzle. A sheet of lightning flashed. In the half-second that it lasted for, that which had seemed limitless became clarified. If time could have paused in that moment, he thought he would be able to take in every detail of the thundercloud, for every wisp and fold of steam became defined in a photojournalist's black and white. When, in the next instant, the world plunged back into darkness, he felt as blind inside as out. He wiped the rain from his eyes and groped around for the lightning rod. His hands were shaking when he seized hold of it. The sense of purpose that had driven him up here had been lost to the darkness like words to spilled ink. He was afraid, he realized. He had never been more afraid.

There was a white light.

And then there was nothing.

# 22

# THE LOVER OF THUNDER

Come morning the storm had died out. It would be a fine day of sunshine, with a pleasant south-westerly breeze tempering the heat.

In Thunderstown, men and women stood dumbfounded in their doorways, staring at the cyan sky reflected in the floodwater. Otherwise they used buckets and tubs to bail out their houses, shaking their heads and cursing Old Man Thunder. Canaries alighted on the weathervanes, or were yellow blurs chasing each other between the chimneys.

On the belfry of the Church of Saint Erasmus, a body lay face down on the stone. It was a man's body, burly and black-bearded. The sunshine had dried off its flesh and hair, but had not yet evaporated the puddle in which it had lain since the storm faded. Every so often the body would give a meek cough or a judder of its shoulder blades, then lapse into another hour of stillness. Now, finally, it groaned and tried to prop itself up. It raised itself an inch before it flopped back into the puddle. It lay there for a little while more, occasionally dribbling up a mouthful of water. Then, finally, with a moan, it rolled on to its back. Sometime later it pulled itself up and sat against the wall. Fluid drooled from its mouth and nostrils.

It tilted its head to drain water from its ears. It rubbed its eyes. After a while more it managed to stand up, as shakily as a newborn calf. When it got the better of its balance it squinted around at the bright rooftops and the dazzling sunshine on the windowpanes of the town. It looked down at itself and sneezed. It rubbed its bearded face.

It stopped very still.

It rubbed its face some more, plying its cheeks and groping at its neck.

'Uhh ...' it murmured, then shook its head. 'I ... huhh ...' It felt again across its cheeks. It twisted its fingers through its drenched black locks.

'I have hair,' it said.

But when it tugged on it, clumps came out on its fingers. It looked at the black scraps in its hands, then tugged experimentally at a part of its beard. This came loose too, pulled free as easily as moss off a stone.

It got down on its knees and leaned over the puddle to view its dim reflection. It reached out a tentative, pointing finger for the face it saw there, then jumped in alarm when the reflection broke into circles.

It kept pulling at its hair. It scruffed it up with both hands and it came free everywhere. It splashed water over its scalp and washed away the last of it until its head was totally bald. It did the same thing to its beard, spitting and slurping when it got a clump of it on its tongue. It rubbed its head, exploring its smooth jaw and crown. Now that the puddle had settled, it inspected its reflection for a second time. It had missed something. Its eyebrows, which rubbed free as easily as chalk off a blackboard.

'Who am I?' it asked of the water. It waited for an answer and when none came it screwed up its eyes and rubbed its head and looked vulnerable and confused.

It got up and staggered to the door. It tripped and nearly tumbled several times as it made its way down the spiral staircase. In the empty church below it paused, because on a pew lay an object it recognized, although it could not tell from where. It picked it up and punched it into shape, then plied for a moment the brim, which was still damp from the storm.

After a minute it remembered. Daniel Fossiter's rain cap. All that had happened came crashing back.

It had begun with a dream of falling, but instead of sleep's darkness everything had been white-hot. Falling for a long time, head over heels, long past the point when the rush of plummeting jerks the dreamer awake. Down and down it had fallen, with a sickening sense of its own weight, until heaviness itself had been the thing to slow its fall. Heaviness had become a kind of gravity, and it had no longer felt as if it were falling but compacting into a nucleus. Eventually it had simply hung, paralyzed by its own solidity. And then it had not been hanging but lying, and it was a prone man on a church belfry.

After a while, the man folded the hat and tucked it into the pocket of his trousers. At one point, during his sensation of falling, he'd sensed another presence, travelling in the opposite direction.

'I will miss you,' he said.

When Elsa woke to the sunlit morning and its postcard-blue sky, she pulled the sheet up over her head. She lay in the narrow bed in the nunnery cell, with the smell of pollen drifting in through the window, and she longed for rain to replace the honeyed burblings of songbirds. She had already cried until her tear ducts were dried out, and she knew she would cry again once they were rehydrated.

She slept the first half of the day away. Daniel was nowhere to be seen. She missed him and began to think he had given up on her. Probably he was holed away in depression in his homestead.

In the afternoon she was able to leave the bed for the first time. Her muscles tightened with each step and she managed only a single lap of the room before she collapsed back on to the mattress.

Sleep gave no relief. She dreamed of rain pouring from the heavens.

When she woke next it was evening. Through the high window of the cell she could see stars emerging, so she turned on the bedside lamp. She didn't want stars. She wanted black skies venting water.

All she had to distract her was a cloud atlas borrowed from Dot. The old nun had warned against it, but reluctantly loaned it to her when Elsa insisted. Now she wished she'd taken Dot's advice, for the moment she opened it and saw the black prow of a cumulonimbus she felt strangled, and threw the book across the room.

She rested her head on the pillow and stared at the ceiling, thinking of her dad, and how ceilings had to be very sturdy things to survive all of the prayers and pleas directed at them.

The moth who had become her cellmate was still up there with its brown wings flattened across the plaster. Now that the bedside lamp was aglow it came alive, dropped from its resting place and zoomed around the aura of the light. When it started throwing itself against the lampshade, it cast elastic shadows across the ceiling and she thought of Finn's mobiles, which would be circling abandoned in his bothy, and she wished she had the paper goose he had made her, or even the paper skyscraper. She had to turn the lamp off and suffer the stars, just to stop the moth from reminding her of them.

A breeze passed by the window.

She sat bolt upright and was rewarded with jarring pains in both sides. This time, however, she had strength to bear them. The wind passed again, with a noise like a tuneless note from a flute, and then died away. She waited impatiently for it to come back, listening to the moth's clicking wings in the interval. When the wind returned it sounded as if it were panting, then faded away into the distance.

When she got out of bed her legs stiffened with pain and she walked as if on stilts to the window. The stars and a sliver of moon made the mountainside light, but at the bottom of the slopes it was as if Thunderstown had vanished, for Finn's storm had cut the power to the streets and they were lost in the gloom.

This time she saw the wind before she heard it. It was patrolling along the length of the nunnery wall, pausing here and there to sniff the mortar before trotting on with its silver tail wagging behind it. She knocked on the window and it looked up at the noise.

'Hey,' she said.

It yapped at her, once, then sprang away as if she had thrown a stick. When it came running back it barked more aggressively, as if it were frustrated that she hadn't followed.

At that she felt as if the lethargy in her bones had run off into the night. She dressed in impatient silence, pulled on her sneakers and her jacket, then slipped out of the door, turning the handle and gripping it on the other side before closing it gently, so that the mechanism lowered silently into the latch and did not cause a sound. She did not want to be stopped by a well-meaning nun.

She padded along the corridor, down the stairs and out into the cloister. The moon was only a crescent, but still it seemed especially bright, glazing the stone walls white.

It was impossible to open the big cloister doors without their beams clunking, but their sounds did not seem to disturb anyone and she swiftly closed them behind her. She was in the antechamber that kept the weather at bay, and only the outer door remained between her and the mountainside. She paused there, wondering whether this was such a good idea. She was in no fit state to wander off on the Devil's Diadem at night.

No sooner had she doubted herself than the wind thumped against the door. Another blustered past, and then another, and then one that whined and one that howled and she listened with her hands around the door handle as the noises built into a great, hollow, gale-force roar. A charm hammered into the wall beside her began to jingle on its hook, until it worked itself loose and smashed against the antechamber floor.

She took a deep breath and opened the door.

Outside, the world lay motionless. She'd thought she'd be immediately overwhelmed by the in-rushing winds, but the air hung still and delicate. More stars than she had ever seen shimmered in the blue night. Together with the moon they paled the dusty mountainside, making boulders into alabaster and the grass into etched silver. And, all down the slope before her, they shone on the fur of at least a hundred wild dogs.

The beasts stood or sat on their haunches as far as the eye could see. Their alert poses made them look more like sculpted statues than flesh and blood creatures. They watched her expectantly. The moon reflected as a white arc in each canine eye.

She waited, unsure of what they required from her. Then, as one, they turned their heads and gazed down the slope.

She had to take a few steps forwards to see what they saw.

A man, toiling up the uneven path to the nunnery.

He had not yet seen her, for all his focus was on his struggle with the steep ascent. Her heartbeat trebled when the moonlight told her he was bald and big-framed, but she would not believe her eyes, since it was impossible for him to be the one she wanted.

Her feet believed them. She stumbled down the slope towards him.

He looked up. He seemed different. Details had altered. He had worry lines on his forehead and crow's feet around his eyes. His physique had become more precise and more world-worn. Yet who else, she thought as she stumbled over the last few paces and halted an arm's reach from him, could have irises that looked like hurricanes? She would recognize him even if half a century had passed between them. He was like a cherished soldier coming home from a long war.

He smiled at her. She threw her arms around him so hard he lost his balance and they fell with an *oof* to the dusty ground.

They were laughing. She was poking his face and pulling at his cheek to confirm it was real. He was grinning. He was nuzzling his face close to hers.

The winds took off in unison and yipped beneath the gleaming stars.

She gave him her lips. They kissed.

And she was in love with the thunder.

# ACKNOWLEDGEMENTS

Thank you to Susan Armstrong for her constant encouragement and her commitment to this novel, to Sarah Castleton, Margaret Stead and Clare Hey for their editorial contributions, and to the Desmond Elliott Charitable Trust.

—

Ali Shaw grew up in Dorset and graduated from Lancaster University with a degree in English Literature. He has since worked as a bookseller and at Oxford's Bodleian Library. His first novel, *The Girl with Glass Feet*, was a huge commercial and critical success, won the Desmond Elliot Prize and was shortlisted for the Costa First Book Award. He is currently at work on his third novel.